> ## "I thought she was the nanny!" Bently exclaimed.

"Let's try that description again," Detective Wood said, rolling his eyes. "Hair. What color?"

"Wheat."

"Like they make bread out of?"

"Like a field of it in the sun," Bently corrected.

"Anything else?"

"Yeah, she had—"

"Great legs," the detective filled in.

"Well, they were long and she had on these well-worn jeans…" When Bently saw the detective suppress a smile, he lost his barely controlled temper. "My seven-month-old daughter's missing! And the woman I'm describing took her! I barely saw her and I doubt I'd know her if she walked in the door." Bently pointed at the door of the station house just as it opened.

A very beautiful—if angry—young woman stormed inside.

"That's her!" Bently yelled. "And that's *my* baby!"

ABOUT THE AUTHOR

Nikki found her first creative outlet in a humor
column on teen life called "It's What's Happening,
Baby." (No kidding, it was the sixties, okay?) She
married young and kept on pursuing her dream of
being a writer. After reading her first Harlequin
novel, Nikki knew she had found a home for the
stories running around in her head. She filched
her teenage daughter's electric typewriter and
began to pound out her first romance. Nikki lives
in Milwaukee with her husband, Ron, the man
who taught her to believe in romance, and who
helps make *all* her dreams come true.

Books by Nikki Rivers

HARLEQUIN AMERICAN ROMANCE
550—SEDUCING SPENCER

Don't miss any of our special offers. Write to us at the
following address for information on our newest releases.

Harlequin Reader Service
U.S.: 3010 Walden Ave., P.O. Box 1325, Buffalo, NY 14269
Canadian: P.O. Box 609, Fort Erie, Ont. L2A 5X3

Nikki Rivers

DADDY'S LITTLE MATCHMAKER

Harlequin Books

TORONTO • NEW YORK • LONDON
AMSTERDAM • PARIS • SYDNEY • HAMBURG
STOCKHOLM • ATHENS • TOKYO • MILAN
MADRID • WARSAW • BUDAPEST • AUCKLAND

To my persistent, opinionated sister Bobbi—it really paid off this time!
Thanks for believing.

ISBN 0-373-16592-7

DADDY'S LITTLE MATCHMAKER

Chapter One

"Holy cow," Raine muttered. Pulling up in front of a row of elegant condos, she checked the address again. This was the place. And Deirdre's contact at the Bundle of Love baby store was never wrong—somewhere behind the fancy door with the scrolled number 220 was a baby. And where there was a baby, there were diapers—lots of them. Raine sincerely hoped that in this case they were disposables, because then she could launch into her sales pitch. Her Cotton Tails Diaper Service could use the kind of client who could afford to live in a place like this.

The grinding of protesting metal split the hush of the morning as Raine pushed the door of her tired old van open and climbed out. Sidestepping the rivers of melted snow from the late-winter thaw flowing across the sidewalk, she mounted the two shallow brick steps and thumped the ornate brass knocker on the front door.

The man who opened the door looked even less like Raine's idea of a father than the condo looked like her idea of a home. Once again, the word *elegant* came to mind. And sexy—sexier than anyone's daddy had a right to be. But he was also angry. Despite the gurgling bundle he held in his arms, his darkly elegant, absurdly handsome face was taut with controlled anger.

"Mr. Pierce?" Raine asked reluctantly, instantly reminded that although they proved to be the most effective way of drumming up new business, she hated doing cold calls.

"Yes, I'm Bently Pierce," answered the man. "And you're late," he bit out. "I sincerely hope this is not a habit of yours, or we will most surely find it impossible to do business together."

Raine stood in the doorway and stared.

The man shifted his weight, raising the baby higher against his shoulder, the action doing nothing to relieve the obvious tension in his body.

Raine merely stood there silently.

"Well?" he demanded, rolling his dark eyes toward the black brows slashing his forehead. "You *are* here about the child?" he added in those same, biting, arrogant tones.

"Well—yeah, I am. But—"

"Then, please—" He moved aside and gestured toward the foyer behind him. Raine stepped past him.

The baby squealed and gurgled, its chubby little arms waving in welcome. Raine couldn't help smiling at the adorable sight she made with her thick, curly dark hair and full pink cheeks.

"Hi, kid, how ya doin'?" she asked, holding out a finger for the baby to grasp.

Making Plans to Leave

Returning the Green Glasses

Chapter 10
The Search for the Wicked Witch

Dorothy and her friends were led to the gates of the Emerald City. The Guardian of the Gate removed their green glasses and put them back in the green box. He wished them good luck and reminded Dorothy that the Wicked Witch was very mean and would try to make them her slaves.

After they had said good-bye to the Guardian of the Gate, they began to walk towards the West. Soon the hot sun made Dorothy and the Lion very tired. They lay down on the cool grass and fell asleep, while the Tinman and the Scarecrow kept watch.

While Dorothy and the Lion were sleeping, the Wicked Witch of the West was watching them. She had only one eye, but it was as powerful as a telescope, and she could see everything. So, as she sat by the door of her castle, she happened to look around, and she saw Dorothy lying asleep with her friends beside her.

The Wicked Witch was angry to find them in her country. She blew on a silver whistle that hung around her neck.

In a few seconds, a pack of wolves came running to her. They had long legs and fierce eyes and sharp teeth.

"Go to those people," said the Witch, "and tear them to pieces."

"Aren't you going to make them your slaves?" asked the Leader of the Wolves.

"No," answered the Wicked Witch, "one is made of tin, one is made of straw, one is a

The Wicked Witch Calls Her Wolves.

little girl, and one is a Lion. None of them is fit to work, so you may tear them to pieces."

"Very well," said the wolf. And he dashed away at full speed with the rest of the pack.

But the Scarecrow and the Tinman were wide awake, and they heard the wolves coming.

The Tinman grabbed his axe, and as the Leader of the Wolves ran towards him, he swung his arm and chopped off the wolf's head. As soon as each wolf came close, he killed it with his sharp axe. Soon forty wolves lay dead in a great heap.

When the Wicked Witch saw what the Tinman had done, she became even angrier than before. So she blew her silver whistle twice.

In a few minutes, a great flock of wild crows came flying towards her.

The Wicked Witch said to the King Crow: "Fly at once to the strangers and peck out

Forty Wolves Lie Dead.

their eyes and tear them to pieces."

The wild crows flew towards Dorothy and her friends. When she saw them coming, Dorothy was afraid.

But the Scarecrow said, "This is my battle. Lie down beside me and you will be safe."

So everyone but the Scarecrow lay down on the ground. The Scarecrow stood up and stretched out his arms. When the crows saw him, they were frightened and did not dare to come any closer.

But the King Crow said:

"It is only a stuffed man. I will peck his eyes out."

The King Crow flew at the Scarecrow, who caught it by the head and twisted its neck until it was dead. As each crow flew at the Scarecrow, he twisted its neck. Soon there were forty crows lying dead beside him.

When the Wicked Witch saw all her crows lying in a heap, she went into a terrible rage

The Scarecrow Frightens the Crows.

and blew her silver whistle three times.

This time a great swarm of bees came flying to her. The Wicked Witch told the bees to sting Dorothy and her friends to death.

But the Scarecrow saw the bees coming. He scattered his straw over Dorothy, Toto and the Lion. This way, the bees flew at the Tinman, and their stingers broke off against the tin. The Tinman was not hurt, but all the bees died. Their bodies lay scattered in the field.

The Wicked Witch was so angry when she saw her bees lying in little heaps that she stamped her foot and tore her hair and gnashed her teeth. Then she called a dozen of her slaves, who were the Winkies, and gave them sharp spears. She told them to find the strangers and destroy them.

The Winkies were not brave people, but they had to obey the Wicked Witch, so they marched away.

The Wicked Witch Is Angry.

When the Lion saw them coming, he gave a great roar. The poor Winkies were so frightened that they ran away as fast as they could.

When the Wicked Witch saw what had happened, she made up her mind how to act.

She went to the cupboard and took out her Golden Cap. This Cap had a special charm. Whoever owned it could call three times upon the Winged Monkeys. These creatures would obey any order they were given. But no one could command the Winged Monkeys more than three times. The Wicked Witch had used the charm of the Cap twice before, so this was her last wish.

She put the Golden Cap on her head and stood on her left foot. Then she recited a secret charm. Soon, the sky darkened and a low rumbling sound could be heard. In a few minutes, the Witch was surrounded by a crowd of monkeys with huge and powerful

A Great Roar!

wings on their shoulders.

The Wicked Witch ordered the Winged Monkeys to destroy the strangers except for the Lion. She wanted him brought to her so she could make him her slave.

"Your commands shall be obeyed," said the leader. Then the Winged Monkeys flew away.

When they found the Tinman, the Monkeys grabbed him and carried him through the air. When they were over some sharp pointed rocks, they dropped the poor Tinman. He fell a great distance to the rocks, where he lay so battered and dented that he couldn't move.

The rest of the Monkeys caught the Scarecrow, and with their long fingers pulled all of the straw out of his clothes and his head. They made his hat, boots and clothes into a small bundle and threw it into the top branches of a tall tree.

After they had done this, the Monkeys threw pieces of rope around the Lion and

The Monkeys Drop the Poor Tinman.

wound many coils around his body, head and legs. When they were sure he was unable to bite or scratch, they lifted him up and flew away with him to the Witch's castle. At the castle, he was placed in a small yard with a high iron fence, so that he could not escape.

But Dorothy was not harmed at all. She stood with Toto in her arms and watched what the Monkeys did to her friends. The Leader of the Winged Monkeys flew up to her. His long hairy arms stretched out, and his ugly face grinned terribly. But when he saw the mark of the Good Witch's kiss on her forehead, he stopped short and motioned the others not to touch her.

"We dare not harm this little girl," he said to them, "for she is protected by the Power of Good, and that is greater than the Power of Evil. All we can do is to carry her to the castle of the Wicked Witch and leave her there."

So, they carefully lifted Dorothy in their

Behind a High Iron Fence

arms and carried her to the castle.

The Wicked Witch was surprised and worried when she saw the mark on Dorothy's forehead. She knew that she could not hurt the girl in any way. When she saw Dorothy's silver slippers she began to tremble in fear, for she knew what a powerful charm belonged to them.

But the Wicked Witch was also very clever. She knew that Dorothy did not know the true power of the silver slippers. So the Wicked Witch laughed to herself and thought, "I can still make her my slave, for she does not know how to use her power." Then she said to Dorothy:

"Come with me; and see that you mind everything I tell you, for if you do not, I will make an end of you as I did of the Tinman and the Scarecrow."

The Witch led Dorothy through the castle until they came to the kitchen. Here, the

The Wicked Witch Is Worried.

Witch made Dorothy clean the pots and pans, sweep the floor, and feed the fire with heavy logs.

While Dorothy was hard at work, the Witch would go into the courtyard and harness the Lion like a horse. She wanted the Lion to pull her cart and take her wherever she wished to go. But as she opened the gate the Lion gave a loud roar and bounded at her so fiercely that the Witch was afraid and ran out and shut the gate again.

"If I cannot harness you," said the Witch, "I can starve you. You shall have nothing to eat until you do as I wish."

So after that she took no food to the imprisoned Lion. Every day she came to the gate at noon and asked, "Are you ready to be harnessed like a horse?"

And the Lion would answer, "No. If you come in this yard, I will bite you."

The reason the Lion did not have to do as

The Lion Will Not Pull the Cart.

the Witch wished was that every night, while the Witch was asleep, Dorothy carried him food from the cupboard. After he ate, Dorothy would sit beside him, and they would talk of their troubles and try to plan some way to escape. But they could not find a way to get out of the castle, for it was always guarded by the yellow Winkies, who were the slaves of the Wicked Witch and too afraid of her not to do as she ordered.

Dorothy worked very hard during the day, and her life became very sad. She knew it would be difficult to return to Kansas. Sometimes she held little Toto in her arms and cried bitterly.

Now the Wicked Witch had a great longing to own Dorothy's silver shoes. She knew the power of these shoes would make her more evil and feared than she already was. She watched Dorothy carefully to see if she ever took off her shoes, thinking she might steal

They Talk of Their Troubles.

them. But Dorothy only removed them when she took her bath at night. The Witch was too afraid of the dark to dare enter Dorothy's room at night to take the shoes, and her fear of water was even greater than her fear of the dark, so she never came near when Dorothy took her bath. The old Witch never touched water and never let water touch her in any way.

But the Wicked Witch was very clever, and she finally thought of a trick so that she could get Dorothy's silver shoes. She placed an iron bar in the middle of the kitchen floor. Then she used her magic to make the bar invisible. In this way, she knew Dorothy would trip over the bar and loose her shoes.

But when Dorothy tripped over the invisible bar, she only lost one shoe. The Witch quickly snatched it and put it on her own foot. When Dorothy saw what had happened, she grew very angry and said, "Give me back

Dorothy Loses One Shoe!

my shoe!"

"I will not," laughed the Witch. "Now it is my shoe, not yours. And someday I shall get the other one from you too."

This made Dorothy so angry that she picked up the bucket of water she had been using to wash the floor and threw it over the Witch.

Instantly the Witch gave a loud scream and then, as Dorothy looked in wonder, the Witch began to shrink and melt away.

"See what you have done!" she screamed. "In a minute I shall melt away."

"I'm very sorry," said Dorothy, who was truly frightened to see the Witch melting away like brown sugar.

In a few minutes the Witch turned into a brown, melted, shapeless mass and began to spread over the kitchen floor. All that was left of the Witch was the silver shoe. Dorothy picked it up, cleaned it, and put it back on

The Witch Begins to Melt!

her own foot.

Then, being free at last, Dorothy ran out to the courtyard to tell the Lion that the Wicked Witch of the West had come to an end, and that they were no longer prisoners in a strange land.

Dorothy Comes to Free the Lion.

A Holiday!

Chapter 11
The Rescue

The Lion was very happy to hear that the Wicked Witch had been melted away, and Dorothy unlocked the gate of his prison and set him free. Next, Dorothy gathered all the Winkies together and told them that they were no longer slaves.

The Winkies were very happy, for they had been made to work hard for many years. They made the day of their freedom a holiday and spent the time feasting and dancing.

"If only our friends the Scarecrow and the Tinman were with us," said the Lion, "I would be totally happy."

"Don't you think there is some way we could rescue them?" said Dorothy.

"We can try," answered the Lion.

So they called the Winkies and asked them to help rescue their friends. The Winkies said that they would be delighted to do something for Dorothy since she had set them all free. So a group of Winkies traveled that day and part of the next until they came to the rocky plain where the Tinman lay, all battered and bent. His axe was next to him, but the blade was rusted and the handle broken off.

The Winkies lifted him and carried him back to the castle. When they reached the castle Dorothy asked the Winkies if any of their people were tinsmiths. She found that there were several Winkies who were skilled tinsmiths. In a little while they came to the castle with baskets of tools. They looked the

The Winkies Carry the Tinman.

Tinman over carefully and told Dorothy that they thought they could mend him so he would be as good as ever.

The Winkies worked for three days and three nights. They hammered, twisted and pounded at the legs, body and head of the Tinman. At last he was straightened out into his old form, and his joints worked as well as ever.

When at last he walked into Dorothy's room and thanked her for rescuing him, he was so happy that he cried tears of joy. Dorothy and the Lion were so happy to see their friend that they danced and celebrated all day.

"If only we had the Scarecrow with us again," said the Tinman, "I would be truly happy."

"We must try to find him," said Dorothy.

So she called the Winkies to help her, and they walked all that day and part of the next

Tears of Joy

until they came to the tall tree where the Winged Monkeys had tossed the Scarecrow's clothes. The Tinman quickly chopped the tree down, and Dorothy and the Winkies carried the Scarecrow's clothes back to the castle. As soon as they entered the castle, the Winkies began stuffing the clothes with nice, clean straw. Soon the Scarecrow stood before them—as good as ever! He thanked them over and over again for saving him.

Now that they were reunited, Dorothy and her friends spent a few happy days at the castle, where they found everything they needed to make themselves comfortable.

But after a few days, they all decided that it was time to return to Oz and ask for the things that they had been promised.

So they sadly said good-bye to the Winkies and packed food and blankets for the journey back to the Emerald City.

The Winkies Stuff the Scarecrow.

"We Have Lost Our Way."

Chapter 12
The Winged Monkeys

The next morning, Dorothy and her friends began their journey to the Emerald City. They walked a long way and still could not see a sign of the Emerald City. And since they had been carried to the castle by the Winged Monkeys, they were not at all sure in which direction they should walk.

Days passed, and they still saw nothing but the fields and forests. The Scarecrow began to complain.

"We have surely lost our way," he said, "and unless we find it again in time to reach the Emerald City, I shall never get my brains."

"Nor I my heart," said the Tinman.

"And I do not have the courage to keep tramping forever, without getting anywhere at all," said the Lion.

Dorothy sat down on the grass to think.

"Suppose we call the field mice," she suggested. "They could probably tell us the way to the Emerald City."

"To be sure they could!" cried the Scarecrow. "Why didn't we think of that before?"

Dorothy blew the whistle that the Queen of the Field Mice had given her. In a few minutes they heard the pattering of tiny feet, and many of the small grey mice came running up to her. The Queen herself came up to Dorothy.

"What can I do for my friends?" she squeaked.

"We have lost our way," answered Dorothy.

Dorothy Blows the Whistle.

"Can you tell us where the Emerald City is?"

Certainly," answered the Queen, "but it is a great way off, for you have had it at your backs all the time." Then she noticed Dorothy's Golden Cap and suggested that Dorothy use the Golden Cap to call the Winged Monkeys, who would carry everyone to the Emerald City.

So Dorothy recited the magic words that were written inside the Golden Cap. In a few minutes she heard the chattering and flapping of wings, as the band of Winged Monkeys flew up to her. The King bowed low before Dorothy and asked:

"What is your command?"

Dorothy explained that they had lost their way, and wished to be taken to the Emerald City. No sooner had she spoken than the Monkeys picked up Dorothy, Toto, the Tinman, the Scarecrow and the Lion, and carried them in their long hairy arms all the way to

The Winged Monkeys Fly to Dorothy.

the Emerald City.

The journey took a very short time. When they reached the gates of the Emerald City, the Monkeys set them all down carefully. Then the King bowed to Dorothy and flew swiftly away, followed by all his band.

"That was a good ride," said Dorothy.

"Yes, and a quick way out of our troubles," answered the Lion. "It certainly was lucky that you remembered to bring that Golden Cap!"

The Monkeys Set Them Down.

The Guardian of the Gate Greets Them.

Chapter 13
Oz the Terrible

Dorothy and her friends walked up to the gate of the Emerald City and rang the bell. After they rang many times, the Guardian of the Gate answered the bell.

"What! Are you back already?" he asked in surprise.

"We certainly are!" answered the Scarecrow.

"But I thought you had gone to find the Wicked Witch of the West," said the Guardian of the Gate.

"We did find her," said the Scarecrow, "and Dorothy melted her away."

"Melted! Well, that is good news," said the Guardian of the Gate.

He led them into his little room and gave them all green eyeglasses just as he had done before. Then they passed through the big gates into the Emerald City. When the Guardian of the Gate told the people that Dorothy had melted the Wicked Witch of the West, they all gathered around the travelers and followed them in a great crowd to the Palace of Oz.

Once they reached the Palace gates the soldier with the green beard greeted them and carried the news of their arrival to the Great Oz. Dorothy thought that once he heard the news, the Great Oz would send for her at once, but he did not. Dorothy and her friends waited for many days, but still heard nothing from the Great Oz.

The waiting was tiresome, and at last they grew angry at Oz for treating them so badly.

A Great Crowd

So the Scarecrow sent a message to Oz which said that if he did not see them at once, they would call the Winged Monkeys to help them and find out whether he kept his promises or not. When the Wizard was given this message, he was so frightened that he sent word for them to come to the Throne Room at four minutes after nine o'clock the next morning. Oz had met the Winged Monkeys once, and he knew their power. He was very afraid of meeting them again.

The four travelers found it difficult to sleep that night. Each thought of the gift Oz had promised to give them. Dorothy fell asleep dreaming of Kansas and her Aunt Em.

At nine o'clock the next morning, the soldier with the green beard came to escort them to the Throne Room.

Dorothy, the Tinman, the Scarecrow and the Lion all expected to see the Wizard in the shape he had taken before. They were all

Dorothy Dreams of Home.

surprised when they saw that the room was empty.

Soon they heard a Voice that seemed to come from somewhere near the top of the great dome, and it said solemnly:

"I am Oz the Great and Terrible. Why do you seek me?"

They looked again in every part of the room and still saw no one. Dorothy asked, "Where are you?"

"I am everywhere," answered the Voice, "but if you wish to talk with me, walk near the Throne."

So they walked toward the Throne and Dorothy said:

"We have come to claim our promises."

"What promises?" asked Oz.

Dorothy repeated the Wizard's promise to send her back to Kansas, and to give the Tinman a heart, the Scarecrow brains, and the Lion courage.

"We Have Come to Claim Our Promises."

"Is the Wicked Witch really destroyed?" asked the Voice.

"Yes," answered Dorothy, "I melted her with a bucket of water."

"Dear me," said the Voice, "how sudden! Well, come to me tomorrow, for I must have time to think it over."

This made the Scarecrow and the Tinman very angry, and they began to shout at the Great Oz, and they demanded that he keep his promises to them. The Lion thought that he might as well frighten the Wizard, so he gave a large, loud roar. This was so frightening that Toto jumped away from him and tipped over a screen that stood in the corner of the room. As it fell with a crash they looked and saw a very strange thing. For, standing in just the spot the screen had hidden, was a little old man with a bald head and a wrinkled face. The man seemed just as surprised as Dorothy and her friends. The Tinman raised

The Lion's Roar Frightens Toto.

his axe and rushed towards the little man and shouted, "Who are you?"

"I am Oz the Great and Terrible," said the little man in a trembling voice, "but please don't hit me—please don't—and I will do anything you want."

Dorothy and her friends were surprised and upset.

"We thought Oz was a Great Head, a Ball of Fire, a Terrible Beast, or a Beautiful Woman," said the Scarecrow.

"No, you are wrong," said the little man. "I have been making believe."

"Making believe!" cried the Tinman. "Are you not a great Wizard?"

The little man hung his head in shame and confessed that he was only a common man who was able to perform some clever magic tricks. He asked Dorothy and her friends to sit down while he told them his strange story.

The Little Man Hangs His Head.

The Wizard Begins His Story.

Chapter 14
The Magic of the Great Oz

Dorothy and her friends sat down in some comfortable chairs while the Wizard told them this story:

"I was born in Omaha. When I grew up I became a ventriloquist and learned how to throw my voice, so it seemed to come from many places at once. I was well trained by a great master. I can imitate any kind of bird or beast." Then he mewed like a kitten, and Toto pricked up his ears and looked everywhere to see where the sound was coming from.

"After a while I got tired of doing that and decided to become a balloonist. A balloonist is someone who goes up in a balloon on circus day and attracts a crowd of people who pay to see the performance. Well, one day I went up in a balloon, and the ropes got so twisted that I couldn't come down again. The balloon went way up above the clouds, and a current of air struck it and carried it many, many miles away. For a day and a night I traveled through the air, and on the morning of the second day I awoke and found the balloon floating over a strange and beautiful country.

"My balloon came down gradually, and I was not hurt. But I found myself among strange people. They had seen me come out of the clouds and thought I was a great and powerful Wizard. Of course I let them think this, because they were afraid of me and promised to do anything I asked them to.

"So I ordered them to build this City and to

Floating Over a Beautiful Land

construct this Palace. They did it all willingly. Then, I thought that since everything in this country was so green and beautiful, I would call it the Emerald City. To make the name fit even better, I put green eyeglasses on all the people. This way everything they saw was green."

"But isn't everything here green?" asked Dorothy.

"No more than in any other city," answered Oz. "But when you wear green glasses, of course everything looks green to you. The Emerald City was built many years ago when I was a young man. I am very old now. But the people here have worn green glasses for so long that most of them think this really is an Emerald City. I have been good to the people here, and they have been good to me. But since this palace was built I have shut myself up, and I have refused to see anyone.

"One of the things I have feared most is

"Isn't Everything Here Green?"

the evil power of the Witches. Since I have no magical powers at all, I knew that their powers could destroy me. I have lived in deadly fear of them for many years. I was very happy when I heard that your house fell on the Wicked Witch of the East. When you came to me, I was willing to promise anything if you would only do away with the Wicked Witch of the West. Now that you have melted her, I am ashamed to say that I cannot keep my promises."

"I think you are a very bad man," said Dorothy.

"Oh, no, I am really a very good man, but I will admit that I am a very bad Wizard," said Oz.

"Can't you give me some brains?" asked the Scarecrow.

"You don't need them. You learn something every day. Experience is the only thing that brings knowledge."

"I Am a Good Man, but a Bad Wizard."

"That may be true," said the Scarecrow, "but I will be very unhappy unless you give me brains."

"Well," Oz said with a sigh, "I am not much of a magician, as I said, but if you come to me tomorrow morning I will stuff your head with brains."

"Oh, thank you—thank you," cried the Scarecrow.

"But how about my courage?" asked the Lion anxiously.

"You have plenty of courage. All you really need is some confidence in yourself. Every living thing is afraid when it faces danger. True courage is facing danger even when you are afraid, and you already have that kind of courage."

"Maybe I have," answered the Lion, "but I am scared just the same. I would like you to give me the sort of courage that makes me forget to be afraid."

"Oh, Thank You!"

"Very well, I will give you that sort of courage tomorrow," said Oz.

"What about my heart?" asked the Tinman.

"I think you are lucky not to have a heart, for the heart is what makes most people unhappy," said Oz.

"That is your opinion," said the Tinman. "For my part, I will bear all the unhappiness without a word if you will give me the heart."

"Very well," answered Oz meekly. "Come to me tomorrow and you will have your heart. I have played Wizard long enough. I may as well continue for a little while longer."

Then Dorothy asked Oz how he would get her back to Kansas. The Wizard confessed that her request would take a little longer to fulfill. He asked them all to stay in the Palace for a few more days while he thought of a way to get Dorothy back to Kansas. In

"What About My Heart?"

the meantime, he asked them to keep his secret.

They all agreed to say nothing about what they had learned and went back to their rooms in high spirits, for they were all sure their wishes would be granted.

Their Wishes Will Be Granted.

The Wizard Sits by the Window.

Chapter 15
Oz Grants Three Wishes

The next morning, the Scarecrow went to see Oz and get his brains. He went to the Throne Room and knocked at the door.

"Come in," said Oz.

The Scarecrow went in and found the little man sitting by the window.

"I have come for my brains," said the Scarecrow.

"I have not forgotten," said Oz. "But I must take your head off in order to put your brains in their proper place."

"That's all right," said the Scarecrow. "You

are quite welcome to take my head off, as long as it will be a better one when you put it on again."

So the Wizard unfastened the Scarecrow's head and emptied out the straw. Then he went to the back room and mixed a cup of cereal with many pins and needles. He shook the mixture again and again. Then he filled the top of the Scarecrow's head with the mixture and stuffed the rest of the space with straw to hold it all in place.

When he fastened the Scarecrow's head back on his body again, Oz said, "From now on, you will be a great man, for you have brains."

The Scarecrow was pleased and proud, and he thanked the Wizard again and again.

When Dorothy saw the Scarecrow with all the needles and pins sticking out of his head, she was very surprised.

"How do you feel?" she asked him.

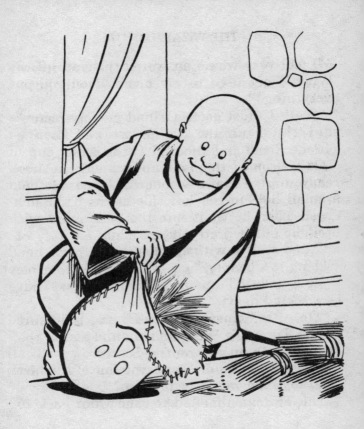

The Scarecrow's Brains

"I feel very wise," answered the Scarecrow. "When I get used to my brains I will know everything."

"Well, I must go to Oz and get my heart," said the Tinman. So he walked to the Throne Room and knocked at the door.

Oz welcomed the Tinman and said he was ready to give him a wonderful heart. He cut a small hole in the left side of the Tinman's chest. Then he went into the back room and brought out a pretty heart made entirely of silk and stuffed with sawdust.

"Isn't it a beauty?" Oz asked.

"It is indeed!" answered the Tinman. "But is it a kind heart?"

"Oh, very!" answered Oz. He put the heart in the Tinman's chest and then replaced the square of tin he had removed.

"There," he said. "Now you have a heart that any man would be proud of."

The Tinman thanked Oz and went back to

The Tinman's Heart

his friends. Everyone wished him joy and good luck with his new heart.

Next, it was the Lion's turn to get his courage. He walked to the Throne Room and knocked at the door.

"Come in," said Oz.

"I have come for my courage," announced the Lion as he entered the room.

"Very well," said Oz, "I will get it for you."

He went to a cupboard and took down a square green bottle. He poured the contents into a green dish. He placed this in front of the Lion, who sniffed at it as if he didn't like it. Then the Wizard said:

"Drink."

"What is it?" asked the Lion.

"Well," answered Oz, "if it were inside of you it would be courage. You know that courage is always inside. So this cannot really be called courage until you have swallowed it. I think you should drink it as soon

Oz Takes Down a Square Green Bottle.

as possible."

The Lion did not hesitate and drank until the dish was empty.

"How do you feel now?" asked Oz.

"Full of courage," answered the Lion. Then he went back to tell his friends of his good fortune.

Oz smiled to think of his success in giving the Scarecrow and the Tinman and the Lion exactly what they thought they needed. It was easy to make them happy, because they imagined that he could do anything. But Oz knew that it would be much more difficult to take Dorothy back to Kansas, and he was very worried because he was not at all sure how it could be done.

The Lion Drinks.

Ready to Face an Army

Chapter 16
How the Balloon Was Launched

For three days, Dorothy did not hear from Oz. This made her very sad and worried. The Scarecrow was very happy with his new brain and told everyone about the wonderful thoughts he had. The Tinman could feel his heart rattling around in his chest when he walked. He told Dorothy that in only a few days he had discovered how to be tender and kind. The Lion declared that he wasn't afraid of anything on earth, and that he would gladly face an army of men or a dozen fierce beasts.

Each one had his wish granted except for Dorothy, who wanted more than ever to return to Kansas.

After four days, Oz sent for Dorothy. When she entered the Throne Room, he said pleasantly:

"Sit down, my dear. I think I have found a way to get you out of this country."

"And back to Kansas?" she asked.

"Well, I am not sure about Kansas, since I am not really sure where it is. But the first thing to do is to cross the desert, and then it should be easy to find your way home. And there is only one way to cross the desert. I have been thinking the matter over, and I believe I can make a balloon which will carry you over the desert.

"How do you make a balloon?" asked Dorothy.

"A balloon," said Oz, "is made of silk, which is coated with glue to keep the gas in

"Sit Down, Dear."

it. There is plenty of silk in this city but there is no gas to fill the balloon so that it will float."

"If it won't float," said Dorothy, "it cannot help us cross the desert."

"True," answered Oz. "But there is another way to make it float. We can fill it with hot air. Of course, hot air is not as good as gas, for if the air should get cold the balloon will come down in the desert, and we will be lost."

"We!" cried Dorothy. "Are you going with me?"

"Yes, of course," said Oz. "I am tired of being such a fake. I don't want my people to discover that I am not a Wizard at all. I'd much rather go back to Kansas with you and be in the circus again."

So Dorothy and Oz cut the strips of silk and sewed them neatly together. When they finished this, Oz sent one of his soldiers to search for a large clothes basket. He tied the

Sewing the Silk Strips

basket to the bottom of the balloon with many ropes. He explained to Dorothy that they would ride in the basket.

When the balloon was finally finished, Oz sent word to his people that he was going to make a visit to a great brother Wizard who lived in the clouds. The news spread through the city, and everyone came to see the wonderful sight.

Oz ordered the balloon carried out in front of the Palace, and the people looked at it with curiosity. The Tinman chopped a big pile of wood and then made a fire of it. Oz held the bottom of the balloon over the fire so that the hot air rising from it would be caught inside. Soon the balloon swelled out and rose into the air, until finally the basket just touched the ground.

Then Oz got into the basket and said to all the people:

"I am going away for awhile. During the

The Curious Balloon

time that I am gone the Scarecrow will rule over you. I command you to obey him as you would obey me."

By this time, the balloon was tugging at the rope that held it to the ground. Since the air inside was hot, it was much lighter in weight than the air outside the balloon. The balloon was beginning to rise into the sky.

"Hurry up, Dorothy!" cried the Wizard, "or the balloon will fly away."

"I can't find Toto anywhere," answered Dorothy. Toto had run into the crowd to bark at a kitten. When Dorothy finally found him, she picked him up and ran toward the balloon.

She was only a few steps away, and Oz was holding out his hands to help her into the basket, when the ropes went—crack! The balloon rose into the air without her.

"Come back!" shouted Dorothy.

But it was too late. Oz was already riding

"Hurry Up, Dorothy!"

in the basket, rising farther and farther into the sky.

And that was the last any of them saw of Oz. No one ever knew if he reached Omaha safely, but everyone remembered him lovingly, and they were very sad to see him go.

Oz Drifts into the Sky.

Dorothy Is Very Unhappy.

Chapter 17
The Journey to the South

At first Dorothy was very unhappy about missing her chance to return to Kansas. She cried a lot that first day. But when she thought it all over, she was glad she did not go up in a balloon, although she also felt sorry about losing Oz.

The Scarecrow was now the ruler of the Emerald City. Although he was not a Wizard, the people were all proud of him. They bragged that there was not another city in all the world ruled by a stuffed man.

The morning after the balloon went up, the

four travelers met in the Throne Room to talk matters over. The Scarecrow sat in the big Throne, and the others sat in soft chairs beside him.

"We are all very lucky," he said, "for this Palace and the Emerald City belong to us, and we can do just as we please. When I remember that a short time ago I was up on a pole in a farmer's cornfield, and that now I am the ruler of this beautiful City, I am quite happy with what has happened to me."

The Tinman and the Lion expressed their satisfaction with the rewards Oz had granted them, and they too said they were content. Only Dorothy was still unhappy. She told her friends that although she loved them all very much, she still wanted to return to her home in Kansas.

The Scarecrow decided to think. He thought so hard that the pins and needles began to stick out of his brains.

The Scarecrow Sits in the Big Throne.

"Why not call the Winged Monkeys and ask them to carry you over the desert?"

"I never thought of that!" said Dorothy. "I'll go get the Golden Cap."

When she brought the Cap into the Throne Room, she spoke the magic words, and soon the band of Winged Monkeys flew in the open window and stood beside her.

"This is the second time you have called us," said the Monkey King. "What is your wish?"

"I want you to fly with me to Kansas," said Dorothy.

"That cannot be done," said the Monkey King. "We belong to this country alone, and we cannot leave it. There has never been a Winged Monkey in Kansas, and I suppose there never will be. We just do not belong there. We will be glad to serve you in any way we can, but we cannot cross the desert. Good-bye."

The Winged Monkeys Fly In.

The Monkey King bowed and then flew away through the window, followed by all his band.

Dorothy was almost ready to cry, she was so disappointed.

"I have wasted the charm of the Golden Cap for nothing," she said, "for the Winged Monkeys cannot help me."

The Scarecrow began thinking again, and his head bulged so much that Dorothy was afraid it would burst.

"Let's call in the soldier with the green beard," he said, "and ask his advice."

When the soldier entered the Throne Room, the Scarecrow asked him if he knew how Dorothy might cross the desert. The soldier explained that he knew of no one except Oz who had ever crossed the desert.

"Is there no one who can help me?" asked Dorothy.

The soldier thought a minute. Then he said:

The Scarecrow's Head Bulges.

"Perhaps Glinda can help you. She is the Good Witch of the South. She is the most powerful of all the Witches and rules over the Quadlings. Besides, her castle stands on the edge of the desert, so she may know a way to cross it."

"How can I get to her castle?" asked Dorothy.

"The road is straight to the South," he answered, "but it is said to be very dangerous for travelers."

When the soldier left, the Scarecrow said:

"It seems that in spite of the dangers, the best thing Dorothy can do is to travel to the Land of the South and ask Glinda for help. This will be the only way Dorothy will ever get back to Kansas."

The Lion, the Tinman and the Scarecrow thought for only a second, and then all said they would go with Dorothy. The journey would be long and dangerous, and they could

"How Can I Get to Glinda's Castle?"

not let their friend go all by herself.

Dorothy thanked them all, and they decided to return to their rooms and get ready for their long journey, which would begin at sunrise the next morning.

Dorothy Thanks Her Friends.

Sleeping on the Grass

Chapter 18
The Fighting Trees

The next morning, Dorothy and her friends said good-bye to the Guardian of the Gate and left the Emerald City.

The first day's journey was through the green fields and bright flowers that stretched around the Emerald City on every side. That night they slept on the grass and looked up at the velvet sky filled with bright stars.

In the morning they traveled until they came to a forest. The forest was very thick, and there seemed to be no way to go around it. So they looked for the place where it would be the easiest to get into the forest.

The Scarecrow discovered a big tree with wide-spreading branches that would allow everyone to pass underneath. But just as he came under the first branches they bent down and twined around him. The next minute, he was lifted from the ground and thrown through the air. This did not hurt the Scarecrow, but it surprised him, and he looked dizzy when Dorothy picked him up.

"Here is another space between the trees," called the Lion.

"Let me try it first," said the Scarecrow, "for it doesn't hurt me to be thrown around." He walked up to another tree. But immediately its branches grabbed him and tossed him back again.

"This is very strange," said Dorothy. "What shall we do?"

"The trees seem to have made up their minds to fight us and stop our journey," said

Grabbed by the Branches!

the Lion.

"Let me give this a try," said the Tinman. He put his axe on his shoulder and walked up to the first tree that had thrown the Scarecrow in the air. When a branch bent down to grab him, the Tinman chopped it in half. The tree began shaking in pain, and the Tinman walked safely under it.

"Come on!" he shouted to the others. "Hurry up!"

They all ran forward and passed under the tree without being hurt. The other trees did not try to stop them. So they decided that only the first row of trees could bend down their branches, and that these were the police force of the forest, who tried to keep strangers away.

The travelers walked to the edge of the forest. Then, to their surprise, they saw a high wall which seemed to be made of china. It was smooth like the surface of a dish, and

The Tinman Chops the Branch in Half.

much higher than their heads.

"What will we do now?" said Dorothy.

"I will make a ladder so we can climb over the wall," said the Tinman.

"I Will Make a Ladder."

The Scarecrow Watches the Tinman.

Chapter 19
The Dainty China Country

While the Tinman was making a ladder from wood which he found in the forest, Dorothy lay down and slept. She was very tired from the long walk. The Lion also curled up to sleep and Toto lay beside him.

The Scarecrow watched the Tinman while he worked and said to him:

"I cannot figure out why this wall is here or what it is made of."

"Rest your brains and do not worry about the wall," answered the Tinman. "When we have climbed over it we will know what is on the other side."

After a while the ladder was finished. It looked clumsy, but the Tinman was sure it was strong and would serve the purpose of getting them over the china wall. The Scarecrow woke Dorothy, Toto and the Lion. He told them that the ladder was ready. The Scarecrow climbed up the ladder first, but he was so awkward that Dorothy had to follow close behind to keep him from falling off. When he got his head over the top of the wall and could see, he said, "Oh, my!"

"Go on," shouted Dorothy.

So the Scarecrow climbed further up and sat down on the top of the wall, and Dorothy looked over and cried, "Oh, my!" just like the Scarecrow had done.

Then Toto came up and immediately began to bark, but Dorothy told him to be quiet.

The Lion climbed the ladder next, and then

Up the Ladder

the Tinman. Both of them said, "Oh, my!" as soon as they looked over the wall. When they were all sitting in a row on the top of the wall they looked down and saw a very strange sight.

Before them was a great stretch of land. The floor of the land was as smooth and shining and white as the bottom of a big plate. Scattered around were many houses made entirely of china and painted in bright colors. These houses were very small. The biggest one reached only as high as Dorothy's waist. There were also tiny barns painted red with china fences around them. There were cows, sheep, horses and pigs, all made of china.

But strangest of all were the people who lived in this unusual country. There were milkmaids and shepherdesses, who wore red and yellow blouses and skirts with golden spots. There were princesses with beautiful dresses of silver, gold and purple. The

Houses Made Entirely of China

shepherds were dressed in short pants with pink, yellow and blue stripes on them. Their shoes had golden buckles. There were princes with jeweled crowns and ermine robes. There were also clowns in ruffled gowns with round red spots on their cheeks and tall, pointed caps. But the strangest thing of all was that all these people were made of china. Even their clothes were made of china. And they were so small that the tallest one was no higher than Dorothy's knee.

At first, none of the little people even looked at the travelers. One little purple china dog with an extra-large head came to the wall and barked at them.

"How can we get down the other side of this wall?" asked Dorothy.

The ladder was so heavy they couldn't pull it up, so the Scarecrow fell off the wall. Then the others jumped down on him so the hard floor would not hurt their feet. They were

Tiny People Made of China

very careful not to land on his head and get the pins stuck in their feet. When they were all safely down, they picked up the Scarecrow and patted his straw back into shape.

"We must cross this strange place in order to get to the other side," said Dorothy, "for we really must continue going South."

They began walking through the country of the china people, and the first thing they came to was a china milkmaid milking a china cow. As they came near, the cow gave a kick and over went the stool, the pail and even the milkmaid herself. Everything fell on the china ground with a great clatter.

Dorothy was shocked to see that the cow had broken its leg off, and that the pail was lying in several small pieces. Even the milkmaid had a nick in her left elbow.

"See what you have done!" cried the milkmaid angrily. "My cow has broken her leg, and I must take her to the mender's shop

Over Goes the Milkmaid!

and have it glued on again. What do you mean coming here and frightening my cow?"

"I am really very sorry," said Dorothy. "Please forgive us."

But the milkmaid was too angry to answer. She picked up the leg and led the cow away. The poor animal limped on three legs.

Dorothy felt very bad about what had happened.

"We must be very careful here," said the kind-hearted Tinman, "or we may hurt these little people so they will never get over it."

A little further on Dorothy met a beautifully dressed Princess. The Princess stopped short when she saw the strangers, and she started to run away.

Dorothy wanted to see more of the Princess, so she ran after her, but the china girl cried out:

"Don't chase me! Don't chase me!"

She had such a frightened voice that

The Princess Starts to Run Away.

Dorothy stopped and asked, "Why not?"

"Because," answered the Princess, "if I run, I may fall down and break myself."

"But you could be mended, couldn't you?" asked Dorothy.

"Oh, yes; but one is never as pretty after being mended, you know," answered the Princess.

"I suppose not," said Dorothy.

"Now there is Mr. Joker, one of our clowns," continued the china woman, "who is always trying to stand on his head. He has broken himself so many times that he is mended in a hundred places and doesn't look at all pretty. Here he comes now, so you can see for yourself."

Indeed, a jolly little clown came walking by, and Dorothy could see that in spite of his pretty clothes of red, yellow and green, he was completely covered with cracks. It was clear that he had been mended in many

The Clown Is Covered with Cracks.

places.

Dorothy felt sad for the poor little clown. Then she turned to the beautiful Princess and said:

"You are so lovely, I am sure that I could love you dearly. I am going back to Kansas. Won't you let me carry you back in my basket, so when I get back home I can stand you on Aunt Em's mantelshelf?"

"That would make me very unhappy," answered the china Princess. "You see here in our own country we live happily and can talk and move around as we please. But whenever any of us are taken away our joints at once stiffen, and we can only stand straight and look pretty. Of course, that is all that is expected of us when we are on mantelshelves and cabinets and living room tables. Our lives are much more fun here in our own country."

"I understand," said Dorothy, "and I would

"Our Lives Are Fun Here."

not want to make you unhappy for anything in the world, so I will just say good-bye."

"Good-bye," answered the Princess.

They walked carefully through the china country. Little animals and people scampered out of their way, afraid they would be broken.

Soon they reached the other side of the country and came to another china wall. It was not as high as the first one, and by standing on the Lion's back they all managed to scramble to the top. Then the Lion gathered his legs under him and jumped the wall. Just as he did this he upset a china house with his tail and smashed it to pieces.

"That was too bad," said Dorothy, "but I think we were lucky that we did these people so little harm. They are all so delicate!"

"They certainly are," said the Scarecrow, "and I am thankful I am made of straw and cannot be hurt so easily. There are worse

Scrambling to the Top

things in the world than being a Scarecrow."

"They are so afraid of outsiders," said the Tinman. "They must have been treated badly by those who did not understand them."

Dorothy nodded her head in agreement as she took her last look at the china wall.

Before them lay a gloomy forest.

Dorothy Nods in Agreement.

A Steep Hill

Chapter 20
The Country of the Quadlings

The four travelers passed through the forest safely. When they came to the edge of the forest they saw a steep hill covered from top to bottom with large pieces of rock.

"This will be a difficult climb," said the Scarecrow, "but we must get over this hill."

So he led the way and the others followed. They had just reached the first rock when they heard a voice cry out, "Keep back!"

Then from behind the rock stepped out the

strangest man any of them had ever seen.

He was short and stout and had a big head which was flat at the top and supported by a thick, wrinkled neck. He had no arms at all. The Scarecrow saw this and did not think that such a helpless creature could prevent them from climbing the hill. So he said, "I am sorry not to do as you ask, but we must pass over this hill whether you like it or not."

As fast as lightning, the man's head shot forward, and his neck stretched out until the flat part of his head hit the Scarecrow in the stomach and sent him falling over down the hill. Then the creature's head returned to the body, and he laughed and said, "It is not as easy as you think!"

A chorus of laughter came from the other rocks, and Dorothy saw hundreds of the armless Hammer-Heads on the hillside.

They realized that it was hopeless to attempt to fight these strange creatures.

The Hammer-Head

"Let's call the Winged Monkeys," said the Tinman.

So Dorothy put on the Golden Cap and said the magic words. In a few minutes the Monkeys stood before her. Dorothy ordered the King of the Monkeys to carry them over the hill and into the country of the Quadlings.

At once, the Monkeys picked them up and flew away with them. As they passed over the hill the Hammer-Heads yelled with anger and shot their heads high in the air, but they could not even come close to the Winged Monkeys.

After they had been set down in the country of the Quadlings, the King of the Monkeys said good-bye to Dorothy and quickly flew away.

The country of the Quadlings was rich and happy. The fields were full of wheat, and there were pretty rippling brooks and well-paved roads. The houses were all painted

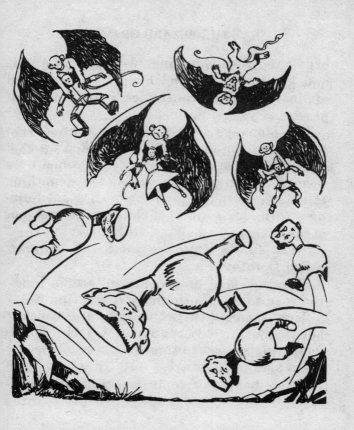

The Hammer-Heads Cannot Catch Them.

bright red. The Quadlings were short and fat and looked chubby and happy. They dressed all in red, which contrasted with the green grass and yellow grain.

The Monkeys set them down near a farm house, and the four travelers walked up to it and knocked at the door. It was opened by a farmer. When Dorothy asked for something to eat, the woman gave them all a good dinner, with three kinds of cake and four kinds of biscuits, and a bowl of milk for Toto.

"How far is it to the Castle of Glinda?" asked Dorothy.

"It is not far," answered the farmer. "Take the road to the South and you will find it."

They thanked the woman and walked until they saw a very beautiful Castle. Three young girls stood in front of the gates. One of them said to Dorothy:

"Why have you come to the South Country?"

The Quadlings

"To see the Good Witch," she answered. The girl asked them to wait a moment and went inside the Castle to tell Glinda they had come.

The Girl Asks Them to Wait.

A Beautiful Witch

Chapter 21
Glinda Grants Dorothy's Wish

After a few moments, the girl came back to say that Dorothy and the others were to be admitted to the Castle at once.

Before they went to see Glinda, they were taken to a room where they washed and fixed themselves up.

When they were all quite presentable they followed the girl into a big room where the Witch Glinda sat upon a throne of rubies.

She was a beautiful Witch. Her hair was a rich red and fell in curls and waves over her shoulders. Her dress was pure white, but her eyes were blue, and they looked kindly upon Dorothy.

"What can I do for you, my child?" she asked.

Dorothy told the Witch her long story. She left out nothing. She talked for a long time.

"My greatest wish now," she added, "is to get back to Kansas, for Aunt Em must be very worried."

Glinda leaned forward and kissed Dorothy's face.

"Bless your dear heart," she said. "I am sure I can tell you how to return to Kansas. But if I do you must give me the Golden Cap."

"Of course!" said Dorothy. "It is of no use to me now, and when you have it you may command the Winged Monkeys three times."

Glinda smiled knowingly, and Dorothy handed her the Golden Cap. She turned to the Scarecrow and asked, "What will you do

Glinda Kisses Dorothy.

when Dorothy has gone back to Kansas?"

"I will return to the Emerald City and be the ruler there," he answered.

Then Glinda asked the Tinman and the Lion where they would go after Dorothy had returned to her home. The Tinman thought for a moment and answered that he wished to return to the Land of the Winkies, and the Lion wanted to go back to his forest and be King of the Beasts.

Glinda knew that the journey back to these places would be long and difficult. So she explained that she would use the power of the Golden Cap to grant the Scarecrow, the Tinman and the Lion their wishes. The Winged Monkeys would carry them safely to their destinations.

The Scarecrow, the Tinman and the Lion thanked the Good Witch for her kindness. Then Dorothy said:

"You are certainly as good as you are

They Thank the Good Witch.

beautiful! But you have not yet told me how to get back to Kansas."

"Your silver shoes will carry you over the desert," answered Glinda. "If you had only known their power you could have gone back to your Aunt Em the very first day you came to this country."

"But then I would not have gotten my wonderful brains!" cried the Scarecrow.

"And I would not have received my kind heart," said the Tinman. "I might have stood and rusted in the forest forever!"

"And I would have always been a coward," said the Lion, "and no beast in all the forest would have a good word to say about me."

"This is all true," said Dorothy, "and I am glad I could help my friends. But now that they have got their wishes and are happy, I think I would like to return to my home in Kansas."

"The silver shoes have wonderful powers.

"Your Silver Shoes Will Carry You."

They will take you any place in the world in just three steps. All you have to do is knock the heels together three times and command the shoes to carry you wherever you wish to go," explained Glinda.

"If that is so," said Dorothy, "I will ask them to carry me back to Kansas."

She kissed the Lion, the Tinman and the Scarecrow good-bye. They all cried and hugged her tightly.

Glinda stepped down from her throne and kissed Dorothy good-bye. Dorothy thanked her for her kindness.

Then Dorothy took Toto in her arms, said one last good-bye to her friends, and clapped the heels of her shoes together three times and said:

"Take me home to Kansas!"

In a few seconds she was whirling through the air so fast that all she could see or feel was the wind whistling past her ears.

Whirling Through the Air

Happy to Be Home Again

Chapter 22
Home Again

Aunt Em had just come out of the house to water the cabbages when she looked up and saw Dorothy running toward her.

"My darling child!" she cried, as she held Dorothy in her arms and covered her face with kisses. "Where in the world did you come from?"

"From the Land of Oz," said Dorothy. "And here is Toto too. And Aunt Em, I am so happy to be home again!"

ILLUSTRATED CLASSIC EDITIONS

ILLUSTRATED CLASSIC EDITIONS

ILLUSTRATED CLASSIC EDITIONS

Mr. Bently Pierce frowned. "Please—Catlin is not a *kid*," he intoned with the air of long-suffering distaste. "She is a little girl, and thanks to your tardiness, we are running late. So if you would—"

Somewhere beyond the formally appointed foyer, the phone rang and the man made an impatient, imperious sound in his throat. Unfazed, Catlin laughed and made a grab at his nose. The man smiled, a quick breathtaking flash of white teeth, and then it was gone.

"I'll have to get that. Would you mind?" He held the baby out and Raine automatically took her. Nestling comfortably in Raine's waiting arms, the baby settled in as if she'd been there a hundred times before.

"You're a cutie, you know that?"

Catlin obviously did. She squealed her delight, shoving her fists into her mouth, making Raine laugh as she gummed her tiny fingers. She smelled of Ivory Soap and talcum and the faint, grainy smell of the baby cereal still stuck to her fingers.

Behind them, the man who sounded even less like a father than he looked, barked into the phone. "Yes, of course...I'm on my way.... Look, it wasn't my idea to move the meeting up. If I'd been informed earlier..." Then, through an obviously tightened jaw, "I *said* I'd be there."

Raine felt Catlin's little body jump as he slammed the phone down, a startled expression stilling the animation of her face for just an instant before she grinned again and held out her arms to her approaching father.

The man took one chubby hand and kissed it. "Sorry, pet, I've got to run. You be a good girl for Ms.—ah—" He sent a raised brow Raine's way.

For the beat of a few seconds she was silent as she stared at his darkly handsome face. He made a sound in his throat, and she pulled herself together. After all, he was hardly her type. Sexy? Yes, in an angry sort of way. Good-looking? No doubt about it—if you liked dark suits and expensive haircuts. But Raine was used to her men in baseball caps and T-shirts. Bently Pierce was out of her league. Way out.

"Ah—Rogers," she finally supplied. "But—"

"Look," the man began as he retrieved a briefcase from the foyer table, stuffing papers inside on his way to the door, "I know this is irregular, but I really have no choice. The interview will have to wait until I return." He stopped long enough to cast an uneasy glance over Raine, sparing time for a disapproving frown at her jeans and oversize sweatshirt. Tapping a finger against his generous, mobile mouth, he gave Raine a narrow-eyed appraisal. "The agency did recommend you, so I suppose—" With an impatient movement he shrugged and moved toward the door once again.

Raine started after him. "Wait—I think someone goofed here. I'm not—"

"Please Ms., ah, Rogers, bear with me on this. I should return in an hour or two. We can settle things then."

Shifting the squirming baby in her arms, Raine looked helplessly at the closing door. "Here, kid," she muttered, placing the baby on the floor, "stay put a minute.'' She yanked the door open in time to see the man slide into a sleek black car. "Wait!" she called, but out of the corner of her eye she saw Catlin start to crawl rapidly toward the living room. Any baby who could move that fast could get into all kinds of trouble in a matter of seconds. Raine gave up and slammed the door, hurrying after the retreating rump of baby Catlin, suddenly glad that she hadn't had the chance to inform Mr. Bently Pierce of the small lump of baby cereal Catlin had managed to deposit on the end of his long, aristocratic nose.

BENTLY BATTLED a mild sense of unease as he fought for position in the stream of Milwaukee morning traffic. The woman hadn't looked anything like his idea of a nanny. But then neither had the last one the agency sent over. It had taken him only one week to figure out that the woman was more interested in watching soap operas on his twenty-seven-inch stereo TV than she was in taking care of Catlin. When he'd opened the door this morning he'd hoped to see a comfortably cushioned older woman who would know Dr. Spock by rote and wear homely little jersey dresses in absurd floral prints. A grandmotherly type who would fall immediately in love with Catlin, dote on her every coo and follow her every crawl. He definitely hadn't pictured a tall, raw-boned woman whose blunt-cut chin-length hair had a disconcerting habit of hiding half her face and whose long, slender legs looked terrific in blue jeans.

Bently chuckled to himself. Now where had that thought come from? He'd barely had time to notice the woman's age, yet a picture of those long legs in tight, faded denim was planted firmly in his mind. Still, the fact remained that she wasn't his idea of anyone to entrust little Catlin to. And maybe he wouldn't have, but this morning he'd had no choice. His job was on the line. Oh, no one had said so in so many words, but the implications were there. This was one meeting he had better not miss. What with trying to find a suitable nanny, he'd missed far too many. Ever since his little girl had been born, his priorities had changed.

Once, his position as legal counsel in acquisitions and mergers at Wesley and Harper was the most important thing in his life. It was everything he'd worked for, everything he'd wanted when he'd chosen corporate law way back in law school. The killing triumph of a takeover, the excitement of a profitable merger— being the best, getting the best. And the money. Caroline had understood it all, had shared it all. But Caroline hadn't understood how he'd felt when he'd learned of the life they'd created together growing inside her—and in the end, she hadn't wanted to share in it.

So little Catlin was his and his alone. And in the seven months he'd watched her grow, the rest of his life had paled by comparison. The need to prove himself to a father now long dead, the need to succeed at all costs—all this and more were shattered by that first heart-piercing cry, that one tiny smile, the love he already saw in his little girl's eyes. Nothing would ever mean as much again.

Bently pulled off the road and drove the short distance to the parking garage beneath one of the twin glass towers on Milwaukee's northwest side—the home of Wesley and Harper. The buildings rose like two mirrored monoliths, reflecting the vastness of the Midwestern sky and the flat, empty land that surrounded them; land purchased and hoarded with the creation of an empire in mind.

He strode through the modern lobby with its hushed tones of mauve and gray, glancing at his watch as he entered the empty elevator. Fifteen minutes late. Once he'd have been appalled to be late at all. Now he congratulated himself on his timing. But when he reached the twentieth floor and opened the conference-room door to ten nearly identical suits, ten similar haircuts and ten frowning faces, he knew that his days of power at Wesley and Harper were numbered.

He opened his mouth to explain—which was when he caught sight of his reflection in the high polish of the conference table. What on earth was that on the end of his nose?

RAINE GROANED. "What am I gonna do with a baby?" she muttered. Not that Catlin didn't appear to be a perfectly delightful baby—she did nothing but smile and gurgle with pleasure as she rode Raine's hip while Raine sped aimlessly through the condo looking for some clue what to do.

Raine loved babies. She truly did. It was the main reason she'd started a diaper service in the first place, to have some sort of contact with the babies she would never be able to have. But she had a business to run, a route to deliver. Mothers were waiting for diapers. She pictured babies' bottoms all over Milwaukee, powdered and ready—and bare. She couldn't afford to lose any business. People counted on her to deliver when she said she would. It was one of her main selling points that her diapers would always be there. Aside from the grisly facts on how disposables messed up landfills, this was the most successful part of her sales pitch.

Raine's pointless wandering came to an end in Catlin's well-appointed nursery. Surveying the modern equipment, the colorful toys and the adorable bunny wallpaper, she muttered, "Geesh, your old man must really be loaded, kid." Catlin gurgled her assent. "Where's your mom this morning, huh?" Catlin looked at her blankly, her pouty little baby mouth sucking her fist. Indeed, except for the cloyingly feminine decor in the living room and foyer, Raine had seen no evidence of a maternal presence. Maybe the kid didn't have one. Maybe she was a motherless child, just as Raine had been.

"Poor thing," she murmured, nuzzling the baby's soft dark hair. If little Cat had no one for comfort but an arrogant, overbearing old man who seemed only too ready to dump the poor kid on a perfect stranger, then all the toys and doodads in the world wouldn't make up for it. Nothing made up for growing up with a father who couldn't care less—how well Raine knew that. If fate hadn't taken away her chance to be a mother, she would never have left her baby's side. Not for a minute.

"Well, why not?" she mused. If she had a baby, she'd most likely take it to work with her. So that's exactly what she'd do with little Cat.

She shifted the baby again and peered at her watch. "Time's a-wastin', kid. Looks like you're gonna have to go for a ride."

After a little rummaging, Raine located a car seat—state of the art, of course—and a folding stroller in a closet. She stuffed Catlin into a pink quilted snowsuit, shoved a knitted cap on her head and managed to get everything out to the van in one trip. By the time she figured out how the car seat worked, Catlin's sunny disposition began to crumple, an impatient wail distorting her sweet little mouth.

Raine slid into the van beside her. "Come on, kid, give me a break. I haven't had much practice at this, y'know." Catlin wailed on, punching her little fists into the air. "Hey, don't blame me. Blame your old man." Catlin ignored this plea, sending Raine rummaging frantically in the glove compartment for anything that looked as if it might amuse a baby. She came up with a cellophane-wrapped package of soda crackers—when was the last time she'd had chili to go? Raine shrugged. "Beggars can't be choosers, kid." She tore open the package and thrust a crumbling cracker into Catlin's hand.

The wailing stopped immediately as Catlin eyed the cracker with interest. After only two shaky tries, she located her mouth and began sucking on the salty square.

Raine sighed in relief and started the van.

"Ms. ROGERS?" Bently called as soon as he'd unlocked the door of the condo. The place seemed altogether too quiet. "I'm back!" he called out with false cheer when his query was met with silence.

He made his way to the kitchen, refusing to acknowledge the spear of foreboding piercing his gut.

Empty. Clean as he had left it that morning. No half-empty baby bottles on the counter. No dirty coffee cup in the sink.

"Catlin?" he called. Despite the knowledge that a seven-month-old could hardly answer, he hoped something—her little laugh, a happy gurgle, an angry cry—would announce her presence.

In the silence, he ran to his study and flung open the door. The leather sofa was empty, the television cold. He ran to the doorway of the living room, his gaze sweeping the white-and-gold splendor of Caroline's idea of decorating. But the room was empty and chilly, as always.

He started for the nursery—then stopped, willing himself to walk, to take his time. It was the last, the only place she could be. If her crib was empty—then what?

Then he would know he was right. He should never have entrusted the only thing that mattered to him in life to a woman like Ms. Rogers.

Quietly, slowly, he opened the nursery door.

Light streamed in the open curtains at the window. The crib was empty.

"Hell," he muttered, "what now?" He ran once again through the condo, checking for unseen notes. He flung open closet doors—checking for he knew not what. Anything, *anything* to tell him where they were—to tell him Catlin was all right.

He went outside. The terrace off the kitchen was empty, the alley behind the condo deserted, gloomy with a winter reluctant to give way to spring.

Inside again, he grabbed the phone to call the agency. That's when he saw the flashing red light on the answering machine.

Of course, he thought, a message. They'd taken a drive, she'd had car trouble. She did have a car, didn't she? He tried to remember how she'd arrived, what had been parked outside when he'd left in such a hurry. How could he have been so stupid, so unthinking about something that concerned the welfare of his daughter?

He pressed the playback on the machine, trying to still the pounding in his chest.

But it wasn't Ms. Rogers's voice he heard.

"Mr. Pierce? This is Mrs. Allen down at Wee Care. The applicant we promised you this morning has taken ill—"

That was all he heard before he snatched up the receiver and punched out the Wee Care number.

"Mrs. Allen? You sent another applicant out this morning, didn't you?"

"Mr. Pierce? Is that you?"

Bently squeezed his eyes shut and prayed for patience. "Yes—yes, it's me. Just tell me you sent someone else this morning."

"But, Mr. Pierce, we didn't. Didn't you get my message?"

"Yes." Bently looked at the machine. "I mean, no—look, that's not important. Just, please, tell me you sent someone else."

"But we didn't. Mr. Pierce, is anything wr—"

Bently slowly lowered the phone, the clatter it made as it hit the cradle the only noise in the silent house.

His baby had been stolen! Kidnapped by a woman he'd never seen before! A woman whose first name he didn't even know! He had no idea of what kind of car she drove, or a license number. Nothing. Nothing at all to tell the police, he thought as he picked up the phone.

He gripped the receiver till his knuckles turned white. What could he say? *Officer, I handed my baby over to this woman... No, I don't know who she was, but she had these great legs and—*

He slammed down the receiver and strode to the front door. "To hell with a phone call!" he shouted to the silent, empty house. "I'm going down to the police station myself." Maybe they had pictures he could look at. Maybe this wasn't Ms. Rogers's first kidnapping.

As he whipped out of the driveway and squealed down the street, he fervently hoped that mug shots included legs, because that was about all he remembered—those terrific damn legs!

"SO YOU'VE FINALLY done it. You've kidnapped a baby!"

Raine looked up from the stack of diapers she was wrapping to find Deirdre Marsh leaning in the doorway, then glanced at Cat, who was dozing peacefully in her stroller. "I'm just baby-sitting—sort of."

Deirdre raised a perfectly arched brow. "How do you baby-sit sort of?"

Raine shrugged. "It's a long story."

"Well, you couldn't have chosen better—she's a precious little thing."

"I didn't *choose* her, Dee. She was just kind of dumped on me."

"Really?" Dee drawled, a lilt of disbelief in the word.

"Yes. Really."

"Well, can I hold her?"

"Geesh, Dee, can't you see she's asleep? Besides, she might drool on your Armani."

Dee looked down at her red suit. "It isn't Armani. It's Donna Karan, darling. But you're probably right," she added with a little grimace of distaste.

Deirdre Marsh owned a boutique, playfully called Marshland, and took full advantage of buying wholesale. Her own best customer, she always looked impeccable, from her short, sleekly sophisticated black hair, to the tips of her scarlet nails, to the curve of her silk-clad legs.

Raine rented space from Dee behind the boutique for Cotton Tails, along with a room above that she called home. Despite the fact that the two women seemed to be exact opposites, they'd become friends.

When the last of the diapers was wrapped and loaded on the truck for the next round of deliveries, Raine followed Dee into the boutique to cop some of the imported coffee she kept brewed for her customers.

Sipping a cup, she watched Dee sort among a silver tray jumbled with jewelry, looking for something Cat, now wide awake and starting to fuss, could play with.

"Ah, here." Deirdre held up a pink-ice tennis bracelet. "This should do."

Raine grabbed it before her friend could hand it to the baby. "Dee, for heaven's sakes, you can't give a kid something like that to play with."

Deirdre's eyes were wide. "Whyever not? Look, I know pink-ice is a little tacky—"

"It's not a matter of taste, Dee."

Dee gave her a quelling look. "What could be more important than taste?"

"Choking, Dee. That thing will slide right down little Cat's throat. Haven't you got a scarf or something?"

Dee ran her manicured hands through a rack of colorful silk. "Here." She grabbed a square of shocking pink and chartreuse. "It's been on clearance for ages. Nobody seems to want it."

Cat clutched the silk in her tiny fist, the colors riveting her attention.

"Well, Cat likes it."

"Yes," Dee drawled, "the child has appalling taste. Good thing Auntie Raine brought you to me, precious. Lord knows you'd never learn anything about style from her." She gave the gurgling baby a pat on the head, then turned her attention back to Raine. "So—are you going to tell me who you kidnapped her from?"

"I told you, she was dumped on me by a hunk of ice in an expensive suit who doesn't deserve to be called Daddy."

Dee raised her brows. "Expensive suit? Ralph Lauren, maybe?"

Raine rolled her eyes ceilingward. "How should I know? I can't tell a Ralph Lauren from a Lauren Bacall. The point is, the guy doesn't deserve a kid like Cat and it would serve him right if someone *did* steal her!" Raine handed her empty cup to Dee. "And when I take her back, I just might tell him so!"

Raine piloted the stroller out of Marshland and strapped Cat, still clutching the silk scarf, into the van. The baby gave a huge yawn, stuffed her tiny fist under her chin and promptly fell asleep.

Raine stroked Cat's downy cheek with her finger and smiled softly. She felt her heart swell with love as she watched this little girl she'd only known a matter of hours. What was it about Cat that got to her so? Since she'd started Cotton Tails, her days were scattered with babies. They came and went in her life, in her arms. A poor substitute perhaps for the children she could never have, but so far they'd managed to fill that void, to keep her heart from breaking. But none of them had clamored at her heart the way Cat did. True, even as babies went, she was exceptionally beautiful, with her dark curly hair and huge brown eyes, her round rosy cheeks and her pouty little mouth that so easily broke into a grin. But it wasn't just the perfect picture of her that was carving out what felt like a permanent place in Raine's heart.

Was it the absolute trust the baby seemed to place in her? All day, every time she awoke from a doze, Cat's big, brown eyes surveyed her surroundings soberly, until they found Raine. And then the eyes would light up like the sun, the mouth would giggle and gurgle—and Raine's heart would open a little more. She only hoped that one day with this little angel wasn't going to leave a hole that could never be filled again.

Raine eased the van to the curb in front of the condo. The driveway was still empty. "Looks like Daddy's still not home," she muttered under her breath.

Catlin slept peacefully in her car seat, sated by the bottle of milk Raine had begged from one of her customers. Her sweet little face scrunched up, her head lolling to one side, she was a tiny angel with a smear of milk drying on her cheek, clutching a pure silk scarf in one of her sticky little hands.

Raine got out of the van and sauntered up to the condo, punching the doorbell repeatedly with her finger. Maybe Daddy wasn't back yet, but Cat's invisible mom might have returned from her bridge club or clothes fitting—or wherever ladies who lunched went after lunch. But nobody came.

Raine strode angrily back to the van. The man said he'd be back in a couple of hours. It was now late afternoon. What could he have been thinking of, to just dump his kid on a perfect stranger and then disappear?

And what if he was gone for good? What if he had really abandoned Cat and was never coming back?

The baby stirred when Raine climbed back into the van. Raine watched her. She'd only known Cat a matter of hours and already she was hating the thought of giving her up. How could her own father?

An impossible scenario skittered through Raine's mind. What if she started the van and went home? What if she just kept the baby for herself? And if *Mr.* Bently Pierce had second thoughts about abandoning his daughter to a complete stranger it would be his tough luck.

She'd have the baby she always wanted.

Raine reached out and touched Cat's cheek again. "I wish you were mine, Cat," she whispered. "But I could no more kidnap a sweet little thing like you than I could pitch for the Milwaukee Brewers."

Cat opened her eyes and yawned, moving her head to take in her surroundings, her pouty little mouth breaking into a smile when she spotted Raine.

Raine swallowed the lump in her throat and started the van. "Say, kid," she said to Cat, "did I ever tell you about my fast ball?"

BENTLY TORE into the police station. "My baby's been kidnapped!" he yelled.

The place suddenly became very, very quiet.

"Well, well." A big man who seemed to be in charge ambled over to the nearest desk, rubbing the back of his neck. "Don't get many kidnappings out here in the suburbs." The desk chair creaked tiredly as he lowered himself into it. "Name's Wood—Detective Wood. And you're . . . ?"

"Bently Pierce."

"Well, now, Mr. Pierce, why don't you take a chair and tell me all about it."

Bently sat and started to talk. At the end of his tale, the least he expected was a force of not less than six men to strap on their weapons and head for the door. But the entire room remained silent, seemingly chained to their desks and going nowhere. Except for one young uniformed officer, who strode over to lean on the nearest desk, his mouth twisted with slight amusement. Bently felt like punching him in the nose, but Detective Wood was asking another question in his slow, maddening manner, his fingers curling around the lapel of his rumpled brown suit.

"I told you," Bently answered, "I thought she was from Wee Care. The nanny agency," he added when he saw the puzzled frown on Detective Wood's face.

The detective scratched his head, running his hand over his thinning gray hair then clamping it around the back of his neck, just as he had the first time Bently had told his story. "But she wasn't?" he slowly asked.

Bently was losing patience. "No," he bit out, "she wasn't."

"Well, then, who was she?"

"If I knew that I wouldn't be here—I'd be out finding her myself!"

Detective Wood scratched his head again, and Bently started to wonder if it was made out of the same substance as his last name.

"Let's try that description once more..."

Sighing heavily, Bently ran his hands through his hair. "I told you, I don't remember much about her.

She had this way of dipping her head so her hair covered her face."

"Hair? What color?"

"Wheat," Bently replied immediately.

The detective wrinkled his brow. "Wheat? You mean like what they make bread out of?"

Bently nodded enthusiastically. "Wheat," he stated again with more determination. "Like a field of it in the sun."

Detective Wood shifted his look to the uniformed officer leaning on the next desk. The officer rolled his eyes.

Wood wrote on the sheet before him. "Anything else?"

"Just that she had—"

The detective looked down at the sheet again. "Just that she had great legs," he filled in, a grin twitching his mouth.

The uniformed officer snickered and Bently felt the need to explain himself. "Well, they were long, and she had on these worn jeans—"

Detective Wood's grin grew wider, and Bently stood up abruptly, pushing his chair back with such force that it skittered across the floor, bounced off an unoccupied desk and landed on its side, causing more than one cop to jump to the ready. Wood shook his head and they settled down again.

"Look," Bently clipped out, his barely controlled temper darkening his eyes, thinning his mouth, "my daughter is missing! *She is only seven months old!* What possible difference does it make what kind of legs the woman had?"

Detective Wood scratched again, apparently unfazed by Bently's outburst or the quick trip one of his chairs had taken. "Well, Mr. Pierce, if you could give us more to go on—like what kind of car she was driving."

"I told you, I never saw her car! And I didn't exactly take close inventory of what she looked like. I doubt I'd know her if she just this moment walked through that door!" He pointed at the stationhouse door just as it opened.

"That's her!" he yelled. "And that's *my* baby!"

Chapter Two

Raine froze just inside the doorway, tightening her hold on Cat as Bently rushed toward her.

"Oh, no you don't!" she shouted, twisting away from him, shielding Cat with her body.

Catlin looked startled, then her face creased into a smile and she giggled, peering over Raine's shoulder with huge, glowing eyes.

"Catlin, are you all right? Come to Daddy." Bently held out his arms, but Catlin simply buried her face against Raine's shoulder and giggled again.

Bently turned helplessly to Detective Wood. "Aren't you going to do anything? That's my baby and that—" he pointed at Raine again "—is the woman who stole her! I demand that you arrest her for kidnapping at once!"

Detective Wood ambled over, patting his paunch, giving Raine the once-over. "Well, she's got the legs, all right."

Behind him, the uniformed officer snickered.

Bently thrust his hand into his hair. "This is preposterous! This woman waltzes off with my child and—"

Raine had heard enough. "Hold it, Pierce. I didn't exactly waltz off with her. You gave her to me—*dumped* her on me, in fact."

Wood looked from Raine back to Bently. "That true?"

"I told you, I thought she was the new nanny! She totally misrepresented herself so she could make off with my child."

Wood took his time thinking it over, scratching his head and rubbing the back of his neck. "Well, Mr. Pierce, if that's so, what's the lady doing here? Seems to me a police station is the last place she'd wanna be." He turned to Raine. "Just what is it brings you here, ma'am?"

Raine raised Cat higher on her hip, gave Bently a self-satisfied look and strode boldly forward. "I'm here to report an abandoned baby," she stated calmly and emphatically. Then, throwing another look at Bently, she added, "And a clear case of child neglect."

Detective Wood shook his head, opened a drawer and slipped out another sheet of paper, handing it to Raine. "Okay, lady. Give us your statement and we'll get in touch with Child Protection."

"Wait just a minute!" Bently grabbed the paper from Raine's hand. "You can't do this!"

Raine snatched the paper back. "Watch me."

"Look, Detective Wood." Bently leaned frantically across the desk, fixing the detective with a dark-eyed, intense look, his words slow and heavy with conviction. "I have never neglected my child—ever. I left her in good faith with a woman who totally misrepresented herself as a nanny sent by the agency I'd contracted."

Raine elbowed Bently aside. "That's *his* story! Ask him why he never gave me the chance to explain that I wasn't who he thought I was. Ask him why he was in such an all-fired hurry to get to his *big meeting*—" her tone dripped sarcasm as her eyes flashed briefly at Bently "—that he barely took the time to ask my name."

Catlin gurgled, sucking on a finger and looking at her father as if waiting for the answer herself.

Wood scratched again. "Took the time to notice your legs, though."

"What?"

Bently rushed in before the detective could say more. "Why hasn't this woman been arrested? I'm telling you that's my baby and she's the one who took her!"

Raine thrust her chin out. "Tell you what, Pierce, I'll turn myself in just as soon as I file this complaint against you—and then I'll see you in court." She stalked over to the uniformed officer, grabbed a pen out of his shirt pocket and started to write, all the while holding a spellbound, wide-eyed Catlin on her outthrust hip.

"She can't do that, can she?" Bently asked in a panic.

Wood shrugged. "Sure can. In fact it's her civic duty to do so."

Raine shot Bently a triumphant look, then resumed writing.

"This is going too far!"

"Yup," Wood said, "I'm inclined to agree with that. In fact, if you'll turn the little lady over to me—"

Raine reluctantly handed Cat over. But when Bently smiled and held out his arms, Wood stood his ground. "Not so fast, Mr. Pierce."

"Look, I can prove she's mine." He dug in his pocket for his wallet. "I have papers, pictures—"

"Oh, I believe she's yours, all right. Even Ms. Rogers here doesn't dispute that. I just think you can save yourselves—and the county—lots of time, not to mention money, if you straighten this thing out yourselves."

"And just how do you propose we do that?" Bently bit out.

"Wilson," Detective Wood ordered, turning to the officer, "stick 'em in holding cell number two. Let 'em cool their heels a bit." He chucked Catlin under the chin, beaming like a grandfather. "I'll take care of the little lady here."

Officer Wilson could barely contain his glee. "Yes, sir!" he rang out. Before either Bently or Raine could recover from the shock, he had each of them by the arm and was dragging them out of the room.

"Wait just a minute!" barked Bently. "You can't do this! I demand a lawyer—wait a minute, I *am* a lawyer!" His voice louder, all bite and bark, he amended, "I *demand* a phone call!"

"Yeah!" Raine said, trying to dig her heels in and slow down the whole darn process. "I want a phone call, too! On TV everyone always gets a phone call!"

Wood chuckled. "That's only if I'm arresting you. And I ain't—I'm just holding you."

Bently craned his head around to gape disbelievingly. The last thing he saw before being dragged out the door to the holding cell was Catlin, a happy grin on her sweet little mouth, an atrociously colored scarf waving from one tiny fist.

THE CELL DOOR clanged shut.

"Unbelievable," Raine muttered as she started to pace.

Bently watched her angry strides, his gaze drifting helplessly down to study her legs. His mind hadn't tricked him; they were every bit as great as he'd remembered. A truly unforgettable pair.

They stopped right in front of him and his gaze moved leisurely up her body to her face.

"What do you think you're looking at?" she demanded.

He almost smiled. "Do you always have such a chip on your shoulder?"

"Being falsely accused of kidnapping tends to make me mad." Slowly, her lips moved into a dangerous little grin. "I don't know—guess I'm just funny that way."

His face sobered; his mouth tightened. "You think I like being accused of child neglect any better?"

She let her look trail down to his gorgeously tailored chalk-stripe suit and dark silk shirt—continen-

tal, a little dangerous—and back up to his eyes, more
dangerous still. Raine had always thought of brown
eyes as friendly—warm and inviting. Bently Pierce's
eyes were another matter entirely. Huge and deep, they
glared at her from beneath thick-lashed, heavy lids.
His dark hair, gleaming like black silk in the harsh
glow of the bare bulb swinging slightly in its wire cage
overhead, swept away from his forehead to fall longer
in back, curling up against his collar. His nose was
long, straight, his mouth full and, at the moment,
grim.

Her eyes fixed on his again, holding his gaze with
the sheer force of her anger. "Well, now, Mr. Pierce,
guess you should have thought of that when you
abandoned Cat to a perfect stranger this morning."

Pewter, Bently thought nonsensically. Her eyes were
the color of pewter, an arresting contrast to the color
of the hair that nearly obscured them. Autumn wheat
touched with gold, as if the sun shone on her even in-
doors, even in the dismal holding cell of a jail. He'd
been right about her hair, but how had he missed the
color of those eyes? Almond shaped, ringed with
thick, sooty lashes, they were at odds with the tone of
her hair and paleness of her skin. Her mouth, naked
of artificial color, bloomed wide beneath a nose that
was large and slightly bony, the bump down the center adding to the impression she gave of being a
fighter.

Her long legs were braced, her hands thrust into her
pockets, and the defiant look on her face told him that
she was prepared, and more than willing, to fight for
his daughter's welfare.

He stared into her eyes, willing himself back to anger that he suddenly suspected might be misplaced. "Her name is Catlin," he clipped out in quiet tones, "and I *did not* abandon her. If you had only told me you weren't from Wee Care, I never would have left her at all."

"So we're back to that—back to it being my fault!" She flung her head sideways, stuffing her hands into her pockets. "And sure, why not? After all, I'm the one wearing an old pair of jeans. You're the one in the designer suit."

Bently grinned without humor. "Your chip is showing again, Ms. Rogers."

Her hands came out of her pockets and fisted on her narrow hips. "You want chip, Pierce, I'll give you chip! While you were out gallivanting around town, earning another million, I was trying to keep my business together with a baby I knew nothing about attached to my hip! While you were out living life on the fast track, I was doing the work of three people and entertaining *your kid* at the park—"

"You took Catlin to the park?" Bently interrupted in quiet astonishment.

Her hands relaxed, diving into her pockets again, and she dipped her head and shrugged. "It was near one of my stops."

"Did you put her on the baby swings? She loves the baby swings—"

Raine grinned. "Yeah, you should have seen her. She squealed loud enough for two kids."

Bently sank onto the bunk against the wall. "Don't you just love her laugh?" He'd been away from his daughter all day and was missing far more than her laugh.

"Oh, yeah," Raine drawled, walking over to sit on the bunk beside him. "You should have heard her on the merry-go-round."

Bently raised his brows. "You put her on the merry-go-round?"

"Well, we were the only ones and I held her the whole time."

"She didn't get sick?" he cut in.

"No, I went real slow. She loved it. The kid's a real trouper, Pierce."

Bently beamed with pride. "Catlin's special."

"She sure is," Raine agreed.

"Do you have children of your own?" Bently asked.

The question brought her head around, the pewter eyes nailing him before she jumped to her feet.

"Knock it off!"

"What?" he asked, wondering what had changed her mood so abruptly.

She was back to her pacing. "I know what you're doing—you're trying to charm me. You're attempting to use your daughter and your sex appeal to charm and manipulate me into not filing a complaint."

Bently stood. "It's called conversation, Ms. Rogers." A grin teased at his lips. "And I have absolutely no control over the fact that you find me charming and sexy."

She stopped pacing, crossed her arms and gave him a haughty look. "In your dreams, Pierce."

The grin solidified. "You said it, Ms. Rogers, not I."

Yeah, she'd said it, but she hadn't meant it—not the way he'd taken it, anyway. He stood there, suit jacket thrust back by the hands in his pants pockets, his tie still perfectly knotted, silk shirt stretched across his muscled chest. Yeah—some women might find him sexy. Some women might find him charming. Not her. She was too smart to be manipulated by a fancy suit and a few muscles.

She turned away from him, walking to the bars that held them in together, wrapping her hands around them, leaning her forehead against the cool steel.

"Listen, Pierce, I just want to get out of here. Spending the night in a one-bunk cell with Mr. Suburban Milwaukee isn't my idea of paradise."

Paradise. Bently scanned her long legs and thought there just might be something to the word—jail cell or not. She started to pace again and he found himself wondering what all that emotion and energy could yield if she decided to put a smile on some guy's face.

What was he thinking of? Pulling her down on the bunk and whiling away the hours of captivity with a little carnal activity? That should surely convince her of his fitness as a father!

This was no time to indulge in fantasies about Ms. Rogers—and it was definitely time they got out of there.

He moved in front of her, forcing her to stop her restless pacing.

"There's only one way we're ever going to get out of here."

She crossed her arms again and cocked her hip. "This better be good, considering you're the one who's the lawyer."

"Tell me why you showed up at my door this morning."

"What?"

"Convince me you had a legitimate reason for being there. After all, when I asked you if you were there about Catlin you said you were."

"I was!" she shot back.

"So tell me why." He took a step closer to her, his gaze going from her pewter eyes to her full, defiantly tilted mouth, and back up again. "Convince me," he demanded quietly.

His voice was soft, intimate, putting a secret spin on the words. Or was it her imagination? Despite her disdain for his type, was she subconsciously entertaining thoughts of a fast little roll with Mr. Bently Pierce on the narrow cot shoved against the wall? Those huge, dark eyes watched, waiting. She stared at his mouth for a moment, remembering the flash of strong white teeth that morning when he'd smiled at his daughter. The lips were full, mobile, expressive. No longer in a grim, disapproving line, they looked soft, yielding. With a mouth like that, the guy was probably a great kisser.

What's your problem, Raine? she said to herself. *The guy's a jerk. And the sooner those bars locking you in with him get opened, the sooner you get away from him, the better.*

She uncrossed her arms, pulled herself up straighter, shoved a hand into the back pocket of her jeans and drew out a card, thrusting it at him.

He took the card from her, read it, then looked up, his dark brows twisted in question. "Diapers?"

"Yeah, Pierce, diapers. Cloth ones. Those disposables you put on Cat are poison to the environment. They account for over four percent of all solid waste and take up to five hundred years to decompose. *Five hundred years.* Think about it. And eighteen billion of them are used each year—little Cat alone will go through about ten thousand herself. They're a solid-waste nightmare." She began ticking points off on her fingers. "They contaminate groundwater. They cause more diaper rash. And they're gonna be around long after you and me and little Cat are history. On the other hand, cloth diapers take one to six months to decompose—and that's after they've been used again and again." Pausing for breath, she reached out and tapped the card with her finger. "I can put Cat in natural pure cotton for probably less than you're shelling out to pollute the environment. And I pick up and deliver."

Bently grinned.

"Something funny?"

"That was quite a speech."

Raine shrugged. "It's my sales pitch. I make cold calls just about every day. And that, Pierce, is what I was doing at your house this morning."

Bently nodded and looked at the card again. "Raine Rogers, Cotton Tails," he murmured. "You *were* there to sell diapers."

"Exactly. Now what about you?"

He looked up, his words carefully cautious. "What *about* me?"

"Your turn, Pierce. Convince me that you're a good-enough daddy to raise a kid like Cat and maybe we'll get out of here before midnight. Go on," she said with a lift of her chin when he remained silent, "convince me."

The anger was back in his dark eyes, as was the grim set of his mouth. "I don't see why I should have to explain myself to you."

"Because that's the game, Pierce, and you set up the rules." Her wide mouth tilted up at the corners. "Unless, of course, Daddy and Mummy *do* have something to hide. By the way, Pierce, where *is* your wife? Just how does Catlin's mother fit into all this?"

"I haven't got a wife," he said curtly. "And Catlin hasn't got a mother."

Her gaze moved automatically to his hands. No ring. "Okay, so you're not married, but everyone has a mother. Some of us may not have her for long..." Not liking the sudden dryness in her throat, she let her words trail off.

"Well, Catlin never had one at all!" he almost yelled before his voice quieted, saddened. "Caroline skipped town as soon as she got out of the hospital." He sank down on the cot, subdued, brooding.

"Holy cow," Raine murmured. "But how...how could she just leave her own baby like that?" But even as Raine uttered the words, she knew how. By just walking out the door and never looking back, that's how. It probably happened every day, but that didn't make it any easier to swallow.

"You'd have to know Caroline," Bently murmured before suddenly coming out of his brooding and getting to his feet. "The point is, I've raised Catlin from the beginning. I'm the one who has walked the floor with her at night. I'm the one who was there when she first sat up, when she first turned her little fist into a wave, when she ate her first piece of banana, when her first tooth split through her gums. I've laughed at her antics, worried over her cries, stood over her crib and watched her sleep. I'm there in the morning when she opens her eyes, and I'm there at night when she closes them. If I had my way, I'd be there for all the hours in between—and I'd have brothers and sisters for her, lots of them. I have no intention of bringing up Catlin as an only child. But there's such a thing as earning a living, Ms. Rogers. And that's what I was trying to do today."

He closed the short distance between them, getting too close for Raine's comfort. She backed away from him, her eyes never leaving his face, until she hit the cold bars of the cell.

Still he kept coming, stopping only when he had to, when his body was all but pressing into hers. He brought up his arms and gripped the bars on either side of her head.

"I made a mistake today, Raine." His voice was low, mesmerizing, and she got a quick flash of what he might be like convincing a jury. "A mistake that but for your kindness and obvious love for children could have been disastrous. But that's all it was—a mistake. I love Catlin more than I love my life. I would never willingly do anything to hurt her or neglect her." He stopped talking for a moment, letting those deep, dark eyes communicate for him before going on, his voice even lower than before. "I *am* a good father, Raine. I can promise you that."

Bently Pierce was turning out to be a regular hothouse of persuasion. Raine had told Dee that morning that he was a hunk of ice. Hunk, maybe. Ice, no way. When he got going about something he cared about, you could practically see the flames shooting out of his dark eyes. He obviously cared about his baby daughter. And wasn't the happy baby Cat herself further proof?

So, okay, Bently Pierce was a good father—but he was also a man. A man who at that moment was holding his body just inches from hers. And fancy suit or no, it had definite hunky possibilities.

It was time they got the hell out of there.

She wiggled around, careful not to touch his body with her own, and started to rattle the bars. "Hey, Wood!" she shouted. "We're ready to confess! Now let us the hell out of here!"

THEY WERE FREE and Catlin was once more in his arms. Bently stepped out of the police station, his face lifted to the dreary sky. A light drizzle was falling, dusk was closing in and the slight wind held a bitter chill. Still it felt like heaven.

Catlin giggled at the raindrops hitting her cheeks.

He heard the station door bang shut behind him and turned to see Raine coming down the wet cement steps, a definite swagger in her step.

"Um-na, um-na!" Catlin squealed, holding out her arms, her little fists opening and closing with excitement.

"She wants you to take her," Bently said.

Raine tossed her head, her sunny wheat hair catching the light from the street lamp above them. "And what do *you* want, Pierce?"

Holding his baby daughter in a damp drizzle, he looked at this woman he'd accused of kidnapping only a short time ago; he looked at her eyes, glinting silver, he looked at her mouth, wide and cocksure, he looked at those long, long legs in worn and faded denim—and he got turned on. Astonishing as it seemed, against all odds, at that moment, he knew what he wanted.

But this feeling pulsing in him had to be just another aberration in an extraordinary day. He didn't even know the woman, wasn't sure that he liked her— except for her fierce protective instinct toward his baby daughter. And he'd never been the type of man to succumb to a great pair of legs and a haunting pair of eyes. He cleared his throat. "I want you to take her, too," he finally answered.

Raine sauntered over and held out her arms, and Bently put his child in them.

They seemed to communicate on some level he'd never seen Catlin reach with anyone else. They gurgled and giggled, rubbed noses and snuggled.

After several minutes during which Bently felt decidedly left out, Raine handed his daughter back to him. "Guess you better get her out of the rain," she said.

He watched her long strides as she walked to a broken-down van bearing the legend Cotton Tails on its pitted side. She climbed in and he felt an odd touch of loss. Then she rolled down the window and stuck her bright head out.

"Hey, Pierce," she called.

He hurried over, heart inexplicably lifting. "Yes?"

"Take care of her, Pierce. There'll always be another deal, another million to make or lose. But there'll only be one Cat. Sometimes with people you don't get another chance."

She stared at him for a moment, her eyes dark and black as the rain, then the van sputtered to life. But before she pulled out, she called down to him again.

"I see you got the baby food off your nose all right, Pierce, but you better do something about the lump hanging off your tie," she said, her mouth cocked insolently. "What would the boss think?"

Chapter Three

"I'm sorry, Mrs. Cramer," Bently said, opening the door for the short, rotund woman, "but I really don't think it would work out."

The woman looked almost relieved, hoisted her huge tote filled to the brim with Pepperidge Farm cookies and Stephen King novels and waddled out the door.

Bently, holding Catlin, stood watching her. "I don't know, pet. Do you think I'm being too particular?"

Catlin squealed and banged her moist fist into Bently's temple.

"Me neither," he said, closing the door. "After all, Mrs. Cramer could very easily start reading Stephen King aloud to you, all the while rotting teeth you don't yet have with bits of Mint Milanos. We can't have that."

Catlin loudly agreed.

Bently carried her into the study, slipping her into her four-wheeled walker. The walker was a fairly new development, but she'd managed to attain an astonishing skill and speed with it in almost no time at all.

With the study door closed, she used the room as though the walker were a bumper car: ramming into things, squealing with delight, backing up and starting all over again. Bently had long since child-proofed the room and this is where they spent much of their time.

Often, while he was supposed to be working, he found himself watching her instead, thinking her the most intelligent, best humored, most charming baby in existence.

No wonder it was proving impossible to find just the right woman to take care of her.

But he *had* found the right woman. The perfect woman.

He sat down at his desk, but instead of picking up the contract he was working on, he picked up a business card.

Raine Rogers.

He shook his head. How crazy. How absolutely crazy that the woman he'd thought had stolen his child was now the one, the only woman he was convinced could care for his child. Since the day he'd been locked in that holding cell with her, he'd interviewed three applicants. None of them could measure up to Raine Rogers.

"None of them had legs to compare to hers, either," he murmured.

Catlin let loose with a stream of babbles.

"You're right, pet. Her legs have absolutely nothing to do with this." Nor did her silver almond eyes, or her sunny, thick hair, or her mouth that—

He stood up abruptly and paced to the window, drawing back the drape to peer out at more gloomy drizzle. None of those qualities had anything to do with his desire to have Raine be Catlin's nanny. What mattered was that she'd taken his baby along to work with her, that she'd made the time to take her to the park, that she'd kept her safe, warm and secure, throughout a long day of missed connections.

What mattered was that despite his earlier misgivings, he now felt she was the only woman he could trust with his child.

He sat down at his desk again and picked up the card. "What harm would it do to ask her?" he said aloud.

"Um-na, Um-na," Catlin answered before shoving her tiny fist into her mouth and sending her walker careering toward the leather sofa.

Bently chuckled. "I quite agree, Catlin my little love. No harm at all." He picked up the phone. No answer.

He tried three times more that evening, getting only her answering machine. In frustration, he finally left a message on the third try.

But at the office the next day, after being forced to leave Catlin at a day-care center, when he got Raine's answering machine again, he lost all patience.

"Gretchen!" he bellowed. When his secretary poked her head around the door, he said in a clipped voice, "Find me an address for a Cotton Tails Diaper Service or a Raine Rogers, would you?"

"Is that Milwaukee, sir?"

"Yes—wait, no. I mean, I don't know. The Milwaukee Metro area, surely," he muttered almost to himself.

"I'll find it," Gretchen said with her usual brisk efficiency.

"Oh, and Gretchen?"

She halted. "Yes, sir?"

"See what you can dig up about disposable diapers, would you?"

His secretary eyed him owlishly through tortoise-shell glasses. "I beg your pardon?"

"Disposable diapers," he repeated. "Find out what you can about them." She continued to stare, and Bently cleared his throat, almost wishing he'd kept his mouth shut. But he figured he could use anything he could find to get on Raine's good side. "Um, statistics—you know. Ecologically speaking, I mean."

Gretchen stared for a moment more, then went away, leaving Bently positive that this latest bizarre behavior—bizarre for Wesley and Harper, at least—wouldn't go unnoticed at the water cooler.

In fact, Bently was pretty sure that several people at the company were keeping their eye on him. And the other day, the day he'd thought he'd lost Catlin, Jonathan Wesley himself had waylaid Bently in the corridor outside the conference room. More barely masked innuendo about what happens when one ceases to be a team player.

He glared at the papers before him, having absolutely no taste for the latest takeover bid he was engineering.

By midafternoon, when Gretchen came back with an address for Cotton Tails, he was more than ready to take flight.

He shuffled papers into a pile, stuffed the whole thing into his briefcase and stood to leave. So it was only two in the afternoon—let Jonathan Wesley fire him, if it came to that. "You can take this job and shove it," Bently muttered.

Gretchen poked her head around the door. "Did you want something, sir?"

Bently flashed a sudden grin. "Freedom, Gretchen," he answered. And a certain long-legged, smart-mouthed, silver-eyed woman to take care of his child. But for now, a little freedom would do. He brushed past his gaping secretary and headed out to rescue Catlin from day care.

BENTLY PEERED through the front window of Marshland at a pair of very nice legs. Nice, but not great. Not Raine's. The usually efficient Gretchen must have gotten it wrong. This pricey boutique on Milwaukee's east side couldn't possibly have anything to do with Cotton Tails—or Raine Rogers.

Then he remembered the scarf Catlin still clutched in her hand when he'd gotten home from the police station that day. It had felt expensive—had smelled expensive. But the scent, when he'd buried his face in the silk, wasn't Raine's. And somehow, he didn't think the scarf was, either. Aside from the fact that the colors were horrendous, it would do absolutely nothing for an oversized sweatshirt and a pair of jeans.

But maybe it had something to do with this boutique.

"What do you think, Catlin? Should we investigate?"

"Aiy, yea, yea," she answered.

"Yes, I think we should, too," Bently agreed. With Catlin in his arms, he headed around the side of the building, through the alley and around to the back. And there was the wounded van with the Cotton Tails logo on its side.

She was here, somewhere in this building, and he felt a kind of gladness he hadn't felt in a long, long time. For Catlin's sake, he told himself. He was only here for his daughter. He'd ask Raine if she could possibly find the time to take care of his child. And if she said no, there'd be absolutely no reason he'd have to see Raine Rogers ever again.

Bently was brooding over that possibility when one of the back doors to the building suddenly opened, and there she was—the same ragged jeans, the same baggy sweatshirt, the same pewter eyes staring at him. Eyes that had haunted him for the better part of a week.

Catlin broke the silence. "Ki, ki," she said, or something like it. Then she squealed and held her chubby, pink-swathed arm out, opening and closing her fist before shoving it into her mouth and gumming, "Um-na, um-na."

Bently watched the pewter eyes lighten and clear; he watched the wide mouth smile. "Hi, Cat," she said and her voice hit him like an old friend he hadn't seen in a very long time. He started to answer the smile, just a quick flash, before he realized that Raine Rogers's smile wasn't for him. It was Catlin she was glad to see.

She walked over, her movements provocatively slow despite her long stride, and held out her finger for Catlin to clasp. "How's it goin', kid? It's great to see you again."

Her voice was as he'd remembered—deep, a little flat so that words came out with an ironic ring, turning the ordinary somehow intimate. He liked her voice. But what he liked even more was the way she talked to Catlin. He abhorred baby talk, believing that even at seven months his daughter was much too intelligent to be talked down to. Raine Rogers spoke to his child as though she was a person. Somehow he had to find a way to persuade her to become part of Catlin's life.

Raine kissed Catlin's fist, then fixed her gaze on Bently. "What are you doing here, Pierce?" Her wide mouth quirked with insolence. "Somebody steal your *car* this time?" She jerked her thumb over her shoulder toward the van. "As you can see, it wasn't me. I'm innocent this time, too."

"No, Raine, no one's stolen my car—or anything else," he added, although he was aware that his breath could easily be stolen if she kept looking at him like that. He'd never been turned on by a woman with an attitude before, but he was keenly aware that he was close to it, extremely close to it, every time he came near this woman.

"So what is it you want, Pierce?"

He grinned. Raine Rogers would be surprised if she knew what a loaded question that was. Hell, he was surprised himself. He stiffened his shoulders and forced his face to sober up. He'd come here looking for a nanny, after all, someone to meet his *baby's* needs—not his own. He cleared his throat. "Why don't we start with your holding Catlin for a while— she obviously wants you to."

Raine made a move to take her, then stopped. "You sure? After all, the first time you asked me to hold her ended in a kidnapping charge—remember?"

His smile was softer this time. "Only too well. If I recall, it also ended in a charge of child neglect."

"Guess we were both wrong."

Raine reached out to take the baby, but this time it was Bently's smile that made her hesitate. Damn that smile. It did things to his face—and to her insides. The corners of his generous, sensual mouth curved upward gently. His dangerous brown eyes crinkled at the corners, softening them. Softened, too, was the arrogant jut of his chin. But Raine didn't make the mistake of thinking that he was no longer a dangerous man. He was just dangerous in a different way, a way that caused a brief flutter in her lower belly. It had been a long time since she'd felt anything like it. And she didn't want to be feeling it now.

Trying to ignore the sensation, she took Cat into her arms.

"Well?" she asked him once Cat was settled.

"Well, what?"

"What *are* you doing here, Pierce?"

"I have a proposition for you," he said. The flutter went deeper as her eyes locked on his. Amazing, thought Raine, what a word and a pair of dangerous brown eyes could do to you.

"Like what?" she asked, trying to get the image of something hot and physical out of her mind. Eyeing his double-breasted charcoal suit, Raine wondered when she'd started thinking of hot and physical and Bently Pierce in the same neighborhood.

"Do you think we could go inside and discuss it?"

"Sure," she threw out lightly, "why not?"

Bently followed her into a space that could scarcely be called a room. An industrial-size washer and dryer crowded the area, along with cheap metal shelving, a large table heaped with stacks of neatly folded diapers and a giant roll of brown paper.

"This is it?" asked Bently. "This is Cotton Tails?"

Defiance sparked her eyes when she turned to look at him. Her chin thrust upward, her hip jutted out. "Yeah, Pierce," she answered, "this is it. My silver spoon got lost somewhere on the delivery-room floor."

Suddenly he understood just how deep that touch of defiance ran, just how much she was willing to take on in life. This was a woman who would stick it out when the going got rough, a woman who would go the distance. A woman nothing like Caroline. It made Bently want her more than ever—for Catlin's sake. Only for Catlin, he reminded himself.

"And you're it, as well, aren't you?"

Her eyes closed briefly, her wide mouth scrunching sideways. "Excuse me?"

"The whole operation—you run it yourself, don't you?"

She shrugged. "I've got a couple of high-school kids who come in."

The washer flipped into its noisy spin cycle.

"Look," he shouted over the din, "do you have an office? Somewhere we can talk?"

She hesitated for a moment, then motioned for him to follow her through another door, up a narrow staircase and into a room.

But it wasn't an office. It was where she lived.

"Sorry, there's not much room up here. Take a seat, Pierce."

He seemed to have a choice between a dubious-looking desk chair and an unmade bed. Bently stared at the tumbled, flower-sprigged sheets and the room suddenly grew smaller. Clearing his throat, he chose the desk chair.

It creaked when he sat down but seemed sturdy enough.

"Comfortable?" she asked.

"Fine," he answered, his gaze scanning the room. Through a partially opened door he saw a short white terry robe hanging from a hook on the bathroom wall. His gaze moved on but stopped again to alight briefly on a strap of something silky slithering from an over-stuffed drawer. Pale blue. She'd look good in the color. A book lay facedown and open on a bedside table next to a bottle of body lotion. He tried not to picture her wearing the robe, smoothing the stuff over her long, long legs. Or maybe she'd be wearing the silky blue thing, the strap falling off her shoulder—

"Okay, so about this proposition?"

She put the baby on the floor, grabbed the bottom of her sweatshirt, and started to pull it over her head.

This time he did lose his breath. He knew what kind of proposition *he* had in mind, but if she was considering another, more entertaining kind...

But it turned out she was wearing a white T-shirt underneath. Still he couldn't take his eyes off her. The softly worn white cotton clung to her, outlining full, rounded breasts and hugging a flat midriff. She was tall and lean, graceful in an athletic way. She brushed the hair out of her eyes, picked up Catlin again, and he remembered why he was there.

He stood up. "I've thought about you a lot since—"

"Since the day you accused me of stealing Cat," she finished for him, the tilt of her mouth telling him that she was enjoying his discomfort.

He grinned. "Since the day I made a complete fool out of myself."

"Even better."

"Yes, well, the point is, I haven't been able to get you out of my mind."

He seemed to finally be getting through to her because suddenly her silver eyes were glued to him, her wide mouth subdued, softer. The narrow window behind her threw a pale, late-winter light against her, silhouetting her body, making her hair almost a halo. She was beautiful in a way unlike any woman he'd ever known before. With his daughter snuggled in her arms as if she belonged there, she looked both saint and sinner, both sweet and hard as nails.

His gaze flickered toward the tumbled sheets again, trying not to picture her there, amid the cornflowers, moonbeams in her wheat-colored hair. And he knew that the longer he stayed in this room full of her, the harder it would be to remember that Catlin was the only reason he was there.

"I want to hire you to be Catlin's nanny," he blurted out.

Her eyes closed briefly, her mouth twisted. "Excuse me?"

"I said—"

"Oh, I heard what you said, Pierce, I just don't believe it."

She put Catlin down again, grabbed a glossy magazine off the cluttered desk to keep the baby's pudgy hands occupied and strolled slowly toward him. "What do you think I do all day, Pierce, loll around and eat bonbons?"

He couldn't help it, he had to laugh. "As long as it's not Pepperidge Farm cookies."

"I'm more of a Chips Ahoy girl myself."

He laughed again and shook his head. "Raine, you're quite a woman."

"Yes, I am," she said, moving even closer, raising a hand and placing it on his chest, fingering the material. "Nice suit," she said with the rise of a brow, her pewter eyes moving up his chest to his face.

"Thanks," he murmured, wondering if she knew what the slow, languid movement of her hand on his chest was doing to him.

"You know," she said, shifting her weight to her other hip, the movement bringing her closer still, "just because you wear an expensive suit doesn't give you the right to come up here and flaunt your charity. Just because you falsely accused me of kidnapping doesn't mean you owe me anything.'' She stopped caressing him with her hand, grasped his lapel and brought his face down to hers. ''I can take care of myself, Pierce. I don't need your handouts.''

She let go of him so suddenly that he lost his balance and found himself sprawled among the cornflowers.

Her scent was there. Light, fresh. Peaches—and something else. Some sort of light flower. Wild? Maybe. Sweet? Definitely.

She stood close to the bed, glaring down at him with eyes like smoke, and he had the sudden urge to grab her hand and pull her down there with him.

Lord, this was getting out of hand! He didn't know the woman, had no real reason to like her—except for how she was with his baby daughter. But, good God, if that was the only criterion needed for his libido to slip into overdrive, he'd be madly infatuated with Mrs. Gilbert, the little gray-haired lady at the checkout where he did his grocery shopping. No matter how busy she was she always found the time to fuss over Catlin, but he hadn't once fantasized about pulling *her* into bed with him.

He pulled himself up, aiming to get on his feet, to put these uncharacteristic and unwelcome thoughts aside. After all, if he did succeed in hiring this woman to look after his daughter, he could hardly go lusting after her, could he? But unaccountably, when she made to move away from him, he grabbed both of her wrists in his hands, drawing her closer until her legs bumped his knees. She immediately tried to twist out of his grasp, but he held her firmly, determined to have his say.

"What do you think you're doing, Pierce?" she asked him in a low, measured voice that was as sexy as hell. "Is the lord of the manor out to have his way with the serving wench?"

Despite himself, Bently chuckled. "That's quite a mouth you've got on you, Ms. Rogers. Not to mention the greatest pair of legs I've ever seen, the most haunting pair of eyes and a voice that could drive me out of my mind if I let it. But despite all that, I didn't come here intending to have my way with you." Although, Bently had to admit, the idea had some merit.

She was looking down at him with defiance in those pewter eyes, a go-to-hell tilt to her wide, insolent mouth. Briefly, he wondered what it would feel like to have that mouth soften beneath his. No—a woman in his life was the last thing he needed after what Caroline put him through. He didn't need a woman in the bedroom, he needed a nanny in the nursery.

He softened his hold but didn't let go. "I didn't come here to offer you charity, either, Raine. I've never found anyone I've trusted to look after Catlin, not from the day she was born. No one has ever cared as much about her as I do, taken such pleasure in her or been as kind, loving and willing to do battle for her. No one, Ms. Rogers. Not until you. I came here to-day to offer you the job of nanny, not because I think you need the money—but because *I* need *you.*"

Those deep, dark eyes stared up at her. She could feel her pulse tripping against the warm hands encircling her wrists. He needed her. Yes, and she needed that baby merrily tearing apart a magazine on the floor behind her. She'd thought of Cat often in the past days. Too often. They'd been abandoned by their mothers at different ages, and under different circumstances, but the motherless child in Raine's heart cried out for little Cat. Someday, Cat would know that her mother hadn't wanted her—and then the pain would start. And no matter what Bently Pierce did, no matter how different he was from Raine's own reluctant, closed-off father, that pain would chip away at the joy that was now such a big part of Cat's smile.

So why didn't she say yes? Why didn't she do what this man wanted and become Cat's nanny? She could love her, help her build a shield against the pain.

She felt Bently Pierce's fingers shift against her wrists. Felt his thumb move slowly over her pulse. And she knew why. He had a child she could love, but he also had something else. He had the power to make her dream again, had the power to make her want again. They were as different as hot from cold, as night from day, but her body didn't seem to care. It only knew that Bently Pierce had the power to make it come alive again. And for that, she was staying as far away from him as possible.

"The answer is no, Pierce. Now, if you'll let go of me, I'll get back to work."

"As soon as you agree to have dinner with me tonight, I'll let you go."

"Buying me a steak isn't going to make me change my mind. I own a business, Pierce. It may not be much, but it's all mine. And I don't have time for baby-sitting."

Reluctantly, he let go of her wrists and she stepped back. Bently rose from the bed, cleared his throat and ran a hand through his hair. "If you worked for me, you could use your salary to hire someone to do the hard work, make the deliveries. You could just manage the place."

She sighed heavily and shook her head. "You don't give up easily, do you?"

"Not when I want something."

She dipped her head, her hair cascading forward. "It wouldn't be a good idea for me to work for you," she said softly.

He took a step toward her. "But you're fond of Catlin. I know you are."

She looked at him briefly before dipping her head again. "Yeah, you're right. She's a great kid. But, trust me, it wouldn't work out."

"Why?"

She tossed her head and stared at him. He was persistent, she'd give him that. She grinned a little, bending to retrieve Catlin from the pile of scrunched paper on the floor. She gave the baby a final hug, felt her heart give a final tug, then she handed Cat back to her father.

Bringing out her best defense, the only one she had, she tossed her head, cocked her hip, lifted her brow and quirked her lip. "Why?" she drawled. "Because I said so, Pierce."

He grinned and shook his head. "See, Raine, you already sound like a veteran. As a nanny, you'd be a natural."

She pulled her gaze from his grin and gave Cat one last, longing look before strolling to the door and holding it open for him. "Get out of here, Pierce, and let me get back to work."

He started to leave, then paused on the threshold. "I may be leaving, but that doesn't mean I'm giving up."

"You're wasting your time."

His gaze moved slowly over her. "I have a feeling that you would never be a waste of time." His gaze stopped its slow journey, and his brown eyes homed in on hers. "I'll be in touch," he said, then closed the door behind him.

Raine let out her breath and sank down on the bed, curling up, clutching her pillow tightly. *Stop it,* she told herself, *stop feeling love for that little girl and lust for her father. And* don't even think *about accepting his job offer!*

She rolled over on her back. She could just see herself playing Mommy—getting in deeper and deeper. Making more and more room in her heart for a little girl who would never be her own. And the little girl's father? What could *he* do to Raine's heart?

Nothing, absolutely nothing. Because he was never going to get the chance. No one would ever get the chance to do what Mick Rogers had done to her again. She could still see the look in his eyes when the doctor told them that Raine would never give him the son he wanted. She could still remember what it felt like when she'd learned that Mick hadn't loved her enough to heal that disappointment and go on with their lives, still remember the moment she knew that the forever they'd vowed on their wedding day was never going to come. And she could still remember the words that came from Bently Pierce's soft, mobile mouth when they'd sat in that jail cell together. He had no intention of raising Cat as an only child.

Groaning, Raine jumped off the bed and clattered down the stairs. Back to her diapers, back to the babies that weren't her own, back to the life she'd made for herself. A good life. But it would be a life without Cat—and a life without a man like Bently Pierce.

Chapter Four

"Oh, no," Raine groaned. Was that Bently Pierce leaning against the Cotton Tails van?

She kissed baby Schumacher goodbye, handed her back to her mother, bounded down the steps of the Schumacher house and strode up to him. "Are you following me, Pierce?"

"Maybe," he answered lazily, his dark eyes alight with something close to mischief.

"Unbelievable," she muttered. "How did you manage to track me down?"

"Dee said you'd probably be in this neighborhood, so I just rode around till I found you."

"Don't you have a job to go to or a kid to watch or something?"

"Catlin's with my cleaning lady—and my job can wait."

"Well, mine can't." She started around the other side of the van, but he was quicker, stepping in front of her, blocking her way.

"You didn't return my calls, Raine. Is that any way to do business?"

"Diapers are my business, Pierce, not fending off persistent seekers of nannies. When you want to talk diapers, let me know." She started to ease by him, but once again he blocked her way, putting out an arm and bracing it against the van. She bumped up against it. It felt hard, implacable.

"I want to talk diapers, Raine. If you'd returned any of my calls, you'd have known that."

His voice was low, his mouth, forming the words, soft and sensual. And that was exactly why she hadn't returned his calls. She didn't want to hear his voice. She'd thought about him and Cat too much. Far too much. She couldn't risk being persuaded to become some sort of pseudomom.

"What do you *really* want, Pierce?"

Her wheat hair lifted on a stiff breeze, the sunny strands blowing across her remarkable silver eyes, sweeping her scent to his nostrils—the scent that had risen from her tumbled bed. What did he really want? He knew what he might want if the very idea of it wasn't so unlikely, if the thought of getting involved with another woman at this time in his life wasn't so totally unwelcome. No, he assured himself again, he didn't want Raine Rogers for himself. But he did want her for Catlin. Or at least some part of her.

"Diapers, Raine," he finally answered. "What I really want is diapers."

She leaned a shoulder against the van, brow raised, mouth twisted. "No kidding. Since when?"

He smiled. "Since I found out that enough disposable diapers are used every year to go to the moon and back seven times, enough to fill a garbage barge every six hours. And did you know that it costs one hundred million dollars a year just to dispose of them?''

She grinned and he felt absurdly rewarded.

''Yeah, I knew.'' When she dipped her head, the sunny strands of her hair concealed the continuing grin.

Bently was enchanted. Stubborn, tough Raine seemed almost shy.

Her gaze swung back up to him. ''I'm impressed,'' she said.

Giving in to a swift, sudden need to touch her, Bently raised his hand and brushed her hair from her eyes with his fingers, the tips caressing the soft, pale skin of her cheek.

Raine stopped smiling. She stood up straight, pulling away from him. ''What'd you do, Pierce—have your secretary do a little research?''

So, thought Bently, *we're back to insolence and chips on the shoulder.* Okay, he liked that in her, too. Just as much as he liked the shy grin. Maybe more.

He backed her against the van, coming close without touching, just barely holding himself in check. ''I pay for it, Raine. Just like I'm going to pay for you.'' His eyes traveled her face, coming to rest on her mouth. ''I want every-other-day deliveries—including Sundays. Starting tomorrow.'' He brought his fingers back to her face, retracing her cheek, rubbing his thumb along her full bottom lip. He heard the intake of her breath, felt the tautness of her body. If he didn't leave—now—he would surely have to give in to the unaccountable longing to cover her mouth with his own, to feel her body soften in his arms.

He backed slowly away from her, then started for his car.

"Pierce!" she called. "Get your diapers somewhere else!"

"I don't think so, Raine," he called over his shoulder. "The Better Business Bureau doesn't take kindly to discrimination."

Bently chuckled to himself when he heard her kick the side of the van. Just as he reached his car, she yelled, "I don't deliver on Sundays!"

"Then start!" he yelled back, got in his car and drove away.

"DON'T YOU ever work?"

Bently stepped back to allow Raine through the patio doors and into the kitchen. "Funny, I seem to remember my boss saying the same thing just a few hours ago."

Raine plopped a package of diapers on the kitchen table. "Figures. You've been hanging around the house every time I've made a delivery. I thought the agency was sending over another nanny."

"They did."

"And?"

"She had the most appalling habit of cracking her chewing gum, not to mention the worst taste in clothes I've ever seen."

"Come on, Pierce, what difference does it make what she wears? Cat's a little young to start copying fashion trends."

"Any woman who would wear bright orange polyester stirrup pants shows a remarkable lack of good judgment. She would be a bad influence on Catlin all the way around.''

Raine grinned and shook her head. ''Face it, Pierce, you just don't want to go to work.''

''You're right. I'd much rather stay home and play with Catlin. Come and see her. She should just be waking up from her nap.''

Raine hesitated. She knew exactly what Bently was doing. He was trying to wear her down, get her involved in Cat's life despite her refusal to do so. And it was working. Over the past two weeks, Raine looked forward to seeing the baby more and more until it had become the absolute highlight of her day. She'd even rearranged her schedule so Bently's was the last delivery of the day, giving her the freedom to stick around if she was invited, which she always was. Bently seemed to have a knack for being in the midst of some new baby chore whenever Raine showed up. One day it would be playing with Cat while he gave her a bath, the next it would be feeding her an early supper. And usually the phone would ring and he'd ask Raine for help. And of course she gave it, working herself more and more into the routine of Cat's life.

She reminded herself that she'd done most of these things with most of the children along her delivery route at one time or another. Mothers could always use an extra pair of hands, and Raine, liking the contact with babies, had always willingly supplied them. But Bently Pierce's condo was a danger zone, one she felt she had to navigate carefully or she'd step on a land mine that would rip her newly mended heart to shreds. And it wasn't only her feelings for Cat, the motherless child she was coming to care more and more about with every delivery, that were in danger of exploding. Bently Pierce, with his quick flash of a grin and his changeable brown eyes was a land mine all his own.

"Are you coming?" he asked.

He leaned in the doorway, waiting for her, his tie at half mast, his dark hair brushing the shirt collar open at his throat. She thought about the day she'd found him leaning against her van, waiting. More than two weeks had passed, but the touch of his fingers still lingered on her cheek, the rough feel of his thumb still burned on her mouth. Bently Pierce was more dangerous when he smiled at her than when he'd accused her of kidnapping.

"Come on," he said, holding out his hand to her.

And against her better judgment, she went.

She talked to Catlin while Bently changed her. Bently chuckled and Catlin squealed with delight as Raine gave a comic, verbal tour of a day in the life of a diaper deliverer. When Bently left the nursery to get Cat her bottle, Raine held her in her arms, strolling around the room, discussing the bunnies on the wallpaper.

"Would you like to give her her bottle?" Bently asked from the doorway.

Raine knew she shouldn't. She knew she should get out of there before she was so attached to them both that her sneakers sprouted cement soles. Then, taking its usual cue, the phone rang.

"I have to get that—I'm expecting a call from the office." He handed Raine Catlin's bottle. "Be right back."

Raine settled into the bentwood rocker, Catlin in her arms. She liked the warmth of the baby against her body, liked singing to her softly while Cat stared up at her with eyes fighting off sleep. "Cat," she whispered, "you're getting me in trouble here, you know that?"

Catlin sucked and watched.

"You've already got too big a piece of my heart in your tiny little hand," Raine whispered, "I can't afford to lose any more."

Catlin blinked and waved a fist, smiling, milk spilling out of the sides of her mouth. "Ki, ki," she said, then started sucking again, her eyes never leaving Raine's face while Raine started to softly sing again.

How could Cat's mother not have wanted her? It stung Raine's heart, stung that part of her where a motherless little girl still lived. Watching Cat's eyes close for the final time, she whispered, "Sleep tight, little one, I'm here for you."

Yeah, she thought, *right now I'm here for you, but someday I'll be gone—just like your mother. Just like my mother.* "Oh, little Cat," she murmured, "I wish I could be here for you forever."

Bently finished his call and started down the hallway to the nursery. When he was halfway there, Raine's low, soft voice came to him. She was singing to his daughter. John Lennon's "Imagine." Odd choice for a lullaby, he thought. But as he stood in the doorway and listened, he changed his mind. It was a wonderful song to sing to a child. He heard Raine whisper something to her. He couldn't make out the words, but the love in them was unmistakable, and something tightened around Bently's heart.

Raine Rogers was blue jeans and attitude. But she clearly had a deep, untapped well of nurturing and loving. He wanted it for his daughter. But as he watched her, her thick, sunny hair falling into her face, her wide mouth softened into a quiet smile as she gazed down at his sleeping child, he began to wonder if he wanted it for himself, too.

Raine looked up and saw him, saw the soft, deep look in his eyes, saw the gentle lift of his full mouth. She was starting to think that Bently Pierce was a hell of a guy. A guy who put his baby ahead of business, a guy who filled out a simple white shirt and a pair of suit pants like no one she'd ever seen. His dark hair, too long for his clothes, fell over his forehead. His square chin sported the shadow of a beard. He looked tired, but he looked happy. He looked as if he was in love.

Raine abruptly stood, gently laying Cat in her crib, covering her with a soft yellow blanket. Bently Pierce *was* in love—with his baby daughter. And Raine was getting out of there now before she started wishing he was in love with her. Before she forgot that these precious moments with Cat were just that—moments. Borrowed moments.

She brushed past him in the doorway and headed for the kitchen. Bently followed.

"Are you leaving already?"

"I've got work to do, Pierce."

"Stay. Have supper with me."

At the patio doors she turned. "Look, Pierce, you keep dangling Cat in front of me like you can make me give in and take the job. But I won't, so just give it up."

He grabbed her hand before she could leave. She didn't like the contact. It jolted her, his hand warm and masculine, but she couldn't let go.

"I know you don't want the job, Raine."

She looked into his eyes. "Then why do you keep bugging me, Pierce?"

He took a step toward her. "Did it ever occur to you that I just might like spending time with you?"

There was that flutter again, low in her gut. The guy had a pair of eyes on him and a voice that, when he wanted it to, could melt all over you. She yanked her hand out of his. "Right," she said, the words heavy with irony. "Nice try, Pierce. See you when you run out of diapers."

"GOING OUT AGAIN?" Dee asked from the doorway.

Raine threw wet diapers into the dryer. "Yeah, I've still got a delivery to make."

"Let me guess," purred Dee, examining a long burgundy nail, "Bently Pierce." She arched a dark brow. "Right?"

Raine set the dryer to tumble. "No—*Catlin* Pierce. Cotton Tails diapers don't come big enough for daddies."

"Cute. But the two of them do make a perfect little package, don't they? A sexy man and a little baby all rolled up together and tied with a big, bright bow."

Raine leaned on the dryer and crossed her arms. "They're customers, Dee, that's all."

"Ahh, but they're customers who get special late-afternoon deliveries—deliveries that seem to take longer and longer every time."

Raine felt color staining her cheeks, and she dipped her head to hide it. "So? I've always liked spending time with babies. You know that."

"Yes, I do. But so far as I know, you've never hung around to rock the Schumacher baby to sleep. Next thing you know, you'll be discussing silver patterns."

Raine tossed her head. "Get real, Dee. Bently Pierce is interested in only one thing from me—child care. A guy like him wouldn't be interested in someone like me for anything else. And even if he were..." The words, a little wistful, hung in the air.

"And even if he were, what?" Dee asked.

Raine picked up a wrapped bundle of diapers and headed for the door. "And even if he were interested in something else from me, he wouldn't get it." At the door she turned, her hand on the knob. "Catlin is the reason I hang around Bently Pierce's fancy condo— the *only* reason. After Mick, there's no way any guy is getting a stranglehold on my heart ever again."

She whipped out the door before Dee could say more. Dee had a way of chipping away at Raine's soul until something buried fell out. And there *was* something buried there—but it was going to *stay* buried there. Because even if she let it out, what good would it do? A man like Bently Pierce wasn't going to be interested in a woman who delivered diapers for a living. A woman who lived in one small room. A woman whose wardrobe consisted of a couple of pairs of battered jeans and a different sweatshirt for every day of the week.

As she'd told Dee, the only thing Bently wanted from Raine was a little loving care for his daughter. And that's all Raine wanted, too. Catlin was the only thing that mattered.

She drove out to Bently's suburb, parked the van in the alley behind the condo and made her way up the stone walkway to the patio doors, pushing the doorbell and bracing herself for that little flutter in her belly, for that flash of strong white teeth and soft, brown eyes. It was Catlin she cared about. Only Cat. Bently Pierce was just a good-looking guy with a way about him that could get to a woman who'd been without a man too long. Nothing more.

She took in a deep breath and rang the bell again. The man had insisted on every-other-day deliveries— the least he could do was be home to get them! But when the door finally opened, the man standing there wasn't Bently. He was tall and blond, with long hair that curled around a bony face and pale blue eyes lit with humor. He slid the door open with a welcoming smile, a smile that did no more for her than make her relieved it wasn't Bently's.

"Hi, I'm Jack," he said, "free-lance writer, sometime baby-sitter and full-time neighbor. And these must be Catlin's diapers. Come on in."

With relief, Raine stepped past him then turned around for another look. He wore baggy gray sweats and high tops without laces. And he looked altogether more manageable than Bently Pierce.

She was still sitting at the kitchen table with Jack when Bently came home.

"I see you two have met."

A shiver ran along Raine's skin at the sound of his voice. Damn, she should have been gone by now. If she was so relieved that he hadn't been home, why was she still hanging around? Had she been hoping to see him, after all? She half stood, figuring she'd make a quick, clean exit.

Get a grip! she admonished herself. *What are you, afraid of some guy in a suit?* She sank back down again, willing herself to relax.

"We were just discussing the basketball play-offs, Ben. Who's your favorite?"

"Very funny, Jack." Bently walked over to Catlin's high chair, giving her a kiss and a caress on the head.

"Ben here isn't into sports. It might mess up his Armani."

Raine's gaze swung immediately to the dark expanse of Bently's shoulders. Armani. Dee would be pleased with the information. She'd also be pleased to know that Raine was far from immune to noticing how the cloth draped so gorgeously over the hint of muscle underneath it when he picked up Cat and held her high in the air, making her laugh. Oh, Dee would be pleased, all right, *if* Raine told her. Which she wasn't going to.

Damn Dee, anyway. If it hadn't been for their conversation that afternoon she wouldn't be noticing those shoulders *or* those strong, muscular arms. In fact, she usually made it a point *not* to notice.

Bently slipped Catlin back into her high chair, giving her another biscuit to gum, then went to the refrigerator, opening the door and rummaging around. He fished out a bottle and held it aloft. "White wine, anyone?"

"I don't suppose you have anything as plebeian as a beer in there?" Raine asked, in the mood to be a little difficult.

"A beer sounds good to me, too, Ben," Jack said.

Bently fished two out, opened them and handed one to Jack and one to Raine, along with a glass.

Ignoring the glass, she took a swig right from the bottle.

Her hair caught the light from the ceiling fixture as it tumbled away from her face. Bently remembered how it felt in his hands the other day. Looking at her now, a person might think it was the only soft thing about her. She reminded him of one of those girls in high school who were always smoking in the second-floor rest room—a little tough, a little cocky. Those girls had always intrigued him, but not nearly as much as Raine Rogers was intriguing him now.

"So," Jack mumbled in his beer, "How goes it in the rarefied air of the corporate tower? Rip apart any small corporations today?"

"You're a *corporate* lawyer?" Raine asked, interested in spite of herself.

Bently nodded, bringing his glass of wine to the table. "Does that surprise you?"

Raine shrugged. "Guess I always pictured you in front of a jury."

Jack grunted. "That's where he should be. Saving some poor guy from the system, not helping the system screw him. Ben would be good at it, too. He can be very persuasive."

Bently gave Raine a long look. "Well, sometimes." He hadn't persuaded her to come care for Catlin. But four days a week, she was here to deliver her diapers—and he milked the time for all it was worth, placing Catlin in her arms as often as he could. The tactic was working. She was more and more attached to his little girl—just as he'd wanted her to be. But he was beginning to wonder, late at night when Catlin was sleeping and the condo was lonely, if he wanted something more from her—something for himself.

He shrugged out of his jacket and slung it over a chair, sitting down at the table across from Raine, sipping his wine, wishing Jack would leave so they could begin their little early-evening ritual. He'd been thinking on the way home that maybe he could get her to stay for Catlin's bath, so he hadn't exactly been happy to see Jack sitting next to her, all cozy, discussing sports, eating into their time together. Impatiently, he yanked his tie loose, his fingers going to the buttons of his shirt.

Raine watched, her gaze becoming fixed on his hands, strong and blunt fingered, undoing his shirt, revealing a thatch of dark hair curling up to the base of his throat. He ran his fingers through it, moving upward to rub the side of his neck. Her gaze followed and she felt odd, as if she were part of something intimate, something that made her heart trip.

Almost as if she were touching him herself.

She jerked her gaze upward to find him watching. Her face flamed and she dipped her head to hide it, taking a swallow of beer, trying not to choke on it.

Jack scraped his chair back. "Well, I'm off. I'll let you know about those Bucks tickets, Raine."

Raine looked up at him, her smile a little brighter just to be given some kind of diversion. "Great. I'll look forward to it."

"See ya, Ben," he said, then he kissed Catlin good-bye and left.

"You're going out with him?" Bently asked, his voice curt, blunt.

"He said he might get Bucks tickets from a friend."

"I see," he clipped out. "Well, it's time for Catlin's bath. You're welcome to stay, if you like."

Without waiting for an answer, he pulled Cat from her high chair and left the room.

Raine sat on in the darkening kitchen, wondering what Bently Pierce's problem was now. He seemed angry that she might be going to a basketball game, for heaven's sake. The man's idea of a good time was probably orchestra seats at the Milwaukee Ballet. She stared at his half-empty wineglass. Couldn't even lower himself to drink a beer. Raising her bottle to her lips, she gulped the rest of the brew down. It was warm and bitter. She reached for his wineglass, careful to drink from the side that didn't bear the imprint of his mouth. The wine was tart, fruity, still cool. She stroked the rim of the glass with her thumb and the specter of his hands against his skin rose to her mind, the darkness of his chest hair against the white of his shirt. What would it be like to—

She sat up straight in her chair, carefully placing the glass back on the table in precisely the same spot where it had been.

Cat's laughter reached her along with the faint splash of water and the deeper tones of Bently's voice.

Had her father ever bathed her as a baby? She had no memory of it. All her childhood memories seemed to begin the day her mother left, the day her father's thoughts turned inward and he became not much more than a silent presence in her life.

The kitchen suddenly felt lonely. The smart thing to do was to leave. She felt vulnerable, all too aware of her isolation. It was dangerous to stay. Then Cat laughed again and the sound beckoned her, a more powerful pull than her common sense. She stood up and went to find them.

Cat was in the large bathroom sink, pouring water from a plastic cup down her belly, laughing and smacking her hand against her wet skin.

"Cup," Bently said, touching the object. "Catlin's cup."

Cat looked up at him with smiling eyes. "Ka," she said. Then, "Ka, ka," as she swatted the water with her hands, splashing Bently's shirtfront.

"Looks like Cat's not the only one getting a bath."

Bently swung around, giving her a brief, lethal grin. The one that did funny things to her insides.

"You came to help with Catlin's bath?"

She got her mind off that grin. "Looks like you need it," she said, grabbing a towel off the rack.

Cat looked up at her and screeched, showing off by slapping the water with both hands. A sudsy spray arced up and over the rim of the sink, splashing Raine in the face, dribbling down her sweatshirt and soaking Bently's already-damp shirt to the skin.

Raine gasped, wiping soapsuds from her face.

"Apparently, my daughter is in favor of a communal bathtime."

Raine dipped her head, dabbing at his shirtfront with the towel in her hands, trying not to picture what he'd look like lying in a bath, his skin slick and warm from the soapy water.

"You've got some suds right—there."

He'd covered her hand with his own, guiding the towel up to her chin. Her mind was caught up with the feel of his hand on hers, the same hand that had caught her fancy as he'd touched his own flesh earlier in the kitchen; the same hand that held the wineglass and raised it to his mouth, the mouth she couldn't seem to stop staring at now.

He brought up his other hand and pushed a strand of wet hair from her cheek.

"Are you really going to go out with him?" he suddenly asked, his eyes on hers, his voice so low that she thought she hadn't heard him right.

"What?"

"Jack. Are you going to go out with him?"

Raine shrugged gently, her eyes still on Bently's. "Sure, I guess so."

Bently's eyes flickered, breaking the hold he'd had on her. Pulling his hand away, he turned abruptly back to Cat, lifting her out of her bath and wrapping her in a towel.

Raine followed him into the nursery where he laid Cat down on her changing table and patted her dry.

"What's got into you, Pierce?"

"Nothing."

"Right." She watched him struggling with a wiggling Cat, trying to get her into a one-piece sleeper. His muscles bunched beneath his thin, damp shirt. His dark hair brushed the back of his collar, curling up against it. Her gaze drifted lower. He had a pretty good backside for a guy who pushed paper for a living. Tight, rounded. She thrust her hands into her jeans pockets and started to prowl the room, looking at this and that, anything to take her mind off his commendable rear end.

Bently fastened the last of the snaps on the sleeper and hoisted the baby into his arms, then laid her down in her crib.

"You mad about something, Pierce?"

Bently shot her a look. "Maybe."

He headed for the kitchen. Raine was right behind him. She watched him pull a baby bottle from the refrigerator and hold it under the hot water at the sink.

"It's Jack, isn't it? You don't want me to go out with him, do you?"

"No, I don't," he shot over his shoulder.

"Why not? Why shouldn't I go out with Jack?"

Bently shut off the water and placed the bottle carefully on the counter. He turned to face her. "Why shouldn't you go out with Jack?" he asked, stalking over to her, his face dark, his eyes scowling. He put an arm around her waist and yanked her against him.

"Because of this," he ground out, and then his mouth came down to crush hers.

His body was hard, hot beneath the damp shirt. She felt it through her wet sweatshirt as if their skin was touching. His mouth moved on hers, claiming it completely, taking away her breath, taking away her balance. She put a hand on his shoulder—only to steady herself, she thought. But she couldn't stop herself from stealing up to the nape of his neck, from running her fingers into his thick, dark hair.

She heard him moan into her mouth, felt his tongue, rough and ardent against hers. The flutter in her belly grew to an ache, needy, rampant, making her almost sorry when he pulled away.

His breath came hard, his glowering gaze burned into her. "I've fought against doing that for a long time, Raine. In the beginning, I would have sworn that I wanted you only for Catlin—now, I don't know anymore." He took a deep breath, his dark brown eyes softening. "All I know for sure is I don't want you going out with Jack."

They were still staring at each other, still wrapped in each other's arms when Catlin cried out. They jumped apart.

Bently ran a hand through his hair. "I—I have to see about Catlin."

"Yes," Raine muttered, dipping her head. "Of course."

After he left the room, she hesitantly raised her fingers to her lips, surprised when the touch didn't burn. She hadn't felt anything like that kiss since—hell, she'd *never* felt anything like that kiss! "Damn,

Raine," she murmured again, "what are you getting yourself into here?"

Her head came up, her chin thrust out and she gave herself the answer: nothing. She was getting herself into *nothing*—because she was going to be gone by the time Bently came back. She was already falling in love with Cat; the last thing she needed was to fall for her father, too. Dee was right. They were a perfect package: a motherless baby who needed her, a man who could get to her the way no other man ever had. But she didn't kid herself that that kiss had meant anything to Bently Pierce. He needed someone to take care of his daughter. And maybe he needed a woman in his bed. It wasn't going to be her.

She ran for the door, closing it quietly behind her.

Chapter Five

The kitchen was empty when Bently returned. Raine had gone without a word, leaving only the faint scent of peaches behind.

He thrust a hand into his hair, pacing in frustration. Had he just thrown away weeks of coaxing Raine into Catlin's life? *And into his own.* He supposed there was no longer any point in fooling himself. He didn't want Raine just for Catlin. It seemed he also wanted her for himself.

And maybe he had from the very first.

His head came up at the sudden screech of metal out in the night, his heart lifting with relief. Hurrying to the patio doors, he stepped outside.

She was bent over the open hood of the van, peering inside. He strolled over to her with a calm he was far from feeling.

"Having problems?"

She didn't look up at him. "Choke's stuck again—won't start."

"Come inside. I'll call the auto club for you."

She did look at him then. "Look, Pierce, people like me don't belong to the auto club. There's a screwdriver on the front seat. Get it for me, would you?"

Bently found the screwdriver and handed it to her. "What are you going to do?"

"This'll hold the choke open long enough to get it started." She got into the van and started it and, leaving it running, got out again, removed the screwdriver and slammed the hood shut. "It's been running a little rough lately—needs the timing set. I just haven't gotten around to doing it yet."

"Wait a minute—you set your own timing?"

Raine shrugged. "Sure. That and tuneups, oil changes, brake jobs. Little things."

Bently laughed softly. "Not so little, Raine. I'm in awe of anyone who can change their own oil without getting covered in the stuff."

It occurred to Bently that it was very strange standing there discussing motor oil with a woman he'd just shared a devastating, soul-consuming kiss with—a woman he'd just admitted to himself he wanted.

He reached out to touch her hair, but she shrugged away from him.

"Don't," she said.

"Raine—"

"Forget it, Pierce. Just forget that kiss ever happened, okay?"

He grinned a little. "I don't know, Raine. As kisses go, it was pretty unforgettable."

She thrust her chin up. "Well, it's not going to happen again."

"Why? Look, I didn't intend to feel this way, but—"

She tossed her head, her eyes nailing him with anger. "But you're willing to make the sacrifice to get me to take care of Cat."

His eyes narrowed, hardened. "What are you saying? You think I'd seduce you to get you to become Catlin's nanny? What kind of man do you think I am?"

"I don't know, Pierce. What kind of man *are* you?"

He stared at her, her defiant stance, her silver eyes, that hair shooting sparks in the glow of the street lamp. God, she was just about the damnedest woman he'd ever met. Seduce her into taking care of Catlin? He gave a short bark of laughter. Hell, he only wished that was it.

"Look," he said, "forget Catlin for the moment...."

She shook her head. "No way, Pierce. Cat is the only reason you and I are even standing here talking."

"If she's that important to you, why don't you come and take care of her?"

She threw her gaze heavenward, blowing air through her bangs. "Back to that, are we?" Her gaze swung back to him. "Look, I'll be her friend, okay? Or an aunt, a big sister—whatever. I want to spend time with her. But I can't become her nanny. I can't afford to get that close." She tossed her head again, staring off over his shoulder. "It would hurt too much when I had to let her go," she murmured.

Lord, if she'd tried she couldn't have said anything that would hit him harder in the heart. Speechless for a moment, he finally asked, "And will you be *my* friend, too?"

Her silver eyes, brimming, came back to him. Her wide mouth twisted. "You need a friend, Pierce?"

"Don't we all?"

Yeah, she supposed that was true. She nodded. "See you day after tomorrow."

He looked at her bent head. "Drive safely, friend," he whispered, then he leaned closer and kissed her cheek.

At the first touch of his lips, she thrust her head back, but instead of breaking the contact, the action caused his lips to skim down her jaw and lightly touch the side of her mouth. Oh God, he wanted that mouth under his again.

"What the hell was that for?" she demanded, the chip on her shoulder firmly in place.

"Just a little kiss between friends, Raine, nothing to get shook up about."

She yanked open the van door and swung up into the driver's seat. "Well, don't let it happen again!" she yelled.

Slamming the transmission into drive, she peeled out into the alley, swinging into the street, not slowing down until a light changing to red forced her to stop.

"'Nothing to get shook up about,'" Raine repeated to herself loud enough to hear over the knocking of the engine. So why was she? Why was she still so shaken by a small kiss on the cheek?

It wasn't the kiss on the cheek that was the problem. It was that other kiss, the one that stole her breath and sucked at her soul. But her soul wasn't up for grabs. Not by Bently Pierce.

He was white wine and corporate takeovers. She was beer and basketball. Maybe she'd been wrong and he hadn't only been trying to get her for Cat. Maybe he did want her for himself. But he also wanted kids in the backyard. Kids she could never give him.

She pulled into the alley behind Marshland, inching into her narrow parking space, and cut the engine. She sat there while the engine ticked and cooled, thinking about his mouth, thinking about his hands holding her against him.

She threw open the van door. Damn it all, anyway! She'd go to the ball game with Jack, and when the night was over, she'd throw her arms around him and kiss him good and hard. Hard enough to erase the memory of Bently Pierce's mouth on hers forever!

"WHAT DOES IT sound like, Pierce?"

Bently gripped the phone tighter. Hearing her voice for the first time since he'd kissed her threw him. He tightened his jaw against the swift rush of hunger running through his veins. "What do you mean, what does it sound like? It won't start!"

Raine sighed heavily. "I know that. But what does it do? Is it turning over at all?"

"Turning over?"

"Men are supposed to know about these things. You shouldn't be allowed behind the wheel without your auto-club card."

"I was too busy learning the law to figure out how a car works. And I *do* have an auto-club card. In fact, I called them first, but their circuits were all busy and five minutes of Barry Manilow was all I could stand."

"Okay, where are you?"

When Bently told her, she whistled under her breath. "What are you doing in a neighborhood like that?"

"Well, now you know why I don't want to leave the car here and call a cab. So, *friend,* are you going to help me or not?"

"Get yourself another cup of coffee and sit tight. I'll be there in about fifteen minutes. Think you can stay out of trouble till then?"

"Your mouth is giving me more trouble than anything else is likely to."

"You wish," she drawled insolently and hung up.

Bently grinned at the receiver, thinking about that wide, provocative mouth, thinking about the possibility of kissing it again.

Then he remembered that she was going out with Jack that night, and he slammed the receiver down hard and turned back to the diner counter to order another cup of coffee.

It was true the diner and the neighborhood weren't ones he frequented. Needing secrecy, an old friend had chosen it for a meeting. David Lester's company was fighting a hostile takeover, and it looked as if the legal department was in the back pocket of whoever was behind it. David had needed advice—fast, confidential and free.

The ensuing conversation had been stimulating and rewarding, leaving Bently with a feeling of purpose that he hadn't felt in a long while as he waved David off from the parking lot. But when he got into his car to leave, it had refused to start.

He could have waited for the auto club, but as soon as he thought about Raine and her knowledge of cars, it was almost as if some invisible force pushed him toward the pay phone. Once he'd thought of calling her, he couldn't get the idea out of his mind.

The waitress came up and filled his cup again, placing a plump hand on her ample waist. "Refills are free, honey, but I hope you ain't gonna sit here and drain my coffeepot without so much as ordering a piece of pie."

Bently looked up at her. She was a handsome woman, her black complexion enhanced with scarlet lipstick on her full mouth and purple shadow on her big, heavy-lidded eyes.

He gave her a smile. "Pie sounds good. Why don't you bring me a piece of the house specialty?"

"Sure thing, hon."

A moment later she was back, setting a huge piece of peach pie in front of him. "This looks delicious. Thank you."

"Honey, you sure got some nice manners but 'round here we appreciate a nice big tip a whole lot better."

The man on the stool next to Bently laughed. "Lottie here ain't one to mince words. Nothin' like a smart-mouthed woman, I always say."

"I seem to be coming up against the type a lot lately," Bently muttered.

"Can't beat 'em, if you ask me. Now, you take my old lady—"

Bently and the man were thick into a discussion about the pros and cons of smart-mouthed women when Raine arrived. She strode into the Coffee Cup Café with that long, lazy gait of hers, grabbing the attention of every man at the counter.

"Geesh, Pierce, here you sit gossiping and wolfing down pie while I gotta interrupt my workday to rescue you." She picked up his fork, spearing the lone chunk left on his plate and popping it into her mouth.

Bently watched a slice of peach slide over her lips and disappear. "It's the house specialty," he pointed out, his mind on the peach juice glistening on the fullest part of her lip. "Lottie recommended it."

"Is that right? Well," she drawled, looking over his shoulder at the man next to him watching the exchange, "if you can manage to tear yourself away from the patrons and the cuisine, I'd like to get cracking on that car. You and your pals may be of the leisure set, but I've got a business to run."

Bently's neighbor leaned over and asked, "She your woman?"

Bently shook his head. "Afraid not. She's my mechanic."

The man whistled under his breath. "That does it. I'm joinin' the auto club tomorrow."

Bently laughed, threw down a five, waved to Lottie and started to follow Raine out the door.

"Hey, buddy," the man at the counter called out. "Remember what I said about a smart-mouthed woman? When they got legs as long as their mouth is big, well, hell, only a fool passes up a chance like that."

Bently shook his head. "I'm no fool. But the fact is, she's going out with my best friend tonight."

"Well, buddy, if I were you, I'd do something about that."

Bently stared at him for a moment, then he grinned. "You know, maybe I will."

Raine was leaning on the Lincoln Mark VIII, her long legs crossed at the ankle, when Bently came out of the diner. The day was the warmest April had seen so far, and she'd exchanged her usual sweatshirt in favor of a simple white shirt tucked into battered jeans. Her hips were lean, her waist small. But what drew him the most was that wide, brash mouth, ready to give him trouble. He made a decision right then and there. If he had any say at all in it, nobody, not even Jack, was kissing that mouth but him.

"Come on, Pierce. Get a move on."

"In a hurry, Raine?" His mouth twisted. "Ah, that's right. You've got a big date tonight, don't you?"

She fisted her hands on her hips. "Is that what this is about? If you got me down here to mess up my date with Jack and there's nothing really wrong with your car—"

He put up his hands. "You wound me, Raine. I wouldn't dream of doing any such thing. And the car most definitely has something wrong with it. Here, let me show you."

He got in the car and tried to start it. When nothing happened, he unlatched the hood. By the time he got out again, Raine had the hood up and was peering inside, giving a very nice view of her backside and her long, long legs.

He peered over her shoulder, letting his hip brush hers. "Aren't you sorry you doubted me?"

She glanced back at him. "No, I'm not. You forget, I've seen what lengths you'll go to to get your own way."

He watched her pull pliers from her back pocket and unhook some cables.

"Give me your keys, Pierce."

He placed the key ring in her palm and watched her use them to scrape at the surface of the two U-shaped clamps at the end of the battery cables.

Reattaching the cables, she tightened them with the pliers and handed him back his keys. "Okay, give her another try."

The engine turned over smoothly.

Bently got out of the car. "How did you do that?"

She shrugged. "Wasn't hard. Your battery cables were corroded. Your starter wasn't getting any power. Clean the cables, the car starts. Simple."

He stared at her, a smile building slowly. "You are an amazing woman, Raine. Thoroughly amazing."

"Right now I'm a woman with dirty hands. Got anything as low class as a rag in this machine?"

Bently opened the trunk, took something out and handed it to her.

Raine took hold of the neat little square and shook it out. It was emblazoned with rotund golfers, all in bright plaid knickers. "Cute, Pierce. You sure you want to get it dirty?"

Bently grinned. "Be my guest. It's the least I can do for a friend."

She wiped her hands and threw the golf towel into the trunk alongside a gleaming set of clubs in a leather bag. "So you play golf. I guess I should have known."

"A liability of the profession. Cut a deal, play eighteen holes. It's not something I enjoy but it comes with the territory—much the same as you having to smile at babies, I would imagine."

"There's a difference. I *like* smiling at babies. And I like my job. Something tells me you're not nuts about yours."

He slammed the trunk. "You're right. I'm not."

He looked at her leaning against his car, her streaked hair shimmering in the sun, stirring and lifting in the breeze. When it blew in her eyes, she tossed her head and his gaze followed the line of her throat—and lower to the open V of her shirt, the shadow of her breasts against the pristine white lifting slightly with the movement.

Something caught hold of him inside, running through his veins. Something wild, as pagan as the earthy scent of the budding spring on the wind. His mind's eye saw him taking hold of her, forcing her down on the hood of the car, touching her skin, the sun beating on his back while he took and took from that wide, insolent mouth of hers.

She tossed her head again. "Something wrong, Pierce?"

Yeah, he thought. *I can't breathe for wanting to taste your mouth again.* Her scent, her look, the movement of her body filled him with untamed thought, sudden desire. He wanted to offer her carnal knowledge, something hot and sweaty and fast. Something dangerous and crazy and wild from his heart. But he knew she wouldn't let him. So he offered her a piece of pie instead.

"WHAT ARE YOU DOING here, Pierce?"

"What do you mean?"

Raine forked up the excellent pie and took a look around. The café was clean but worn, the orange counter dotted with cigarette burns, the vinyl upholstery on the slightly tilted stools taped. The customers were a mix of races, but one thing they all had in common: not one of them wore a suit like Bently Pierce. "Well," she answered, "the pie is the best I've eaten and Lottie's a real corker, but somehow this place doesn't look like your usual type of establishment."

"I had a business meeting."

"Here? Get real."

"Actually, it was very real. A friend needed some free and confidential advice. He chose the place for anonymity."

"Good choice. You're the only suit in the joint. What did he need? Fake passport? Numbered Swiss bank account?"

Bently took a sip of coffee and shook his head. "Nothing that spectacular. He just needed to know how to keep the sharks from devouring his life's work."

He was silent for a moment, staring out the window at the buses and cars, at the people waiting for lights to change so they could cross the street. Real life—real people. People just like the ones affected every time a company moved south or left the country for cheaper wages, every time a would-be giant like Wesley and Harper ate them up and spat them out. And he helped.

"You know, this afternoon I was giving the kind of advice that could stop a company just like the one I work for from ruining a man's dream, from putting people out of work, families on welfare and unemployment." His gaze left the window and settled on the woman across from him. "It felt good, Raine. Better than I've felt about my profession in a long, long time."

She leaned forward, her elbows on the table, her hair swinging against her cheeks. "Why do you do it, then?"

He thought about that for a moment. "At first it was to prove a point—to make buckets of money. I had visions of showing up my father and becoming a self-made man."

"I figured you for the kind of guy who was born with money."

"You figured right. The proverbial silver spoon in the mouth. Trouble was, I spent a good deal of my youth trying to spit it out. I was an only child, lonely, rebelling against all my father's dreams for me. I guess that's one reason I don't want to raise Catlin as an only child.''

Raine nodded. ''Spread the expectations around a little, huh?''

''Exactly. That and give her someone more to love—someone more to love her.'' He took a sip of coffee. ''The day I left home, there was a big scene. My father told me exactly what he thought of me, none of it good, and what a failure he expected me to become once I'd stopped riding on his coattails. I've spent the years since trying to prove him wrong.''

''But what's the point if it doesn't make you happy?''

''Oh, Raine.'' His voice was weary, defeat fighting at the corners to get in. ''I'm afraid there's even less point than you think. The old man died nearly ten years ago. All these years I've been fighting a ghost.''

He seemed lost, in need of comfort. There was only the width of the booth between them, yet they were a world apart. She told herself she'd better remember that, told herself despite knowing what his mouth could do to her, what his body could make her feel.

She could have said a lot of things, about understanding loneliness, about parents who don't really care. She could have taken his hand. But she knew touching him would be a mistake. Besides the booth that lay between them, there was his law degree, his background, his wanting other children in his life. Yes, touching him, even in comfort, would be a mistake because she knew what she'd feel when she took his hand. And she knew it could lead nowhere—absolutely nowhere.

She put her hands under the table.

"So who taught you about cars, Raine? Your father? A brother, maybe?"

She shook her head. "I've got two half brothers, but they're much older—grown and married while I was still a kid. And my dad—well, he pretty much ignored me. No, I learned about cars from Mick."

Bently raised his brows. "Mick?"

"My ex-husband. We had a trucking company—short haul. I kept the books, scheduled runs, worked on the fleet a little."

Bently smiled. "Where you learned how to jury-rig a choke and the importance of keeping battery cables clean."

She shrugged. "Mick was into cars—fast cars. If you wanted to be with Mick, you learned about cars."

"And you wanted to be with Mick?"

She picked at her unfinished pie with her fork. "Yeah, I wanted to be with him. We got married when we were twenty, just after we started the business. I figured we'd have a family and live happily ever after."

Bently watched her playing with the pie. "What happened?" he asked softly.

She threw the fork down with a clatter. "A cute little pregnant waitress named Trudy happened." She glanced at her watch. "I gotta go. I've still got some deliveries to make before—"

"Before Jack picks you up for your date," he finished for her.

Her pewter eyes nailed him. "Yeah, Pierce. Before Jack picks me up for our date."

Bently sat back, making himself relax against the orange booth. "Fine," he said, smiling affably. "Thanks for your help, Raine. And have a great time with Jack tonight."

Raine stood up. "I'll tell him you said hello."

"Oh," Bently said, beaming up at her, "I don't think that will be necessary."

"HELL OF A GAME," Jack yelled into Raine's ear.

She nodded. "Terrific. And this place is unbelievable."

The Bucks had won, and the pub across from the Bradley Center Arena was filled with overheated bodies and the din of celebration.

"Wanna go someplace else—someplace quieter?" Jack yelled.

Raine shook her head. She needed the noise. She needed any distraction available. Because it wasn't the two players who'd just put in an appearance to the frenzied applause of the crowd that filled Raine's mind. Nor was it the attractive guy at her side, the guy she'd promised herself to kiss senseless until she'd wiped the memory of Bently Pierce's mouth out of existence.

Try as she might, she couldn't focus on Jack. He was cute. He was fun. But she couldn't get Bently Pierce out of her mind. After she'd listened to him in the diner that afternoon, he was becoming more than just some handsome rich guy who happened to have a little girl she was falling in love with. More than a guy who could push her buttons, sexual and otherwise. He was a guy who knew about loneliness, about need, the same as she did.

Jack leaned in close to her, putting his arm on the back of her chair. "You and Ben got something going I don't know about, Raine?"

Raine started guiltily. Was Jack some kind of mind reader? "Of course not," she huffed, trying for the proper amount of disdain. "Why do you ask?"

"Because Ben just walked in the door and this is definitely not his type of hangout."

Raine sat bolt upright, body suddenly alert, eyes darting through the crowd. "Where?"

Jack nodded across the room. "He's at two o'clock and gaining. And no one has ever been that happy to see me."

"Get real," she drawled, forcing her attention back to Jack after one brief, potent glimpse of Bently winding his way through the crowd. "Why should I be happy to see Pierce?"

"I don't know," Jack said into her ear. "Why *are* you?"

Before she could answer, Bently Pierce's voice melted over her, despite the noise. "I didn't expect to see you here," he said.

"Like hell," Jack drawled.

Raine looked up at Bently. His dark hair fell over his forehead. The collar of his long, dark coat was turned up against the black cashmere turtleneck he wore underneath. He looked every inch the dashing lawyer—which was exactly what he was. *What are you doing lusting after someone like him?* Raine chided herself. Jack was the one she should want. Jack, with his team cap backward on his head, his tattered jeans and bagged-out T-shirt, practically her fashion twin, was far more her type.

"How was the game, Jack?" Bently asked, but his eyes were on Raine.

"We won," Jack said, but no one paid any attention.

"Mind if I sit down?"

Only Bently Pierce would ask permission to sit in a place like this. Only Bently Pierce would show up in a sports pub wearing a pair of pressed pants to go with his prep-school manners. "Yeah," Raine answered, thrusting her chin up, "we mind if you sit down."

Bently ignored her, pulled out a chair and sat.

"You're wasting your time, Pierce. I don't think they have Dom Perignon on the menu."

"I'm developing a taste for beer," he said, his dark eyes never leaving hers as he snared her bottle and drank.

Raine watched him put the bottle down. No way was she touching it again. No way was she putting her mouth where his had been. The thought of it waved through her like a kiss, and she licked her lips and broke eye contact, tossing her head and leaning closer to Jack.

"Maybe we *should* get out of here," she drawled, trying to sound seductive while still raising her voice loud enough for Bently to hear. "Go someplace more quiet—more *private*," she added, looking pointedly at Bently.

Jack snaked an arm around her. "If that's what you really want, Raine, baby." He punctuated his words with a light brush of his lips on hers.

Before she could think of how it would look, Raine drew her head back, away from the kiss.

Jack chuckled and put his mouth to her ear. "Yeah, that's what I thought."

"Jack—" she began apologetically.

"Skip it, baby." He kissed her cheek and scraped his chair back.

"Where are you going?"

He leaned down to her. "I'm going over to the bar to get another beer—and give you a chance to make up your mind who your date is tonight."

"Jack!" She tried to call him back, but he was already wading into the noisy crowd at the bar.

Bently quickly slid over, claiming Jack's place, putting an arm across the back of her chair. "Let me take you home, Raine."

"Get lost, Pierce."

He leaned close enough for her to feel his breath at her ear. "Come with me," he murmured. "We'll get lost together."

She pulled away from him and forced a laugh. "Couldn't get me for a nanny, so now you plan on seducing me into a little free baby-sitting, huh?"

His eyes darkened. "If that's what you really believe, then come with me, let me prove you wrong."

The gaze, the words, stopped her for a moment. Or rather, they stopped her brain. Her body was cruising full speed ahead, on some erotic collision course of its own. Where the hell was Jack?

She pushed away from Bently and stood, eyes frantically searching the crowded area near the bar. He was nowhere in sight. "I'm out of here," she muttered.

Bently stood, grabbing her arm. "What about Jack?"

She shrugged his arm off, nailing him with a look. "Tell him I needed some fresh air."

Bently was watching her walk away when Jack came up alongside him and just stood there, sipping a bottle of beer. "Why aren't you going after her?" he demanded.

"Why aren't you?" Jack asked, eyes twinkling.

"Don't you want her?"

"Not the way you do, old pal."

"But that kiss—"

Jack shrugged. "To illustrate a point. The lady hasn't really been mine all evening. I figure it took a lot for you to drag yourself in here amid all these T-shirts and Nikes. For me, she's a diversion. For you, she's an obsession."

Bently didn't like the sound of the word. Probably because it was getting too damn close to the truth. He shook his head. "Damn it, Jack, I don't know what to say."

"Say it quick, pal, and get a move on before some other guy out there gets lucky."

Bently grinned. "I guess I owe you one."

"Big time, pal, big time. Now get going."

"Thanks," Bently said then started to wind his way through the crowd.

Chapter Six

She wasn't in the parking lot. The fine day had given way to a windy night and somber clouds, threatening rain, scudded across the sky. A low rumble of thunder rolled in off Lake Michigan only blocks away, and Bently felt a drop or two hit him on the forehead.

Figuring she'd be just stubborn enough to walk home, Bently climbed into the Mark VIII, maneuvered through the overcrowded parking lot and hit the streets.

Minutes later, he found her heading down Wisconsin Avenue toward the lake. Pulling to the curb, he slowed the car and hit the control for the power window.

"Raine!" he yelled. "Come on. Get in the car!"

"Go to hell, Pierce!" she threw over her shoulder.

"Damn it, Raine! Come on, I'll take you home!"

Whirling around, she yelled, "Get lost!"

She started to run and he took off, careering halfway down the block, pulling into an alley, the car blocking her way on the sidewalk. Throwing open the door, he stepped out just in time to grab her arms before she could start back the other way.

"Let go of me!"

She struggled against him, but his hands were hard on her, giving her a slight shake. "Don't be so damn stubborn, Raine. Get in the car and I'll take you home."

"*Me* stubborn? You knew I was going out with Jack tonight! Don't try to tell me that running into us was a coincidence! You planned it!"

"You're damn right I planned it," he said through a tight jaw. "I don't want you going out with Jack or anyone else. I want you for myself."

"Well, *I* don't want *you!*"

She broke from him suddenly, but he grabbed her arm and swung her around, backing her into the alley and up against the rough brick of a building. "Prove it," he said.

"What?"

He grinned at her and the rain started to fall. "Prove you don't want me, Raine. Because I think you do."

She shook the rain from her face. "Isn't the fact that I'm out with another man proof enough?"

"No, it's not." The rain poured down between them and his grin disappeared, his deep brown eyes focusing on her mouth. "Let me kiss you," he murmured, the sound of thunder nearly drowning him out.

But she heard him, her treacherous body leaping at the words. Doing her best to ignore it, she glared at him. "Are you crazy?"

He shook his head, water flying from his dark hair. "No. Let me kiss you, Raine. And if it's true, if you really don't want me, then you'll feel nothing and I'll leave you alone. What have you got to lose?"

My sanity, she thought. But the offer was tempting. Maybe she could prove to herself *and* to him that there was nothing between them—nothing but Cat. A dangerous gamble, but she decided to take it.

"Okay, Pierce—but just one," she hurried to add. "One kiss and you'll admit that the only thing between us is Cat."

His hands tightened on her arms. "One kiss and if you feel absolutely nothing, I'll admit it."

"And then you'll behave yourself? We'll just be friends, and I'll get to spend time with Cat?"

She caught the flash of his white teeth through the murky night. "I'll behave myself and you'll get to spend as much time with Cat as you want."

"All right." She lifted her face to him, feeling a little as if she was facing her judge, jury and executioner all in one, and closed her eyes.

His mouth touched hers and she clenched her fists, willing herself not to react, not to open her mouth to him, not to open her heart. And for a moment, she thought it was going to be all right.

The thunder rumbled around them, a flash of light blazed against her closed eye lids, and the rain came down, relentless as his mouth. But it couldn't put out the fire that was building inside her body.

She felt her lips soften, felt her body wanting to yield. His tongue slipped into her mouth, hot, restless, its journey raising her to another plateau of need, and she felt an ache—deep, demanding.

She had to stop it, now, before it was too late. She put up her hands, splaying them on his chest, intending to push him away, intending to prove to him that it was Cat that mattered, that it was only Cat she really wanted. But when she felt the heat through his thin, soft sweater, felt the thud of his heart beneath her palms, instead of pushing him away, her fingers curled into the fabric.

Bently felt her touch as it turned into a caress and the sweet victory drove him further. He wanted more, wanted to be closer. Grasping her hands, he tore them from his sweater, forcing them behind her back where he held them with his own, pinning her to him, bending her to the curve of his body. Her body seemed to come alive, and for a moment he thought she might fight against him. Instead she slid her leg up his outer thigh, pulling him in with her knee. A low, animal growl came from his throat, tearing his mouth from hers. It was a sound he hadn't even known he was capable of making.

"Oh, God," he murmured. "Raine, Raine, Raine." And all the while he said her name his lips kept coming back to hers...devouring, owning.

He moved against her, seeking solace for his swollen, heated body, and they slammed back against the side of the building, their bodies pressed together, length for length. She held him there with her upraised knee, he gripped her buttocks with his hand, and they moved together, the ache of his erection homing in against the tight, hot denim between her thighs.

Dry-docking they'd called it when he was a kid. But he was no kid. It didn't seem to matter—nothing in his memory had ever inflamed him like holding this woman, feeling her tongue in his mouth, hearing her soft, throaty cries. The streetlight in the alley spotlighted them for the world to see. The rain beat against his back, dripped off his hair. And he didn't care. He only wanted never to stop.

Somewhere a car door slammed, an engine burst to life. Raine pulled her head back, her eyes dazed and out of focus. He looked at the beauty of her rain-washed face, at the drops clinging to her dark lashes and her sun-drenched wheat hair. His grin came slowly, triumphantly. "I win," he whispered into the rain.

That smug, egotistical smile was what finally made her come to her senses. She twisted her hands free and shoved him away. "All bets are off. You broke the rules."

"Don't be a sore loser, Raine. You know I won."

She held up a resolute finger. "One kiss. It was supposed to be only one kiss. You blew it. I win."

"It *was* only one kiss—one long, sensual, sensational kiss—but one kiss."

She ran a hand through her rain-soaked hair, her wide mouth cocked. "Uh-uh, Pierce. Your lips broke contact with mine more than once. That equals more than one kiss."

"Don't be absurd! The point is, you felt something—you want me, Raine, and you can't deny it."

"*The point is* you broke the rules," she said, thrusting her chin up, trying to control the ache in her lungs as her breath tore through her, trying to ignore the fire in her body. He was right—she wanted him. More than she ever wanted anything in her life. And it scared the hell out of her.

He stood there in the rain, the force of his breath a cloud in the cold night between his parted lips, the light of passion firing his dark eyes. If Mick could break her heart, what could a man like this do to her? And what of Catlin? All she had to do is reach out to touch him and he would be hers—for tonight. Maybe for tomorrow night, too. But, just like Mick, he wouldn't stick around forever. And when he left, he'd take Cat with him. She'd lose them both.

She backed slowly away from him, off the curb and into the street, the wicked tilt of her mouth and the glib words on her tongue like a shield of protection. "Sorry Pierce, but you lose. Looks like you're just going to have to behave yourself." She turned her face to the wind and held up her hand. "Taxi!" As if on cue, a yellow cab pulled in front of her and stopped. She opened the door. "Tell Cat I'll be around to see her tomorrow," she called to him, then she hopped in the cab and it took off into the wet night.

CRADLING CATLIN in his arms, Bently jogged across the alley to Jack's bungalow and pounded on the screen door.

Jack appeared behind the ancient screen, looking even more disheveled than usual, a cellular phone cupped in his palm.

"Hey, Ben—what's up, pal?"

"I know it's short notice, but I've got to get to a meeting. Can you take Catlin for me?"

Jack came out on his porch, took off his baseball cap and smoothed his long, tangled hair before thrusting the cap low onto his forehead again and shaking his head. "No can do. I'm working on a nice fat feature for the Sunday supplement. I'm on deadline. Sorry, Ben."

"Lord, what a mess. I've got a meeting I can't miss in half an hour—the day-care center won't take her without reservations and I can't find my cleaning lady."

"Listen, Ben, you've got to get yourself a nanny."

Catlin squirmed in her father's arms, giving a sharp cry of agreement.

Bently gave her a kiss on the cheek and jiggled her up and down. "You think I haven't tried?" He sighed in exasperation. "I've interviewed dozens but none of them can compare to—"

"To Raine," Jack finished for him. "Well, did you try calling her?"

Bently snorted. "After that stunt I pulled the other night, Raine is barely speaking to me. She comes in with her diapers, spends time with Catlin and then disappears."

Jack's blue eyes sparkled. "Just what happened between you two after she stormed out of the pub?"

Bently's lips twisted sardonically. "Let's just say I lost a bet and now I have to behave myself."

Jack chuckled. "Which you're finding hard to do?"

"Precisely. Which is why I don't particularly want to call her right now and fling myself into the face of temptation if I don't have to."

Jack shrugged. "Then I guess you'll just have to take Catlin with you."

"What?"

"Take her to work with you."

Catlin, crowing loudly and slamming Bently on the chest with her fist, seemed to agree with the suggestion.

Jack's cellular phone jangled. "Hey, I gotta get this."

Jack answered the phone, disappearing into the bungalow again.

"Well, Catlin, my little love, looks like you're going to work."

He jogged back to the condo, threw some things into a diaper bag, filled several bottles with an assortment of juices and milk and was out the door with just ten minutes till meeting time.

"Looks like Daddy's going to be late again," he muttered, starting the Mark VIII and backing down the driveway.

Catlin banged a rattle on her car seat, letting loose a string of baby words, ending with an emphatic, "Ki-ki!"

"Don't think I haven't thought the same thing myself, pet. I'd love to quit my job and stay home with you all day, but there's such a thing as mortgage payments and college funds."

Catlin made a derisive sound suspiciously like a raspberry.

"My sentiments exactly," Bently concurred, keeping up a nearly nonstop conversation with his small daughter all the way to Wesley and Harper.

Once there, he loaded himself down with bags and bottles, strapped Catlin into her umbrella stroller and headed into the building.

Catlin loved the elevator. Her eyes grew wide when the door slid shut and she looked up solemnly at Bently from her stroller. But when she felt the upward motion she giggled, her eyes avidly watching as the numbers changed on the digital floor indicator.

"Just remember to be this charming when old Jonathan Wesley gets a look at you," Bently told her.

The elevator doors slid open and Catlin squealed, turning several heads in their direction. Smiling affably, Bently offered no explanations, merely wheeled her past the receptionist's station to his office.

"You're late," Gretchen accused, her attention on her computer. "Mr. Wesley just buzzed and—" She looked up and stopped dead, the eyes behind her large glasses astounded. "*What* is *this?*" she demanded.

"*This* is a baby," Bently explained patiently. "Surely you've seen one before," he added, although from the look on her face, he doubted any such thing.

"I know it's a baby, but what is *it* doing here?"

"*She* is my daughter and I couldn't find a sitter."

"Well, I hope you don't think that I—"

"I wouldn't dream of it, Gretchen. I assure you I can handle a baby *and* Jonathan Wesley at the same time." Bently piloted the stroller past her into his office.

Gretchen followed, "Mr. Pierce, I'm accustomed to working under professional conditions and lately—"

"Yes?" Bently prodded, his dark eyes narrowed on her. "Lately, what?" he bit out.

Gretchen took a step back, her hand fluttering nervously at the neck of her silk blouse. "Well," she continued, a little less certain, "things haven't been going well around here, as you know. Your behavior has been less than professional on several occasions and—"

"I don't need a lecture on professionalism from you, Gretchen." He picked up a stack of files from his desk. "Now if you'll excuse me. I am, as you pointed out, late."

With all the dignity one could muster wheeling an umbrella stroller, Bently pushed past his secretary and out into the hall, praying that Catlin stayed her adorable self and didn't start to howl during the meeting.

CATLIN STARTED TO HOWL during the meeting. Bently plucked her from her stroller and struggled with her diaper bag, extracting a bottle of juice and fitting it into her mouth. She hiccuped a few times and shuddered, but the crying stopped.

Bently looked into Jonathan Wesley's frowning face and went on just as if he weren't holding a baby in his arms. "I know what the prevailing theory is, Jonathan, but I'm still against liquidating Star Steel."

"Their earnings were down the last three-quarters and the union's got its foot in the door," Jonathan Wesley argued.

Bently dismissed the argument with an impatient shake of his head. "The steelworkers have been trying to organize Star for years."

"Well, they finally made it—they won the vote."

"By a very narrow margin," Bently pointed out. "There's a lot of dissent among the workers. There's a good chance that in a year they'll vote the union out again."

Hank Roberts, senior partner in charge of mergers and acquisitions, looked disgusted. His graying bushy brows were lowered in perpetual frown. "We're wasting time here, Pierce." His beefy, grizzled hand flicked the pages of the report under discussion. "This company's breakup value is higher than its worth as a running business. They've got computerized plasma and flame cutters that are state of the art—worth millions."

"So why not put them to use? With the money you're allocating to ruin Star, Wesley and Harper could turn it around."

Hank adamantly shook his bullet-shaped head. "It's a job shop, Pierce. Has no product of its own. They're losing contracts almost every quarter."

"But not for lack of quality. Their work base is being eroded by companies opening their own fabricating plants down south where labor is cheaper or jobbing out to Mexico."

"So far, Bently," Jonathan interrupted, "you're not telling us anything new. Your facts argue more for liquidation than against. And you're wasting our time. You drew up the contracts, made them airtight as usual. Now in the final hour you come in here with a baby in your arms, spouting bleeding-heart treason.''

Bently looked at his boss, the man he'd always respected, had hoped to emulate. Thin, delicately boned, dapper and well-groomed, he was a visual study in contrasts to Hank Roberts. But the hardness was there, the eye on the bottom line. When had Jonathan changed? Or was it Bently himself who had done the changing?

He tried one more time. "Just hear me out, Jonathan. If we can make the union see reason, accept short-term concessions to provide money for development—''

Hank held up a huge hand. "You're forgetting, Pierce. Star Steel is sitting in the middle of a valuable piece of land, land we've already started developing. The office park, condos and retail center at the heart of what will become Harper Village will be virtually self-contained. It's what people want, Pierce. It's the wave of the nineties.''

Catlin gurgled and pushed the bottle out of her mouth. Bently automatically raised her to his shoulder and started patting her back. "It seems to also be the wave of the nineties to cost hundreds of men their jobs.''

"Harper Village will create *thousands* of jobs,'' Hank retorted.

"Service jobs. Jobs that don't pay enough to support a family. We could turn this company around, make it viable again.''

Jonathan stood up and started to pace.

"All I'm asking, Jonathan, is that you hold off on this, just until I can get some figures together, talk to union and management."

"Hank," Jonathan said, his eyes on the floor, "leave us alone for a few minutes, would you?"

"Sure, Jonathan, anything you say." Hank gave Bently a disgusted shake of the head and left the room.

"You're treading on thin ice here, Bently. You used to be a team player. Used to have killer instincts with the best of them."

"Priorities change, Jonathan."

"And right now your priorities stink. You know what Harper Village means to me. I thought you backed me on this."

"I do, Jonathan. I just think there's a way to do it without shutting down Star Steel."

"Such as?"

"Develop Harper Village farther north. There's farm land lying fallow there. I should think the farmers would be glad to sell out if you offer them enough money."

"We're already negotiating with them, Bently," Jonathan said, a hint of sadness in his voice. "We need that land—all of it. You'd know that if you'd bother to show up for work once in a while."

Bently ignored Jonathan's gibe. What could he say? Jonathan Wesley was right. He was missing work more and more—and caring about it less and less. Saving Star Steel was the first thing he'd cared about when it came to Wesley and Harper in a long, long time. "A few acres won't stop you, Jonathan. The project could still work."

"The kind of people we hope Harper Village will attract won't want to live next to a factory, Bently. Use your head. Or has fatherhood made you so soft you fail to see what's important anymore? How can you expect to conduct business with a baby in your arms?"

Bently's jaw tightened, his brows coming down over eyes that were almost black. "My feelings about Star wouldn't change if Catlin weren't in my arms, Jonathan. You're right when you say that fatherhood has changed me, but wrong if you think I can't see what's important. Quite the contrary. Catlin has made me see what is really important, Jonathan. And it isn't always the bottom line."

"Keeping an eye on the bottom line has made Wesley and Harper what it is today," Jonathan replied scornfully. "And if this is any indication of how you intend to conduct yourself in the future, with a baby on your shoulder and a bleeding heart in your chest, then you had better hand in your resignation."

"This is exactly how I intend to conduct myself in the future, Jonathan," Bently snapped back. "And with a baby in my arms when necessary. And I have absolutely no intention of making it easy for you and resigning."

"Then you're fired."

Catlin chose that moment to burp—loudly. Jonathan Wesley pulled back his well-groomed head, a look of affront on his patrician face, before walking out of the room with his usual dignified air.

Bently hoisted Catlin aloft and looked into her drooling, smiling face. "I couldn't have said it better myself, pet. Thanks for sticking up for your old man."

SPRING HAD QUIT TEASING for once, and the sun was still high midafternoon the next day when Bently, hands buried deep in the pockets of his loose linen trousers, strolled down the alley behind Marshland. Raine was washing the Cotton Tails van, and he slowed his step to watch her. The fresh breeze and bright sun played in her hair, her long, lean legs stretched and flexed against faded denim, and her breasts gently moved in the close-fitting white T-shirt she wore.

Over the rushing sound of the hose, she didn't hear his approach, and he used the element of surprise to assuage the need he had to touch her. Coming up behind her, he slid his arms around her middle and buried his face in her peach-scented hair. "Mmm, you smell like spring," he murmured, a tight spear of desire flashing through him when he felt the surprised leap of her body.

"Pierce! You scared the heck out of me!" She twisted and turned, but Bently's arms remained firmly around her middle, his body pressed far too closely to the back of hers.

"Come on, Pierce, let me go! Can't you see I've got work to do? Besides, you lost the bet, remember? You promised to behave!"

"I *have* been behaving myself—all week! Anyway, you won that bet by default only. You felt something for me that night, and we both know," he growled near her ear, punctuating his words with a light nip of his teeth, "that I can make you feel it again, anywhere, anytime I like."

"Like hell!" She squirmed in his arms, but the action caused the hands splayed across her midriff to brush the undersides of her breasts, her nipples hardening instantly in response. She decided that it was best to stand perfectly still.

"Come on, Pierce, I mean it! Let me go!"

He tightened his hold on her, one hand gliding lower, caressing her belly. When he felt the quick intake of her breath, a thrill of triumph shot through him, adding glory to the sudden spring day.

But this sexual teasing and tangling wasn't why he'd sought her out. He'd woken to the happy sound of his daughter babbling in her crib, and a sudden need to see Raine. But he wanted more than he'd asked of her before. He wanted someone he could talk to, someone who would understand.

"Relax, Raine," he murmured into her ear. "I'm not planning to throw you to the concrete and ravish you. You're always going on about being friends— well, today I need one."

His hold had slackened and she spun out of his arms. "Something's happened. What is it? Is it Cat?"

He put up his hand, brushing her cheek with the back of his fingers. "No, it's not Catlin who needs you this time. It's me. I got fired yesterday."

Raine dropped the hose. "You're kidding? You? Fired?"

"Me. Fired."

"That's awful! What are you gonna do?"

Bently shrugged. "They say everything happens for a reason."

"Yeah, like me showing up at your front door just when you were desperate for a nanny."

"Damn it, Raine, will you forget that nanny business? Besides, I hardly need one now."

"So why are you here?"

Bently shook his head. "You can be so sweet, so loving with my daughter, and yet when I come to you, suffering, you—"

"Excuse me, Pierce," she interrupted him, "but you don't look much like you're suffering."

His mouth lifted in a half grin. "Well, maybe not now. I guess I did most of my suffering last night, in the dark."

Heedless of the fact that it was still wet, she leaned against the van. "Like most of us do. And did you find any answers in the shadows on the ceiling above your bed?"

He looked at her sharply. "You've been there, I see."

"More than once." She stared at her sneakers for a moment. "You could have called me, you know. I know what it's like to lose."

He looked at her bent head, at the hair falling forward to hide her face, and it came to him that she held on to her emotions as tightly as he always had. There was sweetness there, buried, along with gentleness and caring. She could show it with Catlin. Why was it so hard for her to show it with him?

"What would have happened if I'd called you last night, Raine?" he asked softly.

It took her a moment to raise her eyes to his. "I would have listened. I would have asked you how you felt about it, and if there was anything I could do."

"Ask me now," he continued softly.

"How *do* you feel about it, Pierce?"

He thought for a moment before shaking his head in wonder. "Strangely, after a few hours of soul-searching last night, I feel rather elated. As though I've been set free. As though there's a door opening. I'm not yet sure where it leads, but I have the feeling I'm going to enjoy the journey." He looked away from her briefly, his eyes searching the blue of the sky above, before letting his gaze find hers again. "Does any of that make sense to you?"

"Sure it does. When I left Mick, I left everything. My marriage, my home, my business. I lay around staring at the ceiling for a while, too. Then it suddenly hit me that the world was full of choices. I could choose to lie around and feel sorry for myself, or I could get off my butt and explore what was right for me."

"Why Cotton Tails?" he asked.

"I knew I didn't want to work for anyone else—I wanted to be my own boss. My divorce settlement was enough to start something small. People were starting to think more about the environment and there weren't many diaper services available. And I liked the idea of being around babies."

"You should have some of your own, Raine. You'd make a wonderful mother."

She stared at her sneakers again.

"There's another question you said you would have asked."

She raised her head.

"If there was anything you could do for me?"

Her mouth cocked. "And I'll just bet there is," she muttered, crossing her arms at her chest, fully expecting a request that had nothing to do with friendship.

"Spend the afternoon with Catlin and me."

Surprise replaced the cynicism in her eyes. "That's it?"

"That's it."

"Where *is* Cat, anyway?"

"She's in with your friend Deirdre. She caught sight of us when we pulled up in front of the boutique and came running to claim her."

"They've met before."

"So I gathered," Bently said dryly. "Will you come with us, Raine?"

What would it hurt, she asked herself, an afternoon with the two of them? Her deliveries were done for the day; she'd been planning to tackle some paperwork, but there was nothing that couldn't wait. She was being offered precious hours under the sun with Cat. And Bently? He was only asking for a friend—and maybe she needed one, too.

"Okay," she finally said. "Let me finish rinsing the van then I'll change my clothes and meet you in Marshland."

"Terrific." Bently started down the alley, then turned back. "Raine?"

"Yeah?"

"Thanks."

"Hey," she said, tossing her head, "what are friends for?"

Raine watched Bently walk down the alley, wondering if she was making a big mistake. His baby was firmly in her heart. Often she'd imagined herself taking Cat for long walks on just such a day as this; wheeling her to the park, hearing her laugh on the baby swings again.

But did she imagine Bently beside her? Did she want them both?

Impatient with her thoughts, she picked up the hose and gave the van a quick rinse, stealing one last glance at Bently, his dark hair lifting to the wind, his shoulders broad and strong beneath the white shirt he wore.

It didn't matter if she wanted them both—she couldn't have them both. She looked at the sky.

But she could have today.

Throwing down the hose, she ran to change her clothes.

"YOU DROPPED something, Pierce."

Bently watched Raine stroll into Marshland and bend to pick up the bracelet that had slipped through his fingers and onto the floor.

"Here."

Without looking at it, she handed it back to him, her attention focused on Catlin wiggling in Deirdre's arms. The baby had squealed, reaching out with her pudgy arms at first sight of Raine. Bently didn't blame her. He felt like squealing and reaching out, too.

Raine's legs had been spectacular enough in jeans. In the simple khaki shorts she'd chosen to wear, they were dynamite. Enough to explode a man's heart into overdrive.

The silver bracelet still dangling from his fingers, he watched her move around the boutique, murmuring to Cat. Or rather, he watched her legs. They were long and shapely in a sturdy, athletic way, the skin smooth and pale. Her highly arched feet were bare, a pair of white sneakers dangling over her shoulder by the laces.

"Bently? Did you want to see something else?"

"What?" He turned back to Deirdre. "Uh, no—no this is the one. I'll take it."

"Cash or charge?"

Bently's eyes were back on those legs again, four pairs of them as Raine held the baby in front of a three-paneled mirror, making faces into it, making his daughter laugh.

"Bently?"

"Oh, ah—charge I guess."

Bently whipped out his wallet and extracted a card, smiling faintly when he saw Dee's knowing, amused look. He took the package she held out and shoved it into the pocket of his linen trousers.

"Ready?" Raine asked from behind him.

He turned around to face her. She'd exchanged one white T-shirt for another, this one deeply scooped in the neck, her breasts moving faintly free against the soft cotton. *Yeah,* he thought, *I'm ready—more than ready.* Bently knew exactly how he'd really like to spend this day, and it wasn't a picnic in the park.

No, if he had his way, he'd hand Catlin back to Deirdre, swing this woman up into his arms and carry her off to the small room upstairs, tossing her amid the cornflowers, tearing off his clothes and joining her there to while away the afternoon exploring every inch of that pale skin—tasting her, claiming her.

Had he ever had thoughts such as these? She'd mined something in him that had been buried beneath the cool exterior he'd always shown the world, something hot, wild and needy. He should have felt vulnerable, but what he felt was triumphant.

"Yes," he finally answered, "ready."

Chapter Seven

Bently strapped Catlin into her car seat in the back of the Mark VIII, then climbed in the front next to Raine.

"I thought we'd pick up some food and take Catlin to the park for a picnic."

"Mmm, hmm," Raine murmured absently. She had turned her attention to the wraparound dash of the Mark VIII, fingering the complicated analog gauges, calling the correct time on the voice-activated phone.

Bently leaned back in the leather seat, enjoying watching her play around.

"How fast does this thing go, Pierce?"

"Fast enough."

She sat back. "Somehow this doesn't seem like your type of ride. I picture you either in a station wagon or some big gas guzzler with whitewalls and a cruise control."

"Not a very flattering picture. Sounds like you also picture me with a cigar and a paunch."

She shook her head. "Naw, you wouldn't want to get ashes on your suit."

He raised a brow. "And the paunch?"

She gave a hoot of laughter. "Oh, no, Pierce. You're not leading me down that path. Besides, who can tell in those baggy clothes you wear."

"Would it help if I removed my shirt?"

The words, and the soft suggestive tone of them, shot a blade of something white and hot through her. "Forget it, Pierce, I'm not interested. But I am interested in driving this car. How about it?"

"Nothing doing." He turned the key and started the engine, pulling away from Marshland.

"Why not?"

"If I know you, you'd have us out on the freeway doing ninety."

"Come on. I wouldn't do that. Not with Cat in the back seat." She slumped down, crossing her arms. "Of course I wouldn't tool around town at a sedate thirty miles an hour, either."

"See? My point exactly. You can't be trusted."

"Square," she muttered.

"Sulky child," he muttered back.

She thrust out her chin. "I *am not* sulking."

Bently chuckled. "I'll let you drive it someday—just not when we have Catlin along."

She sat up straighter. "And why would we ever not have Cat along?"

Bently braked for a red, letting his gaze sweep over her legs. They *were* spectacular. Eyeing them, he could think of plenty of reasons not to have his baby daughter along.

"You're staring at my legs, Pierce."

"You're absolutely right, Raine. I'm staring at your legs."

"Well, I don't like it."

"You've got great legs. It's hard not to take a look."

"You're doing more than taking a look. Friends don't look at friends' legs that way."

There was a honk from behind. The light had changed and the cars were piled up behind the Lincoln. Bently swore under his breath and stepped on the gas. As soon as they were through the intersection, he pulled to the curb. Turning to Raine, he stretched his arm along the back of the seat, letting a finger trace the shoulder seam of her shirt. The balmy breeze wafting through the car window stirred the sunny strands of her hair, like fresh wheat blowing in a field.

She shrugged her shoulder away from his touch. "What did you stop for?"

"Remind me again why we should be just friends."

She hadn't expected the words, simple, loaded. "What do you mean?"

He laughed softly. "Come on, Raine, I'm not blind, deaf and dumb. And neither are you. Every time we get close it's like a fire storm."

She tossed her head. "It'll pass."

"Why let it, Raine? Why keep putting the fire out?"

She stared at him as he raised his hand to brush the hair from her cheek, his fingers lingering, stroking. The sun beat in through the windshield—that was the reason for the sudden heat of her skin. The traffic streamed past, fumes wafting into the car on the warm breeze. That was the reason for the flutter in her belly, she told herself, for the slight light-headedness.

"Start the car, Pierce."

He shook his head. "After you remind me why we're just friends."

She took a deep breath and looked away from him, staring straight ahead. "I don't think you have any idea how important Cat is to me."

"Look at me, Raine."

She didn't want to. She wanted distance—from the father, at least, if not from his daughter. When she stayed still and rigid, he placed two fingers under her chin and gently turned her to look at him. The gentleness of those fingers made a lump rise in her throat, made it impossible not to do as he asked and meet his eyes. It'd been so long—too long—since anyone had been gentle with her.

"I told you I wasn't blind, Raine. Every other night I watch you with her, listen to your voice when you talk to her. Do you think I don't know what you feel when you hold her in your arms? When you tuck her in and kiss her good-night? You feel what I feel, Raine. You feel what her own mother should have but couldn't."

His palm replaced his fingers, caressing her face, gentle as the breeze stirring the spring day. "For some reason, you seem to think that your bond with my daughter should explain why we shouldn't want each other. But, Raine, don't you see? It only makes me want you more."

Her voice was edged with anger. "And if we give in to this... this desire that seems to keep sparking between us, when it's over what will we have? And what will Cat have?" She closed her eyes briefly and swallowed hard. "My mother walked out on me, too, Pierce, when I was only seven years old. There was another man—he didn't want me along for the ride. I guess she decided she could live without me easier than she could live without him."

His hand slid to the back of her neck. "Oh God, Raine, I'm sorry. No wonder you felt so much for Catlin right from the start."

"Cat's luckier than I was. She has you. After my mother left, my father just sort of closed down. It was like I lost them both."

His hand tightened, caressed. "And no wonder you were so ready to do battle for her, to accuse me of being an unfit father."

She moved her head restlessly, as much to get away from his warm caress as to try to sort out her feelings. "My father practically became a recluse. There wasn't anyone else, Pierce, no substitute mother to sing me to sleep, to care for me or to laugh with."

"And is that what you see yourself as, a substitute mother?"

She shook her head. "I see myself as Cat's friend, as someone who wants to be there for her to help fill that empty space she's going to feel someday. Because she's going to feel it, Pierce. No matter how much you love her, someday she's going to know that her mother didn't want her."

His breath came out in a long sigh, and he swung his head to look at Catlin in the back seat. She was gurgling quietly to the soft terry-cloth doll she held in her hands. "I guess I haven't wanted to face that possibility. I guess I've always hoped that by then there would be someone else in my life." He looked at Raine, adding softly, "Someone who would love her as much as I do."

Those dark eyes threatened to expose her soul, and it was a moment before she could trust her voice again. "There *will* be someone—someone to give you that yardful of kids you want so Cat won't grow up alone. But I still like to think that I could be in her life. If I was Daddy's ex-lover, it'd be pretty hard. Not only on us, but on whoever becomes the mother of the rest of those kids."

He reached out to her again, his thumb brushing her mouth, tender as the words that followed. "And what makes you so certain that woman couldn't be you?"

The lump in her throat almost choked her. She thrust her chin up. "Come on, Pierce, we're not working on a forever kind of thing here. I think we both know that."

"*How* do you know it, Raine?"

She looked at him again, her eyes steady, her heart far from it. "Because, besides everything else we've got going against us, I'd never be able to give Cat those brothers and sisters she needs. I'd never be able to give you the other children you want. I can't have kids, Pierce. Mick couldn't handle it, and I have no intention of trying to make any other man try."

Bently swore, loudly and angrily. He tried to take her into his arms, but she pulled back. "No violins, Pierce. I've known it for a long time. I've come to terms with it."

"But, Raine, you of all people should be a mother. You should have a houseful of kids to bully and love."

"You're right, Pierce. I deserved those kids I'll never have. But I won't let it ruin my life—not like it ruined my marriage. Now do you understand why she's so important to me?"

He took her hand and pressed his lips to her palm. "Yes, Raine, I understand. You're important to her, too. And to me," he added softly.

Her smile was a little weak, a little uneven, but she wouldn't cry. She'd meant it when she told him that she'd come to terms with it, she'd moved on. Dreams died, but you couldn't waste your life mourning them. "Start the car, Pierce."

"You're a hell of a woman, Raine."

She snatched her hand back and tossed her hair, making light of it. "Right now I'm a starving woman. Let's go get that food."

They drove the two blocks to Sendik's Market, one of the most popular mainstays of Milwaukee's east side. The store was bustling with afterwork shoppers. Raine carried Cat while Bently pushed a shopping cart. They stopped at the deli first for a pound of tortellini salad. The aroma of chickens roasting on a spit behind glass filled the air. Cat watched with fascination as they turned round and round, their skins sizzling and brown. She crowed with delight when they added one to the cart. Loaves of fragrant fresh bread stacked on bleached wooden shelves against red brick were too tempting to pass up. A long twist of French bread joined the chicken and the salad.

Bently argued for mineral water and Raine insisted on cola, the kind with caffeine. They bought both. Lingering in the produce aisle, they selected a carton of strawberries, two huge apples flecked with white and bananas for Cat.

Bently watched Raine choose a few jars of baby food for Catlin, finding it impossible not to fantasize that Raine was Catlin's mother of the flesh as well as of the heart. He watched her showing Catlin her choices, stroking the baby's head softly, murmuring to her quietly, and thought *Raine should be someone's mother.*

There was a line at the checkout, and Catlin got tired of waiting. She started to fuss, pulling her body rigidly away from Raine's. Raine comforted and jiggled, but the baby was too impatient not to protest. She let out a wail that turned heads all across the market.

"I'll take her outside while you check out," Raine said, then, without waiting for a reply, excused herself and went to the front of the store. When she stepped on the rubber matting and the exit door swung open, Cat quit wailing, staring openmouthed at the door, twisting to get a look at it closing behind them.

"You faker," Raine muttered. "You just wanted to be entertained, didn't you?"

Cat giggled and pushed two fingers into her mouth, the tears already drying on her cheeks.

"Quite an act you got there, kid." Raine was busy playing bump-noses with a squealing Cat and didn't see the couple coming from the other way until she had practically collided with them.

"Raine?"

Her head jerked upward. She recognized that voice. "Mick and . . . and—" she struggled to say the wom-

an's name ''—Trudy. How are you?'' But she could
see how they were. Pregnant. Again.

Mick held a boy of about two, and Trudy's belly
was heavy with another little addition to the happy
family.

Raine looked with longing at Bently's Lincoln, only
a few feet away. She was almost home free. Maybe she
could just—

''My, my,'' Trudy gushed, ''whose cute little girl is
this? We know she can't be yours, don't we, Raine?''

All of Raine's thoughts of escape fled at the sound
of that sugar-sweet deceptively innocent voice. Maybe
it was time she told little Trudy, and the big lug at her
side, exactly what she thought of them.

BENTLY CAME OUT of Sendik's, groceries in hand, and
saw Raine talking to the couple. The man was big and
blond, muscles starting to go to fat. He had a baseball cap on his head and a little boy on his shoulders.
The woman with him was small, young—and very
pregnant. Bently slowed his walk, letting his gaze
travel over the parking lot until he spotted a pickup
truck with Rogers Trucking printed on its side.

So this was Mick. Bently's jaw tightened with anger, hating the man on sight. When he came within
earshot, he heard the girl say something about Raine
and Catlin. Something about how Raine couldn't
possibly be Catlin's mother. His eyes narrowed, but a
slow, lethal smile spread across his face.

He stowed the groceries in the back seat of the Lincoln, then swept up to Raine, putting his arm around
her waist, pulling her into his side. ''Darling, there you

are! Has our little pet finally quieted down?" Without waiting for an answer, he looked at Mick. "Our Catlin hates waiting even more than her mother does."

Raine's mouth dropped open, but before she could speak, Bently planted a loud, hard kiss on her lips. "Isn't that right, sweetheart?" he murmured, clenching her waist tighter, giving her a meaningful look.

Raine frowned. "Um, yeah. I guess so."

"And you must be Mick," Bently said jovially, putting out his hand for the younger man to shake. Looking puzzled, Mick finally shook it. Bently dropped it and immediately turned to Trudy. "And of course you're Trudy. Raine has told me so much about you both."

Mick's face turned red while Trudy's jaw dropped.

"And this must be your son. Cute kid. Although—" he turned to Catlin, kissing her on the forehead "—he's not as cute as our Catlin. Isn't that right, sweetheart?"

Raine had recovered enough to smile and say, "Well, I guess every parent thinks their own kids are the cutest."

Bently laughed heartily. "Well said, darling." He planted another kiss on Raine's mouth. "Well, we must be off." Hand still at Raine's waist, he started to lead her away, then turned back. "Oh, but there's something I promised myself I'd say to you, Mick, if ever we should meet."

Mick turned red again. "Yeah? What's that?" he asked harshly, his eyes wary, obviously expecting a fight.

Bently threw him off guard, letting go of Raine to take Mick's hand again, pumping it like a politician looking for a vote. "I want to tell you that I'm very happy indeed that you are obviously such a stupid man."

"Hey—" Mick began.

Bently ignored him. "Because, you see, Mick, if you hadn't been so stupid as to let a treasure like Raine go, then I wouldn't have her now. And neither would Catlin." Still pumping his hand, Bently slammed Mick on the back. "So thanks, old boy. Your loss has been my gain."

Mick and Trudy were still staring when the Mark VIII roared past them and out of the parking lot.

By the time they'd pulled into traffic, Bently was chuckling.

"You're outrageous, Pierce. Totally outrageous!"

"Yes, well, you seem to bring that quality out in me, Raine."

She shook her head, laughter sputtering to the surface. "Unbelievable." She was silent for a block, then she said simply, "Thanks."

Bently looked at her sharply. "For what?"

"For what? Come on, Pierce, you saved me back there. You must have known how hard it was for me to see them like that—how hard it was for me to take Trudy's needling. I felt like punching her in the nose, but your way was better. Much better." Seconds passed. "I'm not used to other people fighting my battles. Why did you do it?" she asked softly.

"Your ex-husband is an idiot."

"I won't argue with you, but he's not stupid enough to fall for Cat being my kid."

His jaw clenched again. "Well, they made me mad—both looking so smug. And that little tart was so sure Catlin wasn't yours. And so ready to gloat about it."

Raine started to laugh. "Pierce, you've got to be the only human being in this century that could get away with using a word like tart."

He glanced at her, amusement dancing in his dark eyes. "Would you prefer strumpet?"

"No, actually. Strumpet sounds a little high class for Trudy. Tart is probably just right." She laughed again. "The look on Mick's face was priceless. You confused him, Pierce, that's for sure."

"Let him spend the rest of his life trying to figure it out. Maybe he'll come to the obvious conclusion that he wasn't man enough to give you a child."

"Oh, and you are?"

He picked up her hand and kissed her palm. "I could give you Catlin," he said, the words a soft promise against her flesh.

She pulled her hand away. "Act's over, Pierce. Great performance, but the audience has left the building."

Bently pulled the car into the parking lot of a small park and cut the ignition. "Maybe I liked pretending that you're her mother, Raine."

"But that's all it was, pretending." She got out of the car, unleashing Catlin from her car seat.

Bently stayed in the car, watching her walk with her long lazy stride toward the swings, his daughter in her arms. What he'd said was true, he liked thinking of her as Catlin's mother. He liked the idea of Catlin having Raine on her side forever. He watched her sit down on a swing, the baby in her arms, and swish it gently back and forth. Her streaked hair shimmered in the sun, stirring and lifting in the breeze. It blew in her eyes and she tossed her head. Bently's gaze followed the line of her throat down to her breasts, moving softly under her shirt.

He wanted her. He wanted her for himself. He wanted her for his daughter. But he also knew that she was full of stubborn pride. And she was so sure she knew what *he* wanted, what was important to him. But that yardful of kids, those brothers and sisters for Catlin, faded when he looked at this woman holding his daughter. He had a feeling they would be enough. Catlin and Raine would be enough for the rest of his life.

But how was he going to convince stubborn, hardheaded Raine of it? Even she couldn't deny that there was something physical and powerful between them, even though she did her best to stubbornly resist it.

He was just going to have to wage a little war—a tender, slow, very *warm* war.

Bently smiled and got out of the car, grabbing the groceries from the back seat and a plaid stadium blanket from the trunk. He set off across the grass, smile deepening. She might be stubborn, she might have her defenses firmly in place for protection, but Bently had a powerful ally in that little bundle Raine now held in her arms. Daddy's little matchmaker. Between her love for Catlin and her lust for him, this was one war he was going to win. And, boy, was he going to enjoy every minute of it!

"What are you grinning at?"

"Oh, nothing much," Bently said as he spread the blanket out on the grass. "Just thinking what a splendid day it is to do a little battle."

"Excuse me?"

She was standing before him now, his baby in her arms, a puzzled look on her face. He patted the space on the blanket beside him. "Sit down, Raine. You said you were starving. Let's eat."

They divided the salad and took turns tearing at the chicken with their fingers. Catlin spent some time exploring the perimeters of the blanket before settling on her belly, stabbing a drool-wet finger into the grass, babbling to whatever her curiosity had found there.

"So," Raine said around a bite of an apple, "have you thought at all about where that new door opening is going to lead you? I mean, it's good you're not panicking, Pierce, but you *are* still out of work and places like Sendik's Market are expensive."

He twirled a strawberry by its stem. "I've got some money put away, including a small inheritance from my father that I've never touched."

"You planning on going through the rest of your life as a dilettante?"

He smiled ruefully. "I said *small* inheritance, Raine. I think my father wanted to make sure that if I fell on my face I wouldn't have his money to fall back on. A subtle little way of saying 'I told you so' from beyond the grave."

"Sounds like a nice guy."

"I teethed on the motto that nice guys finish last, which is why I made such a damn good corporate lawyer—or shark, as you so accurately pointed out."

"And now?"

He looked at Catlin, tugging at the grass with her pudgy fingers. "And now I want something better, something I can feel good about doing. I'm thinking of setting up in private practice—hanging out my shingle, as it were. What do you think?"

"That depends on what kind of cases you're planning on taking on."

"I thought I'd be one of the good guys this time. I thought I could start by representing David Lester if he decides to fight for his company. But what I'd really like to do is take on a variety of cases—anything that will help the underdog win for a change."

She grinned. "A real white knight, huh?"

Bently grinned back. "Robbing from the rich to give to the poor."

"Then I think it's a great idea. Little Cat will always be able to be proud of her daddy."

He leaned toward her, brushing the backs of his fingers over her cheekbones. "And you?" he asked, his gaze moving over her sun-dappled face.

"I'll always be proud to have you for a friend."

He laughed and shook his head. "You're a hard woman, Raine."

"Lucky for you." She stood up and fetched Cat, settling her between her crossed legs once she'd sat down again, feeding her from a jar of strained chicken. When Cat had had enough of that, she made another tour of the blanket, stopping every so often to gum a chunk of mashed banana in her fist. Content and exhausted at last, she crawled into Raine's lap and fell asleep.

Raine smoothed Cat's dark hair over and over again. "I don't understand how she could have done it," she murmured.

"Who?"

"Caroline. How could she just leave Cat? Even my mother didn't leave when I was a helpless baby. After holding Cat, after feeding her, how could she just walk out?"

"Caroline never did those things."

Raine's head jerked up. "What?"

"She never held Cat, never fed her. She refused to see Catlin again after she was born."

Raine stared at him, her mouth open. "Totally unbelievable," she finally said.

"Caroline never really wanted children."

Raine's anger was right there, an immediate and profane outrage on behalf of his daughter. Bently fell a little further in love with her because of it.

"Then why did she get pregnant?" she demanded.

"Compromise, Raine. That's why you can't really blame Caroline. I was the one who wanted a child. She did it for me."

"You said compromise—just what did you promise *her*?"

Bently smiled faintly. "Nothing too diabolical. I promised she would never have to consider giving up her career. I promised to take equal responsibility in raising Catlin—emotional, physical and financial."

"But she copped out, anyway."

"It was a difficult pregnancy. Instead of bringing us closer together, it drove us further apart." He paused, grinned a little. "I was one of your typical obsessed fathers-in-waiting. I immersed myself totally in the experience. Read anything I could get my hands on, practically bought out the stores, totally convinced that my baby would need every gadget offered out there." He shook his head. "I drove Caroline crazy. I thought it was the most wonderful, most joyful experience of our lives. She just wanted it to be over." He looked away, plucking a leaf from the blanket, crushing the tender, green shoot in his hand. "And in the end, she just wanted to be gone."

"But to not want to see Cat after she was born!"

Bently nodded. "I know. I was appalled by it, too, but by then there was little more than anger left between us. She refused even to allow me in the delivery room." He paused, his jaw tightening. "I believe I really hated her that day—"

Raine took Cat gently in her arms, careful not to wake her, and placed her on the blanket. Straining forward, she touched Bently's arm. "No one would blame you for hating her. I never laid eyes on her, but I think I hate her right now."

Bently covered her hand with his own. "Don't hate her, Raine. She gave birth to Cat. Without her, Cat wouldn't be here. I wanted my child more than anything. And now—now I can't even conceive of life without Cat in it."

Raine looked down at her hands. *Don't ask,* she told herself. *You don't want to know.* Besides, what difference did it make?

But she asked anyway. "I guess you loved her a lot, huh?"

Bently's head shot up. "Who? Caroline?"

Raine nodded, her eyes on the grass she plucked from the earth with her hand.

Bently reached out and claimed her restless fingers. Getting to his knees, he slowly drew her up in front of him. "Once, a long time ago, I thought I was in love with her. But now I see that I couldn't have been. Because now I know what it really feels like to fall in—"

She covered his mouth with her fingers before he could finish. "Don't, Bently. It won't do any good to say it."

"Why?" he whispered against her fingers.

"Because if you say it, the next thing you know, I'll be believing it. And if I believe it, the next thing I'll do is start thinking forever. But forever has a way of never coming, Bently, not for me. My mother left me, my father might as well have. Mick left me, Caroline left you and Cat. Not very good odds, Bently. Not very good at all."

He grinned against her fingers, making the feel of his mouth far too potent, and she had to move them away.

"You called me Bently," he said.

She sighed in exasperation. "Haven't you heard a word I've said?"

"I heard the only word I wanted to hear. You called me Bently, Raine."

"So?" she threw out with some of the old belligerence. "You've been calling Catlin Cat."

He appeared to be thinking it over. "Yeah, I guess I have. Well . . ." He grinned, the look of his mouth almost as potent as the touch of it had been.

"Well, what?"

"Well, I think this calls for a kiss."

She couldn't move fast enough to avoid his arms going around her and his mouth pressing to hers. And then she seemed to forget that that's what she was supposed to do. For long seconds, she forgot to even try to pull away. It was such a sweet kiss. Gentle, light as the breeze blowing in the tree over their heads. Then it changed. His mouth started to move on hers. His breathing changed, as did her own. Just before sensation completely took over, she managed to pull her mouth away and give him a shove hard enough to land him on his back across the blanket.

Bently pulled up on one elbow, grinning wickedly. "You seem to like me sprawled on my back, Raine. There are easier ways to get me there, you know."

"Don't you ever give up, Pierce?" She shook her head and looked at him, lounging where he'd fallen like something out of *The Great Gatsby,* linen trousers spotless, loose linen shirt whiter than white. Only Bently Pierce would manage to stay wrinkle free after being shoved to the ground. "And don't you own a pair of jeans? I feel like I'm breaking bread with the cover boy for this month's *GQ.*"

Bently caught her hand and dragged her down to the ground with him. "If I dig up a pair of jeans and a flannel shirt," he whispered, his dark eyes intent on hers, his body pressed far too close, "can I kiss you?"

He was damn near irresistible, with that grin and that compact muscular body pressing against hers from beneath his fancy clothes. The man definitely didn't have a paunch, she mused.

"Go ahead," he whispered, his lips so close to hers that she could feel the breath of him against her mouth, "call me Bently again."

She moaned, her body yearned, her senses tried for mutiny. But her common sense won out. "Off me, *Pierce,* now—or I start screaming."

Bently groaned and rolled away from her. "I've never known a woman who enjoys playing hard to get as much as you do."

Raine got to her feet and looked down at him. "I'm not playing hard to get, Pierce, I'm playing it smart. Aside from everything else, I'm blue collar. Yours is whiter than white. We don't fit, Pierce. It's as simple as that."

Bently jumped to his feet and caught her in his arms before she could turn away from him. He ran his hands down her back to her buttocks, pulling her into him. Her breathing changed immediately, ragged, hard. She tried to still it, tried to will her body not to react. But it liked being pressed against his—liked it a whole damn lot. She tossed her head and tried to stare him down.

He spread his hands on her and squeezed gently, and she gasped and closed her eyes.

"I say we fit together quite admirably," he said, a fierce little edge to his voice. Then he squeezed again and let her go.

Simmering, she watched as he gathered up the rest of the food and started for the car. He'd gotten the better of her. Her body had betrayed her, and worse, he knew it. Couldn't he see everything that was against them? Damn the man, anyway.

"It'll never happen, Pierce!" she yelled after him.

But he didn't even turn around, and all she heard was his deep chuckle reaching her on the wind.

Chapter Eight

Bently pulled into the alley behind Marshland and cut the engine. "I have something for you," he said.

Raine had been silently stewing all the way home, so his were the first words spoken in the dark car since they'd left the park. She wasn't sure where the anger was coming from, and whether it should be aimed at Bently for his damn expert mouth and his strong, warm hands, or at her own body for constantly betraying her.

Warily, she watched Bently out of the corner of her eye as he drew a package out of his pants pocket and held it out to her.

"What's that?" she demanded.

"It's a present, Raine. And I promise it won't bite. Here—take it."

She eyed it, deciding she wouldn't be at all surprised if it sprouted teeth and took a nip out of her. "Why would you buy me a present?" she asked, trying to keep the edge of anger, but losing the battle.

"It reminded me of you and I wanted you to have it. Simple as that."

She still didn't want to touch it. It seemed like an awfully big leap from kisses in the park to presents in the dark. She couldn't afford any irrevocable leaps.

She heard his heavy sigh of impatience. Heard the rustle of paper. And then he was grabbing her arm and fastening something around her wrist.

It was cool and smooth, jingling softly in the dark as she raised her wrist to her eyes, peering at it in the darkness.

"You bought me jewelry?"

"Just a little silver bracelet, Raine."

She stared at it. "No one ever bought me jewelry before," she murmured.

"It matches your eyes. I wanted you to have it."

The simple oval links held charms of moons, stars and suns. Raine had seen it before. In fact, she'd even tried it on. But when she saw the price tag, she'd taken it off immediately. She wasn't the charm-bracelet type, anyway, she'd told herself. But if she were, she remembered thinking longingly, this would be the one she'd want. And Bently had bought it for her.

She fingered each charm, the silver warming to her touch. She heard Cat's gentle stirring in the back seat where she slept. She could feel Bently's presence in the small dark space, as if the night breeze blowing through the window carried him to her.

This has got to stop, she told herself. Things had gone far enough between them. Something had to be done—and it looked as if she was going to be the one to have to do it.

She cupped her other hand around her wrist, pressing the bracelet against her skin. "I'm free Saturday night," she said with a brightness that she hoped fooled him better than it did her.

"Raine—"

Her name rushed to her as quickly as his arms pulled her against him, his mouth crushing hers, stealing not only her breath but her resolve. Mustering the dregs of it, she gave him a shove that landed him hard against the car door.

"What? You expected payment for the bracelet?" she demanded.

"Well, you said you were free Saturday night, so I just assumed—"

"I'm free to baby-sit, Pierce. *That's all!*"

He straightened, pulling at the twisted collar of his linen shirt. "I wasn't aware I was going anywhere."

"Get a date, Pierce. Go out and enjoy yourself. It's about time you started dating other women."

He stared at her, his dark eyes more dangerous than she'd ever seen them.

"Tell me, Raine," he snapped, "have you also decided what other woman I should date?"

Raine shrugged and gave him a little grin. "I suppose I could fix you up if you can't find anyone who'll go out with you."

"Don't you dare," he bit out slowly, his teeth flashing as white as his shirt.

Raine laughed. "You don't scare me, Pierce. Find a woman by Saturday night—or I'll find one for you."

CATLIN WAS fussing again.

"Come on, pet," Bently crooned. "Don't you want Daddy to go out?"

The baby protested loudly, slamming Bently on his bare chest with a wet fist. He jiggled her up and down, taking his tenth trip around the bedroom, coming to stop in front of the mirror.

"I'll let you in on a little secret, pet," he whispered to her reflection. Catlin stopped fussing, eyeing her tear-stained image with round-eyed interest. "Daddy doesn't want to go out, either. I'd much rather stay here with you and Raine, curled up on the sofa watching television."

"Ki-ki," Catlin said, reaching out for her image.

Bently laughed and kissed her plump, wet cheek. "I'll tell you another little secret. I'm not really going out on a date. Daddy will be cooling his heels at a diner, eating greasy food and drinking no doubt deplorable coffee until enough time has passed to convince Raine that I'm having a perfectly marvelous time."

The doorbell chimed. "There's Raine, now, Cat my pet. Now remember, you're to act like the sweet little matchmaker you are and not breathe a word of this to Raine. The whole object is to get her good and jealous without saddling me with some female who would bore me to death."

The doorbell chimed again and Bently quickly mussed his hair artfully over his forehead, dashed on a huge shot of cologne and started for the front door. Just before he opened it, he undid the belt of his pants, unbuttoning the button and letting them slide a little lower on his hips. He wanted Raine to get a good, hard look at what she would be missing.

"AREN'T YOU even ready yet, Pierce?"

Raine quickly looked away from all that bare chest. She'd stalled, figuring she'd avoid just such a sight. But here he was, naked from the waist up, his belt undone, his feet bare, Catlin cradled in his arms. The baby wore only a diaper, and the contrast of her pink, softly delicate skin against his darker, hair-sprinkled body was quite a sight. His chest and upper arms were more muscled than she'd imagined, and he looked disturbingly masculine holding a small infant.

"If I didn't know better, I'd say Catlin is in a fit of jealous pique. She doesn't seem to want to let me put my shirt on."

He walked past her and headed down the hall toward his bedroom. Lord, the man smelled good. The thick, heady scent of whatever he had splashed on his body worked on her like a magnet, and before she could think about the wisdom of it, she was following him down the hall and standing at the threshold of his bedroom.

More gold and cream, although Caroline had allowed something of a masculine influence here. The blinds were a dark chocolate brown, as were the twin chairs flanking a far-too-delicate table trimmed in gold leaf. The bedspread, of some metallic gold material, was tailored. It spread over the huge bed, drawing Raine's eye, insisting that her mind flutter briefly on the image of what Bently would look like, his dark good looks, his muscled body, lying back against the glimmering gold.

"Um, Raine, would you mind getting my shirt out of the closet for me?"

Happy for a reason to stop staring at that bed, Raine went to the closet and slid the door open. "Which one?" she asked over her shoulder.

"The white silk."

Swell, thought Raine, silk. And was it her imagination or was his voice an octave or two lower? *Pull yourself together. This is a shirt we're talking about.*

She rifled through the shirt section till her hands slid over something white and cool. Real silk, all right. Smooth and slithery. Nice, very nice. Whoever his date was, he was pulling out all the stops. It had been her idea and she was glad he was going, but did he have to dress so enthusiastically?

She slipped the shirt off the hanger, turned around and held it out to him.

He approached her silently, bare feet sinking into the thick cream carpet, dark hair falling seductively over his forehead, his trousers low enough on his hips for a glimpse of black, sleek-fitting underwear. His scent shifted through the room when he moved. She swore she could taste it when she took in a ragged breath. It was like tasting his skin. Her mind seemed to go blank, except for the idea of that skin. And the temptation to smooth back that hair. And the image of that huge bed just behind her. In fact, if it weren't for the baby in his arms, the whole scene would spell the word *seduction.*

No, no—that was merely a figment of her imagination. He was only coming to hand over Cat so he could get dressed for his date. A date she'd pushed him into going on. The thought of the two of them on that bed together was obviously the furthest thing from his mind.

When she took Catlin from his arms, the back of her hand brushed his chest. Fire shot through her and she gulped. "Here." She thrust the shirt at him. "I'll get Cat out of your way so you can finish getting dressed."

Bently watched her leave, wondering if he'd gotten to her at all. He'd been about as blatant as he knew how to be without coming right out and stripping to the skin, flinging himself on his bed, and screaming *Come and get me!* Yet she'd seemed totally oblivious to his efforts, though she'd certainly gotten to him. The feel of her hand brushing his chest had been electric. She, apparently, had felt nothing.

When he'd planned this farce, he'd wanted to get her so fired up that she'd beg him to cancel his date and stay with her. Now it looked as if he was going to have to go through with this ridiculous faux date, after all.

He finished dressing, then found Raine and Cat in the study. She'd stretched out on the carpet, lying on her side, while Catlin crawled nearby. The spring weather hadn't held and the night was cool, so he wasn't treated to the sight of her in shorts, but her battered jeans couldn't hide the length or curve of her graceful legs. Also not hidden was the fact that she seemed totally unaffected by the thought of his going out with another woman. He stalled, pretending to study something on his desk, hoping for some sort of reaction.

He finally got it when she asked, "So who's the lucky lady tonight?" Her voice was just a little too carefully nonchalant.

He stifled his grin and looked up from a paper he'd been pretending to read. "Oh, no one you'd know."

She rolled on to her back and raised her chin to look back at him. "What's the matter? Has she got four heads and the tongue of a fire-eating serpent?"

"On the contrary. Amber is blond, blue-eyed and quite sexy."

"Oh." She stopped looking at him. "Amber, huh? Sounds like the vapid ex-cheerleader type," she muttered.

"Yes, I believe she was a cheerleader. But she was also valedictorian of her class."

"Figures," Raine grumbled.

"And I suppose if I'd left the choice up to you, you'd have found someone more appropriate. A mud wrestler, perhaps?"

Raine hopped to her feet, scooping Cat up into her arms. "Actually, I had a meter maid in mind. The mud wrestlers I know are way too cerebral for you, Pierce. Now hadn't you better get a move on? Don't want to keep Amber waiting, do you?"

Ask me not to go, he chanted inside his head all the way out the front door. But she actually seemed eager to be rid of him. He started the car and watched the woman he was falling in love with holding his baby daughter and waving him off, then shutting the door without a backward glance. And all the while, he was still hoping that she would call him back and beg him not to go.

THE MAN LOOKED GOOD, thought Raine as she watched him walk away. Too good for anyone named Amber. She shut the door and strolled back to his bedroom, telling herself that she only wanted to check to make sure the light was out. His scent still filled the room.

She caught sight of herself in the mirror over the dresser. "It was your idea, Raine," she told her reflection. Cat looked from Raine to her reflection and back again. She gurgled.

"Yeah, I know," Raine answered. "He'd be here with us if I hadn't been so stupid as to suggest that he start looking for another woman."

Well, she wasn't going to let it spoil her night with Cat. She was going to revel in bathing her, feeding her, playing with her and singing her to sleep. Because for all she knew ex-cheerleader Amber just might become Mrs. Bently Pierce, and where would that leave Raine?

Cat let out a string of baby babble, thumping Raine on the head with her tiny hand.

"You're right, Cat. I did wish that I could always be here for you—and I *will* try. Amber or no Amber." After all, wasn't that the whole point? Stay out of Bently's bed, stay in Cat's life? She turned away from the mirror to look at that huge gold surface again. It was slick, sophisticated—and had plenty of room for Cat and any number of brothers and sisters to cuddle up with their parents on cold winter mornings. Raine definitely didn't belong there.

"Come on, Cat, let's check out the TV schedule. I have a feeling it's going to be a long night."

THE SMELL of freshly popped corn hit Bently as soon as he opened the door. He could hear the low rumble of the television from his study, and the flickering glow of the TV screen was the only illumination pouring from the doorway.

He'd stayed away as long as he could, downed enough bad coffee to give him heartburn for a week and sampled two of Lottie's blue-plate specials—and still it was only ten o'clock. He'd thought of taking in a late movie by himself but took one look at the romantic comedy touted on the marquee of the neighborhood theatre and knew where he wanted to be. With Raine. With Catlin.

He'd thought about them the entire evening. Thought about spending a cozy, quiet evening sharing Catlin's bathtime and bedtime with Raine. Then sharing his own bed with Raine.

Quietly he headed down the hall to the study. She was sitting on the floor, cross-legged, in front of the sofa, a bowl of popcorn nestled between her thighs with Catlin sleeping on a blanket next to her.

He grinned at the wonderful picture they made.

"Some baby-sitter you are—don't you know it's way past Cat's bedtime?" he whispered.

Raine's head shot up. "I didn't hear you come in."

He came into the room. "What's so engrossing?" he asked, sitting on the sofa, his gaze going to the television screen. Humphrey Bogart crying in his gin—ordering Sam to "play it."

"*Casablanca*," he whispered. "I haven't seen this in ages." He shrugged off his jacket and loosened his tie, throwing them both in the direction of a chair.

Kicking off his shoes, he stretched out the length of the sofa, his head close to Raine's, reached over her shoulder for a handful of popcorn and settled down to watch.

He had a hard time keeping his mind on Ingrid Bergman. He could smell the peaches on Raine. She'd leaned back against the sofa and scrunched down a little to rest her head very near his own. Ingrid was beautiful, but she couldn't hold a candle to the way the light played in Raine's hair. He laid his head down so close to hers that he could smell her shampoo. It smelled like the same stuff he used on Catlin. He heard her sigh and felt it all the way to his groin.

"Wasn't Bogey noble?"

Yean, he thought, *a hell of a lot more noble than you, Bently old boy.* But in a way it was Raine's own fault he'd had to lie to her. She was the one who'd insisted he find himself another woman. Besides, even Bogey might agree that all was fair in love and war— even the tender war he was waging on Raine.

Raine sighed again. "Wasn't Ingrid luminous?"

Yeah, luminous, he thought. *But not as luminous as you are, Raine—not when you're holding my daughter with all the love in the world on your face.*

He watched Bogey walk into the fog with Claude Raines, talking about friendship after he'd just given up the love of his life. Maybe once he would have applauded it. Now he thought, *no way.* Because now he knew what really being in love was like. He wasn't giving up the love of his life without a fight.

Raine sniffled. "What a movie." She sighed again and turned toward him. Their noses almost touched. "Oh," she said, but she didn't move away.

"Did you and Cat have a nice evening?" he asked her softly.

She nodded, her eyes on his. "I hated to put her to bed, so I didn't."

"I do that sometimes, too," he confessed. "I like having her near, watching her sleep."

She stared into his eyes for a moment, then blinked. "How was your date?"

"Barely tolerable."

She grinned a little. "I guess Amber's not the one, hey?"

"Definitely not."

Her eyes looked like liquid silver, her hair a mussed cloud of moonbeams, her wide mouth middle-of-the-night soft. He wanted to kiss it, wanted to take her face in his hands and tell her that he'd already found the one for him. But then the liquid silver would turn to hard, cold steel and she would turn stubborn and fight him. He couldn't ruin the moment.

He didn't know how long they sat like that, eyes drinking in each other, breath mingling. Then Catlin stirred and sat straight up, rubbing her eyes and ears, fussing a little at finding herself on the floor instead of in her crib.

Raine pulled her eyes away from his and scooped the baby up into her arms. "Why don't you go get her a bottle while I change her," she whispered.

Bently nodded. "Meet you in the nursery."

In the kitchen, he held a bottle under hot running water, staring out the window into the dark, windy night, smiling at his reflection in the glass. She was here—maybe not for the night, but she was here. And it felt right, so incredibly right. A warm home, a sleeping child, a bowl of popcorn and an old movie on a chilly spring night. All he needed to make it complete was to be able to take Raine in his arms.

When he got to the nursery, Raine was rocking Cat, singing to her softly. He handed her the bottle, then hunkered down to watch. When Cat's eyes finally closed again, they put her in the crib together, Raine smoothing Cat's nightgown, Bently pulling her blanket over her and bending to kiss her cheek.

They stood over her for a few moments, Bently covering Raine's hand where it rested on the crib rail with his own. The ritual was all the more special for having her here to share it. "Stay with me tonight," he whispered.

Without a word, she pulled her hand out from under his and left the nursery.

Bently followed. "Why so shocked, Raine?" he said to her back as she headed for the kitchen. "You know I want you. That hasn't changed."

Once in the kitchen, she faced him. "May I remind you, Pierce, that you've just come from sexy, brainy Amber's arms!"

"A date you insisted I go out on," he bit out.

She thrust her hands into her pockets, tossing her hair. "Yeah, well I don't take leftovers—and I don't need a quick roll in the hay as payment for babysitting, either!"

He stalked up to her, grabbed her arms and pulled her up against him. "Get one thing straight, Raine. If I roll in the hay with you, as you so romantically put it, it won't be a payment of any kind. It'll be because I can't get you out of my mind. It'll be because my body goes hard just thinking about the taste of your lips." His gaze fastened on her mouth, the anger in his words dissolving into urgency. "I love the idea that you're here for Cat. But I'd love the idea that you were here for me even more."

She couldn't think. She couldn't pull away. She was caught in his gaze like a doe in a headlight—and almost as afraid. Yet when his mouth came down on hers, fear was the furthest thing from her mind. God, it felt good. All night, she'd imagined him kissing the faceless Amber like this. All night she'd fought the admission that he should be there, right there with her and Cat.

His mouth pulled away from hers. "Stay tonight, Raine. Stay with me," he whispered through ragged breath and she nearly moaned with longing.

She pushed him away and shook her head. "It wouldn't be worth it, Pierce. A one-night stand wouldn't be worth losing Cat."

He shoved a hand through his hair. "Damn it! I'm not talking about a one-night stand!"

"You talking about forever, Pierce? That wouldn't work, and we both know why."

"God, you're stubborn!"

She almost grinned. "No, I'm just *right*," she drawled as she started for the door.

"Okay, Raine, if you think you're so right, if you think dating other women is the right thing for me, then dating other men must be the right thing for you. Maybe it's time I put some energy into fixing you up."

She spun around to face him. "I don't need anybody fixing me up, Pierce," she shot at him angrily. "I get plenty of dates on my own."

He smiled lazily. "Really? Jack get free tickets to a ball game again?"

She straightened her posture. "Yes, really. And no, not with Jack."

"Who, then, Raine?"

"You want proof?"

He shrugged. "A name and date will do for now."

"Well, now that you mention it, I do have a dinner date coming up."

"A dinner date. My, that sounds respectable. When?"

"What?"

"When? Tomorrow evening? Next week? When, Raine?"

"That's none of your business."

"Sure it is, if it's your business whom *I* date. So tell me, Raine, when?" He took a step toward her.

"Saturday night," she answered in panic. "Are you satisfied now?"

"Who's the guy?"

"I'm not telling you that."

"Because there isn't anyone."

"What—you think I can't get a date? Well, I've got one. Saturday night."

"Hmm, so you said. Dinner, wasn't it?" She nodded. "Where?"

"Where?"

"Yes, Raine, where? A&W? Burger King? McDonald's, perhaps? I know those are some of Jack's favorites."

"It's not Jack and it's not McDonald's! This guy's taking me to the Pfister," she threw out, grabbing the name of the first fancy place that came into her head.

"Ah, excellent. The English Room, I assume?"

She thrust her chin up. "Of course."

His eyes narrowed. "What a coincidence. I have reservations there myself next Saturday night."

He didn't believe her. Tough. She wasn't about to back down now. "Great. I'll probably see you there, then."

"Undoubtedly."

She turned to go, then turned back. "Of course, with your sitter troubles, you may have to cancel. Since I won't be available to take care of Cat, I mean."

"I'll find someone."

She stared at him. "Great. Well, see ya."

"Good night, Raine."

His voice was soft, the smile on his lips enigmatic. She couldn't tell if he was making fun of her or not. "Good night," she finally said. When she climbed into the van and started the engine, he was leaning in the doorway, watching her.

Her big mouth had gotten her into trouble again. Where the hell was she going to get a date for Saturday night?

RAINE HUSTLED DEE into Marshland's office and shut the door. "I've got a problem."

"My, this sounds juicy. What kind of problem?"

"I need a date. Somebody flush enough to afford the English Room at the Pfister. And I need it for this Saturday night."

Dee's eyes positively gleamed. "Ohhh, something I can get my teeth into." Without any questions, she grabbed the Rolodex on her desk and plopped gracefully into her chair. "Let's see." She tapped her front tooth with a long burgundy fingernail, spinning the Rolodex with her other hand. "No...no...ohhh, here's one. Ian Sommersby. Perfect. You've even met."

Raine furrowed her brow. "We have?"

"Of course. Don't you remember? He's the one that was following you like a puppy dog all over Cindy Holstrum's wedding reception."

"You mean sniffing around like I was in heat, don't you? The guy was all hands and ego."

"I don't think you can afford to be too picky on such short notice, Raine. He meets your requirements. He's loaded, quite attractive, and he'll jump at the chance to go out with you, even on such short notice."

"Forget it, Dee. I'm not fighting that octopus off just to show up Bently Pierce."

"Ohhh," gushed Dee, "this gets better and better." She patted the empty chair near her desk. "Tell Dee all about it."

"No time. I not only need a date, I need a dress. Something that'll knock a guy's socks off."

"So you've finally come to your senses. You're out to snare Bently Pierce."

"No way!" Raine protested. "I'm out to convince him that we don't belong together."

Dee gave a puzzled frown. "Then whose socks are you looking to knock off?"

"My date's—the one you're going to find for me." She pointed at the Rolodex. "Keep looking."

"But where are you going?"

"To wade through Marshland for the perfect dress. And I expect a big fat discount."

"Are you kidding? To see you in a dress after all these years, you can have it wholesale!"

"You're on!" Raine yelled then started rifling through Marshland's racks of dresses. She rejected one after the other as too staid, too classy, too boring. She wanted something totally dynamite! Something in slightly bad taste. She should have known Dee wouldn't carry anything of that caliber.

Then she found it. Hidden among the clearance racks was just what she needed. She grabbed it and headed for a mirror.

"You're not seriously considering—"

"You bet I am!"

"A bit overdone for the Pfister, wouldn't you say?"

"That's the point, Dee! If you and I think so, Bently Pierce will definitely think so, too."

"But if you want to make him jealous . . ."

"Are you nuts, Dee? I'm not out to make Pierce jealous, for heaven's sake. I'm out to prove to him how totally wrong we are for each other. When he sees me at the English Room in this—" she held the dress up with a flourish "—he'll be glad that it's not *his* arm I'm hanging on."

Dee was still looking confused. "Let me see if I've got this. He wants you—"

"Well, he thinks he does."

"You're crazy about his baby—"

"Right."

"But you don't want him—"

"Well, yes and no. I do want him, but it wouldn't work."

Dee kneaded her forehead desperately with two fingers. "For heaven's sake, why not?"

"Because," Raine said, holding up the dress again, "I'm the kind of woman who would wear this to the English Room!"

"Don't you mean that you're the kind of woman that can't have children?" Dee asked quietly.

Raine's reflection stared at her out of the mirror. "Cat should have brothers and sisters. It's what Bently wants, too."

"People compromise, Raine, if they love someone enough."

"Mick didn't."

"Bently isn't Mick."

No, thought Raine, staring at her reflection. Not by a long shot, he wasn't. Bently Pierce was like no other man she'd ever met. Was she in love with him? She didn't know. She only knew that she cared enough about him—and Cat—not to want to take any of his dreams away from him.

She looked at the dress in her hands again. She also knew Bently Pierce well enough to know that he was going to hate this dress.

"Yup," she said to Dee, a smile back on her face, "this is the dress I'm wearing to the Pfister on Saturday night. Now find me that date!"

Chapter Nine

"Ah, yes. Mr. Pierce. So nice to have you with us again. If you'll come this way, your table is ready."

Bently and his date followed the maître d' to a table near the entrance. Normally, Bently would have preferred one more secluded, but tonight he wanted front and center. He had no intention of missing Raine's entrance with her mystery date.

He looked at his own date for the evening. "Champagne, Claudia?"

She gave him a serene little smile. "That would be lovely, Bently."

Claudia Hilliard was small, delicate and lovely in a refined, understated way. She fitted right in at the Pfister Hotel's English Room. The place resonated with the sort of hushed tones that only seemed to exist in expensive restaurants, as if the cutlery and china themselves were too well bred to ever actually clink or scrape, rudely intruding upon the discreet chamber music. The richly patterned carpet was thick, absorbing footfalls. The seating areas were divided by leaded glass, affording a certain privacy yet allowing patrons to ascertain at a glance which of their well-heeled acquaintances were noshing that evening on the duck ravioli or the classic rack of lamb.

It was the sort of place Bently used to frequent. Tonight he found it a trifle stuffy, a little boring—just like the woman at his side.

"So, Claudia, how are things with the Milwaukee Symphony?"

Claudia played second violin. It was how Bently had first seen her. She'd struck him as lovely and self-contained, the stage lights softly shining on her light brown hair. They'd dated a few times, pre-Caroline, but nothing seemed to happen between them. The last he'd heard, she'd just broken off with a viola player and was still in mourning. Bently had thought it safe to ask her out to dinner—strictly as a friend.

He half listened to her talk about her music, keeping his eyes as unobtrusively as possible on the doorway, hoping not to miss Raine's entrance.

When she finally showed up, half a bottle of champagne and an appetizer plate of duck ravioli later, it was clear that no one, no matter how hard they tried, could possibly miss her entrance.

Bently had never seen such a dress.

And he was sure that if he had, it would never have looked as spectacular as it was looking on Raine at that moment.

It was a color that could only be described as peridot—a deep yellowish green—in some material that shimmered and glimmered when she walked. The bodice was tight, molded like a second skin from her waist to the high neckline. It was sleeveless, cut to expose her gleaming, wide shoulders, and the skirt flared from the waist to end inches above the knees of her spectacular legs.

And oh, those legs! Bently had never seen them look so glorious as they did that night. The high, silvery heels she wore lengthened them beyond what was good for a man's soul. And even more eye-stopping was the fact that a long, large silver zipper shot up the center of the dress, ending in a huge, rhinestone pull at the neck.

Lord, could he picture what he'd like to do with that zipper.

"Do you know her?" Claudia leaned over and whispered.

He could deny it, but what would be the point? Raine was ignoring the maître d' and leading her date over to Bently's table at that very moment.

"Bently—what a surprise!"

Bently stood, sputtering out a hello while his eyes moved directly to the rhinestone slave bracelet hugging her upper arm, up past her gleaming, bare shoulders and to her silver eyes, smoky and deep, with a soft shadow smudged on her almond-shaped lids. Her hair, sun kissed as always, was artfully mussed, swinging out sassily from her jawline.

She looked tan; she looked healthy; she looked sexy as hell. And she just about took his breath away.

"Bently seems to have forgotten his manners." She held out her hand to Claudia. "Hi, I'm Raine Rogers and this is Richard Collins."

"Oh, yes, of course," sputtered Bently. "This, uh, this is Claudia—ah, Claudia—"

"Hilliard," Claudia supplied for him, taking Raine's hand. "Nice to meet you."

Claudia looked even more subdued next to Raine's bright plumage. Her mauve silk dress was in the best of taste, her brown hair was twisted into a knot at her nape, her only jewelry tiny pearl studs in her shell-like ears.

Richard held out his hand. "We've never met," he said softly, "but I've heard you play. Marvelous."

Claudia took his hand, coloring gently. "Why, thank you."

The maître d' was hovering. "I guess they don't think much of table-hopping here. See ya." Raine waved her fingers at Bently. "Come on, Richie, guess they want us to sit." She grabbed the man's tie and led him away, looking like a disco goddess hauling her prey. Bently wished with everything in him that his was the tie in that tan long-fingered hand.

RAINE PEEKED from behind her tasseled menu. Bently looked terrific. His dark slouchy suit with its low-slung double-breasted jacket worn with a collarless silk shirt and no tie made Richard look more buttoned-down Ivy League than ever. She didn't know what Dee was thinking of, pairing her up with a stuffy stockbroker straight out of Brooks Brothers. The guy was wearing wing tips, for heaven's sakes! For the dress to really have an impact, she should have been paired with some punk-rocker type, not some guy in an oxford-cloth shirt with a thread count even higher than his IQ.

"How do you know Bently Pierce?" Richard asked.

Raine thought fast. "I'm a friend of his daughter's."

Richard frowned. "But I thought his daughter was just a baby?"

Raine lowered her menu. "You know him?"

"Only by reputation. Rumor has it that he was fired from Wesley and Harper."

"Yeah, well, only because they wouldn't listen to reason. Bently was tired of playing the shark, so he told them—"

Richard grinned. "Friend of his daughter's, huh?"

Raine dipped her head and shrugged. "Well, they were wrong—he was right. He's going into private practice, which is what he should have done in the first place."

Richard picked up her hand. "Quite a feisty defense. Do you often champion your friends' fathers?"

Raine put her menu aside. "Never mind Bently Pierce, Richard. Why don't you tell me all about yourself?" She propped an elbow on the table, cupping her chin in her hand, and tried for a look of absorbed interest. Richard was still holding her other hand and it was in danger of falling asleep. So was she. In fact, if she hadn't been so wired by the thought of Bently on the other side of the room, she'd have been nodding off at that very moment.

She stole a look at him, only to find his dark eyes glaring in her direction again. The dress had worked. It was obvious that he was madder than hell to see her there in it. Good. Now maybe he'd see that the two of them couldn't possibly work. Now maybe he'd leave her alone.

Too bad the prospect wasn't making her as happy as she'd thought it would.

"Are you using me to make Pierce jealous, Raine?" Richard's soft voice cut into her reverie. She thrust her chin up and tossed her hair. "No, of course not!"

"Well, either something's up or Deirdre Marsh just played an enormous practical joke on both of us."

Bently was still looking, so Raine playfully put a finger under Richard's chin and gazed into his eyes. "What's the matter, Richard," she cooed. "Aren't you happy with your blind date?"

"I may be a little too dull to appreciate that dress, but I'm far from stupid. It's obvious that I'm boring you to death."

When Raine started to protest, he put up a hand. "Oh, it's not your fault, Raine. Nobody in his right mind would pair the two of us up—not unless it was some kind of joke."

"Well, it's debatable, isn't it, whether Dee is in her right mind?" Raine said sweetly. But the guy definitely had a point. Dee had to know that Bently would take one look at them together and just know that there couldn't possibly be anything between them. And maybe that's why Dee had done it. Maybe she'd been out to sabotage Raine's plan from the first! If so, she had greatly underestimated Raine.

"Okay, Richard, I'll come clean. The idea is to get Bently to see that he and I don't belong together. This dress, my behavior, is supposed to be inappropriate for a place like the English Room. The only trouble is,

Dee sent me a guy who's a hell of a lot more buttoned down than Bently Pierce ever thought of being." She looked at Richard. "Sorry, but you know what I mean."

"I spoil the effect of the dress."

"Exactly. You're appropriate enough to cancel it out."

Richard appeared to be thinking the situation over. "All may not be lost," he finally said.

"What do you mean?"

"Maybe I'd be willing to act a little inappropriately for a good cause."

This was getting interesting. "And that cause being?"

"Get me Claudia's phone number and I'll be inappropriate enough to get us thrown out of here."

BENTLY'S EYES narrowed dangerously. Collins had hold of her hand, damn him. Looked as if they were quite engrossed in conversation, as well. Raine had barely taken her eyes off him since they'd been seated. And here he was unable to think of a thing to say to Claudia. He wondered what Raine could possibly have to say to Richard Collins. Bently didn't know him well, and he'd always seemed like a decent man, but Raine with one of the most conservative stockbrokers in the city? It just didn't fit.

"How do you know her?" Claudia asked.

Bently squirmed a little in his seat before answering, "She's a friend of my daughter's."

"Really? I thought Catlin was less than a year old."

Bently tore his gaze from the couple across the room and looked at Claudia. She had a sweet, gentle grin on her face, but he thought he knew exactly what she was thinking.

"I've been obsessed with the woman ever since she kidnapped my daughter," he blurted out.

There was a genteel gasp from the neighboring table, and Bently turned to look at the silver-haired couple. They both suddenly became very interested in their menus, and Bently's eyes became riveted across the room again.

"I take it," Claudia said in a mild voice, "that this obsession has nothing to do with seeing her brought to justice?"

Confused, Bently turned to her. "What?"

"Having her arrested—you said she kidnapped your daughter?"

Bently found himself explaining the whole messy situation to Claudia, who sat listening with polite, amused interest just as if he weren't discussing the woman he was falling in love with with the woman he was supposed to be dating.

"Just look at them," he said when he'd come to the end of his tale, "laughing, talking." And indeed, he could hear Raine's throaty laugh, spontaneous, earthy—sexier than anything the walls of the English Room had absorbed in all its one hundred years. "What could she possibly see in Richard Collins?"

"He seems perfectly nice to me," Claudia murmured. "But you *are* right—he hardly seems her type, does he? In fact, I should say he's much more my type."

Yes, thought Bently, *definitely more Claudia's type. Not that you'd know it to look at them,* he thought crossly. And now Richard was whispering something in Raine's ear—and Bently had a feeling it had nothing whatsoever to do with the Dow Jones.

And now he was *nibbling* her ear! Only Raine Rogers would neck in a place like the English Room. How totally and absurdly—

Oh, hell, who was he trying to kid? If he were her date, he'd take one look at her in that dress and neck the night away, no matter where they were!

"Bently, you're glowering. Perhaps you'd like to leave?"

Bently looked down at the tiny hand on his arm. "No, of course I don't want to leave. Let's choose our entrées, shall we?"

Bently picked up his menu, but none of the English Room's exquisite offerings could capture his attention. His gaze kept wandering over the top of the menu every time he heard Raine's throaty laugh. Richard Collins had to be quite the comedian.

And what was he doing now? Good Lord! The man was getting down on his knees at Raine's feet! And now he was slipping off one of her high-heeled silver shoes. Who did the man think he was—Prince Charming? And now he was actually pouring wine into Raine's shoe, dribbling it all over the carpet! Damn the man! He didn't even have the sense to know that an open-strapped shoe like that wouldn't hold wine. The whole damn restaurant was staring.

"Richard! Stop!" he heard Raine squeal. "Will you get off your knees and behave yourself! Everyone's looking!"

Well, mused Bently, if they hadn't been, they certainly were now, given the way Raine's voice carried. The silver-haired couple at the next table seemed sincerely scandalized. Even now, they were calling for the maître d', demanding that something be done.

Bently slapped down his menu, giving up the pretense of trying to order. "The nerve of the man," he muttered.

"Your friend seems to need help," Claudia offered.

Bently perked up. "You think so?"

"Well, she's obviously not happy about the commotion Richard is causing."

Indeed, she had stopped laughing. Well, who could laugh with Richard on his knees trying to mop up wine with a linen napkin? In fact, she looked so embarrassed that he suddenly felt like smashing the guy's face in. After all, Raine had obviously gone to a lot of trouble for this date, and then she gets stuck with an oaf who doesn't know the first thing about how to treat a lady.

"Bently, are you all right?" Claudia asked.

"No, I'm not all right," he blurted out. "I'd like to go over there and teach that stock shuffler a lesson. How dare he treat Raine like this—embarrass her like this!"

"Well, then maybe you had better do it."

Bently swung his head around at the sound of Claudia's soft, even voice.

"What?"

"Go ahead, Bently. Rescue your friend. That's where your heart is, anyway."

"You're sure?"

She nodded and he stood and threw down his napkin. Claudia placed a small hand on his arm. "Just one thing, Bently."

He looked down at her. "Yes?"

"When you're through with him, send Richard over."

"You mean it?"

"Why not? I've never had anyone drink wine out of *my* slipper before."

Bently grinned. "You're a very nice woman, Claudia."

"Maybe, but I wouldn't be caught dead in a dress that shade of green—so I guess I'm not for you."

Bently took Claudia's hand and bent to kiss it. When he released it, he turned his full attention on the man at Raine's feet. His brows lowering, his mouth thinning, he stalked across the room, uncaring that nearly every head in the place had swiveled in his direction.

"Get on your feet," he ordered, staring down at Richard's head.

"Mind your own business." Richard shot up at him, licking wine off the instep of Raine's shoe.

"This *is* my business," Bently bit out, hauling Richard up by the arm. "You are embarrassing the lady. Kindly apologize and then leave."

Richard's face had gone white at Bently's tone, and Raine didn't blame him. Despite the fact that Richard was inches taller, Bently looked more than capable of flattening him.

"This is outrageous!" the silver-haired man proclaimed, his wife all a-twitter.

"Uh, Bently—" Raine began, thinking that the whole thing had gone far enough.

Bently ignored her. "Apologize, Richard," he hissed, shifting his grip from Richard's arm to his shirtfront, hauling him closer to his own menacing face, "or I'll gladly take you outside and teach you some manners."

Raine jumped to her feet. "Pierce, for heaven's sake, leave him alone."

"Not until he apologizes."

Richard, his eyes starting to bug, merely sputtered.

"How can he say anything with that stranglehold you've got on him!" She thumped Bently on his arm with her fist. "Besides, the whole thing was my fault. So just let him go!"

Bently loosened his hold. "What do you mean, *your* fault?"

"That's right, old boy. It was all Raine's idea," Richard rasped out. "She wanted to get us thrown out of here."

"She wanted to—*why?*"

Raine pushed between the two men with such force that Richard lost his balance and went sprawling to the carpet. "I wanted to show you that I didn't belong in a place like this, any more than I belong in your life! I wanted to make you admit how different we are—how we just don't fit!"

She thought he'd be angry. Instead, his mouth moved into one of his dazzling, toothy grins. "You mean this date was just a setup?"

"Well, you goaded me into saying I had a date, Pierce. You know you did! And so I had to come up with one, and it seemed a shame to waste the whole damn thing, so I thought—"

Bently interrupted her with a rich, hearty laugh before picking Richard up off the floor, dusting him down and escorting him over to Claudia Hilliard.

"There," he said on his return, pulling out a chair for Raine, "now that that's all straightened out, let's order."

Raine's mouth dropped open. "Of all the arrogant nerve! You think I'm going to just trade dates and go on like nothing happened?"

"Why not? After all, this is how it should have been in the first place."

"No way, Pierce. If you think—"

"Excuse me, Mr. Pierce?"

Bently swung around to face the maître d'. "Yes?"

"We've received just too many complaints about this table, sir. I'm afraid the management feels it would be better for all concerned if you left."

Bently stared. "You're throwing me out?"

The maître d' cleared his throat. "Yes, sir, you and your, um, companion."

Raine expected him to be furious. Instead, he drew himself up haughtily, extracted a bill—a large one—stuffed it into the maître d's breast pocket, retrieved Raine's soggy shoe from the floor and grabbed her hand.

"Come on, Raine," he said loudly enough for their interested audience to hear. "This place is getting a little stuffy even for me."

Raine snatched up her purse, waved to the astonished silver-haired couple and then had all she could do to keep upright as Bently pulled her toward the door.

Up the stairs they went, through the hotel lobby, skirting its ornate pillars and several yuppie-type guests waiting to check in and out into the street, with Raine limping all the way in one high heel.

"Will you stop, Pierce—and give me my shoe!" she yelled.

"And then what?" he said over his shoulder. "Are you going to grab the doorman and start necking with *him?*"

Said doorman looked properly shocked, his hand going nervously to his tie. Raine almost laughed. "No, I'm going to put it on so I can stop hobbling, then I'm going to get a cab home!"

The doorman stepped nervously closer. "The lady would like a cab, sir?"

"No," snapped Bently, "the lady would not. The lady is coming with me so we can resume our date."

"We don't have a date, Pierce! We *never* had a date."

"Then we're starting one *now.*"

"Come on, Pierce, you don't want to go out with me—not in a dress like this! Not with one of my shoes soggy with another guy's wine."

Bently took in a deep breath of the crisp night air. "Get something straight, Raine. No one—" he pulled her closer "—absolutely no one—" he pulled her closer still until their eyes were inches apart "—is drinking wine out of your shoe while you're wearing that dress, except me." The last words were low, ground out between his gorgeous white teeth. His dark eyes mesmerized her for one second more, then he pulled her the rest of the way into his arms. "No one gets you tonight but me, Raine," he murmured in her ear, and then she felt the sharp little bite of his teeth at her lobe.

She moaned and tried to pull away. But he wouldn't let her. "Bently, you promised," she groaned as his tongue traced the whorls of her ear. "You lost the bet, remember? You promised to leave me alone."

"I lost that bet purely by default, Raine. You felt something when I kissed you in the rain that night— just like you're feeling something now."

It was too much. She'd never known her ear to be such an erogenous zone before. His teeth and tongue took turns torturing it, soothing it. Raine felt it in every part of her body; her breasts tingled, her belly more than fluttered—it throbbed—and her muscles turned to jelly...

The beat of her heart seemed to get louder—until she realized it wasn't her heart at all, but a horse-drawn carriage pulling up to the curb in front of the hotel.

"Ahem. Excuse me, sir?"

Bently pulled his mouth from Raine's ear. "Yes?" he asked with all the imperiousness of a man who felt he had a perfect right to stand on the sidewalks of

Wisconsin Avenue under the Pfister's green awning and do anything he liked.

The doorman smiled wanly. "If you wouldn't mind just moving over a yard or two, sir? Some passengers are trying to alight."

"Ah, yes, the carriage. Sorry."

"That's quite all right, sir."

The doorman bowed and Bently led Raine away.

Raine hobbled after him. "Where are we going now, Pierce? Maybe you'd like to neck in front of the Riverside Theater for a while?"

Bently gave a bark of laughter. "Very nice suggestion, Raine, but I think we'll try for somewhere more private this time."

"Never mind private, Pierce. Try for some place with food. I'm starving and you owe me a dinner. And give me my shoe!"

Suddenly, he bent gracefully to one knee before her and she felt the rough warmth of his hand circling her ankle. "What are you doing, Pierce?"

A shock of hair blew across his forehead, and a wicked light gleamed in his dark eyes as he looked up at her. "Your shoe, my lady," he said, lifting her foot, sliding his hand under it.

Raine shivered and closed her eyes as he slipped the shoe in place. But by the time he rose, she had her anger firmly back in place. "What do you think you are, Pierce, Prince Charming?"

The tilt of his smile was as wicked as the glint in his eyes. "Exactly," he bit out, and then he was pulling her along again.

She tried to wiggle her hand out of his while they waited for the walk light to cross to the parking lot, but he wouldn't let go. A car full of teenage boys sped past, one of them hanging out the window, whistling and yelling at Raine. Bently finally let go of her hand, only to snake his arm around her waist and pull her in tight beside him.

"What do you think you're doing?" she demanded.

"Staking my claim. You're advertising your wares in that dress. I'm just making sure that all the window shoppers know the merchandise is already taken."

Secretly pleased at his words, she felt her mouth twist into a wry smile. "I thought you'd hate this dress, Pierce. That's why I bought it."

They were crossing the street now, and he waited until they reached the other side before he looked at her, his dark gaze sweeping from the glittery zipper pull at her throat, across her breasts, waist and hips, down to her long, long legs. "The only way I could like that dress any better, Raine, is if it was pooled on the floor alongside my bed."

"You wish," she drawled.

"Damn right I do."

They'd reached the Mark VIII. Raine moved stubbornly to the driver's door, leaning against it and holding out her palm.

"Give me your keys. I want to drive."

"Nothing doing," he said, taking her arm and escorting her none too gently to the other side of the car.

"Come on, Pierce, don't be such a square. Cat's not in the back seat this time. What have you got to lose?"

"Try my life or my car insurance."

"You don't trust me?" she purred sweetly.

"After the stunt you pulled tonight with Richard Collins? Not likely. Besides," he added with a leer, "that dress is giving me about as much excitement as I can take for one evening. I have absolutely no intention of letting you loose behind the wheel."

Bently unlocked the door and all but shoved her in, circling the car and getting in on the driver's side.

"I don't get it, Pierce. I thought you'd take one look at me walking into a place like the Pfister in a dress like this and realize once and for all that nothing between us could ever work."

He turned toward her in the seat, put his hand behind her neck and drew her face close to his. "Get something straight, Raine. If I'm in love with you, you could wear sackcloth and ashes to the Pfister, or a barrel and suspenders to the symphony, and I wouldn't give a damn."

Sudden pressure from his hand brought her mouth up to his and he kissed her, hard. Then he let her go and started the car.

"If I'm in love with you..." The words caught in her mind like a record with a scratch, playing over and over again. What did he mean *if?* And was she in love with him? Did she love him just as much as she loved his little baby daughter? And if she did, what was she going to do about it? If *he* did, what was she going to do about it?

He had to see that it would never work. He wanted more children; she would never have children. He was used to eating at places like the English Room any night of the week, places that made Raine as nervous as a teenager on prom night—which would be the only night she'd have been likely to set foot in the place, if she'd been the type to go to the prom. The dress was supposed to make him see all that. Instead it was turning him on—

"Where to?" he suddenly asked.

"Huh?"

"You said I owed you a dinner. Where would you like to go?"

Raine decided to seize the opportunity for another chance at showing him how really different they were. "Get on the High-Rise Bridge, Pierce, and head for the south side."

Bently raised his brows. "The south side?"

"That's right, Pierce. I know a place that has oldies on the juke and great burgers. You *do* know your way to the south side, don't you?" she added with as much sarcasm as she could muster.

"Oh, I know my way around the south side, Raine. In fact—" he reached out to run a finger slowly around her ear, flicking at her lobe with his thumb before trailing his fingertips to the pulse at her throat "—you might be surprised at the places I know my way around."

Helplessly watching him, she gulped, her pulse thumping against his fingers. He leaned over, his dark eyes homing in on her mouth.

"I like onions on my burgers, Pierce."

He laughed softly and brushed his lips against hers. "So do I, Raine. So do I."

Chapter Ten

Memories was the kind of tavern Bently never went to. The place was dark, illuminated only by the neon beer signs behind the bar and the cheap red-glass candle holders on the tables. The yeasty smell of beer and the enticing aroma of onions frying in butter filled the air. It was noisy, the jukebox competing with the clink of glassware and the cacophony of voices. While a few couples gyrated on the tiny dance floor, more sat at tables chomping on burgers or eating chicken with their fingers.

"Grab a table, Pierce. I'll order."

Bently sat at the nearest table and watched Raine trot up to the bar and yell something to the bartender. Soon she was back with two tall frosty glasses in her hands.

The beer tasted wonderful, better than the expensive wine he'd chosen at the English Room. It was cold, dark, potent. But not as potent as the sight of Raine, flipping the hair out of her eyes with the toss of her head, her bare shoulders moving to the beat of something from the sixties, that slave bracelet glittering on her arm.

"Where's Cat tonight?" she asked.

"Jack. He's always glad to baby-sit in exchange for freezer and microwave privileges."

Raine nodded and gulped at her beer. The jukebox suddenly went silent and she grabbed her purse and trotted off to punch some numbers. Bently watched her short skirt flipping out around her long legs as she walked. So did half the guys in the bar.

The bartender yelled, "Yo, burgers are up!" and Raine took a detour to the bar, heading back to the table with two red-plastic baskets heaped with steaming food.

He watched her slather ketchup on everything, then dig in. He followed suit then took a huge bite. "This is the best damn burger I've ever eaten. Fantastic," he said around a mouthful.

Swell, thought Raine munching on a fry, *he likes it.* Well, what did she expect? They *were* the best burgers in town, and she supposed that even a guy like Bently Pierce would know a good burger when he bit into one. She'd have to try something else.

She stood up. "Let's dance!" Without giving him a chance to refuse, she pulled his hand, forcing him out on the dance floor. She was almost sure he would hate it. Bently Pierce would never make a spectacle of himself out on the dance floor—and he wouldn't want his date to, either.

Surprise, surprise. "Hey, Pierce, you can dance!"

"Sure I can. Did you think I'd sprung from the womb in a three-piece suit with a briefcase attached to my arm? I was a teenager once, you know."

Yeah, she'd known he was a teenager, but she'd never figured him for the type that knew how to move to Foreigner. When the song ended, another started, and to her surprise, Bently showed no intention of leaving the floor. Before she knew it, Raine was breathlessly enjoying herself, forgetting all about the fact that she and Bently Pierce just did not belong together.

They decided to sit out the fourth song. Bently went to the bar and brought back two more cold ones, stripping off his jacket and tossing it on an empty chair.

"I gotta say it again, Pierce. You really surprise me."

"You think because I wear a suit to work I don't like to have fun? Did you think I was too much of a snob to enjoy eating a burger in a place like this?" He put out his hand and traced the edge of the slave bracelet with a finger. "Did you really think, Raine," he said more softly, the words melting over her, "that my feelings for you could turn on a piece of fabric? It would take a lot more than taste in clothes to convince me that we're wrong for each other. And no matter where you take me next or how you plan on trying to shock me, I intend to enjoy every moment of this night with you."

His finger, barely grazing her skin as he moved it slowly down her arm to her wrist, made her shiver. She watched it moving back and forth before he took her hand in his and just held it. And she let him—she just left her hand in his and tried to forget, at least for a while, all the reasons it shouldn't have been there.

Sipping beer, they started to talk quietly, recalling old memories, favorite tunes. Bently told her about his first dance and how he'd tripped over an untied shoelace and ended up sprawled at his date's feet. "Linda Bennett. We were fourteen years old and I swore I'd never dance again."

"But you did."

He grinned. "Yes, I did. But never again with Linda Bennett."

Raine laughed and told him about the time that she and a girlfriend lied their way into a dance at the university, feeling utterly ridiculous because they'd shown up in fluffy, full, strapless formals while everyone else was in jeans.

"I'm afraid we took our cue from all those Sandra Dee movies we watched on the late show."

Bently took a swallow of beer and told her about a building he had looked at that week on the east side. "I'm thinking about buying it. It'd be a place to hang my shingle and there's a three-bedroom apartment upstairs."

"You'd live there?"

"Definitely. Why do you seem so surprised?"

She shrugged. "I don't know. Guess I never saw you living anywhere but that ritzy condo in the suburbs."

"That was Caroline's choice. I've never liked it, but I just haven't had time to find another place yet." He sipped more beer, then looked at her, his eyes glowing darkly in the light from the candle. "There are two offices, adjoining each other, Raine, and a fairly large storage room in the back. I thought when I looked at it that it'd be perfect for Cotton Tails.''

Raine stared at him. Adjoining offices. Bently going in and out as he pleased, Catlin napping upstairs, maybe playing in her playpen downstairs in Raine's office when Bently was busy with a client. Lord, it sounded good. Too good.

She cleared her throat. ''Are you offering to rent to me?''

''If that's the only way to get you there, yes.''

She stared into those deep, dark eyes, just as dangerous as they were the day she'd met him and he'd branded her a kidnapper. Only this time, he was the one doing the kidnapping—her heart was sailing right out of her chest into his hand.

She pulled her hand out of his. ''No.''

''No? Why not, Raine?''

''It wouldn't work.''

''You keep saying that—''

''I keep saying it because it's true. Now, change the subject or I'm out of here.''

To her surprise, he grinned a little. ''Okay. Then why don't I tell you about a phone call I got the other day. I think I just might have my first client.''

''That's great. Tell me all about it.''

They talked for a long time, through two more beers and a basket of popcorn.

''You're really interested, aren't you?'' Bently asked.

''Of course I am. The law is fascinating—especially the kind of stuff you're getting into now. If you can prove that the guy was unjustly fired because of his age and get him all that back pay—hell, it'll save his life!''

Bently grinned. ''You think I should take the case, then?''

''Absolutely! When I first met you I somehow figured you for a trial lawyer. Just seemed like you were meant to be standing in front of a courtroom persuading a jury.''

''Will you come and watch me if it gets that far?''

''You bet—and I'll bring Cat. She should get the chance to see her brilliant daddy at work.''

''Well, I don't know about brilliant...''

But Raine did. Brilliant was the smile he was giving her, and brilliant was the fire in his eyes when he talked about something that really mattered to him.

Bently couldn't stop smiling. Never had he been with a woman who could get so fired up about his work. Or ask so many challenging questions, seeking so many answers. How wonderful it would be to have her there, in that office next to his. To climb the stairs with her after a hard, exciting day. To climb into bed with her at night, to hold—to love. Damn it, why was she so stubborn?

Someone dropped a coin in the jukebox and a throaty, bluesy wail erupted, spreading a new mood across the room, causing the murmur of voices and the clink of glass to recede and hush.

Raine closed her eyes, swaying slightly. ''Mmmm— I remember this song.'' She opened her eyes. ''When my two older half brothers left home, they left behind this huge box of old forty-fives. This was one of them. I used to dance to it alone in my room.''

Bently knew the song, too. ''When a Man Loves a Woman.'' Percy Sledge. It was a decidedly sexy song for a young girl to be dancing to all alone. He leaned forward, trailing the back of a finger over her hand where it gripped her glass. She gave a little jump, but he kept his finger there, running it up and down, up and down.

''And were you dreaming that a man would someday love you like that?''

His dark eyes held hers, she couldn't look away. He was right, she had dreamed. Still dreamed. Once she'd thought Mick was the dream come true. But he hadn't loved her, not like that. Not in a way willing to risk it all, give it all—forever.

The song ended, and without a word Bently rose to his feet, dug in his pocket for some change and strode toward the jukebox.

The song began again and then he was looming over her, his hand stretched out to her. ''Dance with me.''

She looked at his hand, avoiding his eyes, and shook her head. Not to that song. She would never dance with him to that song.

''Yes, Raine. One more dance—then I'll take you home.''

She let her eyes meet his. It was a mistake. Slowly she stood up and let him take her hand.

They made it to the floor just as Percy Sledge was gonna sleep out in the rain for the woman he loved. Bently pulled Raine into his arms and they started to move with the music.

She wouldn't let him hold her close, but their eyes never parted, and the link between them seemed more powerful than if their bodies had been plastered together. They swayed and dipped—sinuous motion, bodies in rhythm.

She was pliant on the dance floor, giving in to the music as he'd never seen her give in to anything before, welcoming it like a lover, letting it intoxicate her. And she, in turn, was intoxicating. He felt himself becoming drunk with her, his blood filling and heating with her, his desire for her building beyond anything he'd yet experienced.

Raine felt it now—just as she had all those years ago—only stronger. The thrumming. The yearning. And something more. Something wild, waiting to break free. A new beat to her heart. When Bently pulled her closer, she didn't resist, nor did she look away. They were bound in the gaze, bound in the music, their limbs moving together, thighs brushing, hips swaying. It was too much. Too much. She closed her eyes.

The song slid to an end, the last strains of the music beating in their blood. He pulled her closer yet, closing his eyes, too. "Raine," he murmured against her ear, his voice harsh with longing. "I want you, Raine," he whispered. "I want to make love to you until you forget that you were ever lonely. I want to make love to you until the only thing left in your mind, in your soul, is me."

She pulled back from him, ready to run. Ready to deny that she wanted everything that those soft, urgent words promised. But it was too late. Her eyes met his, answering for her. In the end it was she who moved closer again, she who thrust her fingers into the thick, dark hair brushing his neck and covered his mouth with her own.

The kiss was dynamite. An explosion of touch and taste, violence and longing, capitulation and inevitability. She pulled her mouth away. "Let's get the hell out of here."

At the car she could barely wait for him to unlock the door and she was pulling at him, grabbing the front of his shirt and hauling him against her, claiming his mouth again. Then she let him go, pushing him away and then turning to start around the other side of the car.

He pulled her back. "My turn, Raine," he murmured roughly, pushing her up against the car, pressing into her, possessing her lips with an openmouthed kiss, possessing her mouth with a sweeping, sweet tongue, giving her no time to think, no time to stop it.

"My God, Raine, I've wanted you for so long—so long." Overcome, Bently gathered her into his arms and held her. Just held her.

The tenderness was more than she could stand. "No!" she cried. Pushing away from him, she yanked open the car door and slid into the driver's seat, slamming the door shut before he could stop her, holding her hand, palm up, out the window. "Give me the keys, Pierce."

"Raine, I think we should talk."

"No. No talk. Just give me your keys."

He fished in his pocket for them and placed them in her palm. She started the car, gunning the engine, and he rushed to the other side, throwing himself into the passenger seat just as she slammed into drive and took off, swinging out of the parking lot and into the stream of traffic on the highway.

Pulling onto I-94, Raine headed toward downtown. The Mark VIII's 280 horses hugged the road, shooting through a neon-and-billboard jungle, curving onto the High-Rise Bridge. The city lights spread below them, the dark mass of Lake Michigan beyond. The wind whipped into the open windows, blowing the hair around her head, bright as a halo. The speed, the recklessness seduced him. Bently made no protest as she scarcely let up on the speed on the narrow ramp that curved onto I-794, heading through the bowels of the city to the Hoan Bridge. And then they were flying over it, high above Lake Michigan, heading south again.

They soared up the steady incline of the bridge, zooming under the arch. The Port of Milwaukee lay dark and quiet beneath them, ships lit against the pitch of night, hulking masses with secrets of their own.

The freeway narrowed at the Port Exit, the cement retaining walls flying up to cradle the car. The Mark VIII slid to a sudden stop at South Carferry Drive then dived into a left-hand turn, fishtailed and then headed back the way they came. The Firstar Center rose before them, a fluorescent-lit monolith sprouting from the curve of the concrete. The weather light atop the gas company glowed like a flame of blue fire in the distance. They had the road to themselves, and Raine never let up on the speed until they pulled onto the off ramp and hit the streets again.

They twisted and turned through downtown streets that Bently hadn't known existed, past noisy crowds spilling from clubs, past quiet couples leaving restaurants, past clusters of dark faces milling under street lamps. Bently didn't even know where they were until they pulled into the alley behind Marshland.

Without a word, Raine threw open the door of the car and got out. Bently was right behind her. Grabbing her from behind by the shoulders, he pulled her to a stop, sliding his arms around her, his mouth at her ear.

"You can't run away from what's between us, Raine."

He heard her breath go in, heard her release it in a shaky sigh. "I can try."

He smiled against her neck. "You've been trying for weeks—and it's not working." Running his mouth down the side of her neck, he felt a shiver go through her.

"But we don't belong together."

"Yes we do," he bit out, his arms sliding back, giving his hands the freedom to run over her. Splaying his hands across her breasts, he moved his fingers back and forth until her nipples tightened, until he heard her sigh as she threw her head back with abandon.

"Oh, Bently," she moaned, part sigh, part surrender.

"Say it again," he said, his fingers working her nipples through the shimmery cloth that covered them.

"Bently."

"Take me upstairs, Raine, let me make love to you," he whispered, harshly, desperately.

"Yes!"

She fumbled for the key in her purse, fumbled with the lock, until he took the key from her shaking fingers and somehow got the door open.

The back room of Marshland was dark, the Cotton Tails washer and dryer like gleaming pale hulks in the light of the street lamp outside the small window. Raine started for the stairs, but Bently found he couldn't wait any longer to taste her mouth again.

He spun her into his arms, capturing her surprised cry with his lips. When he pulled his mouth away, she gave him a small smile.

"I thought you wanted me to take you upstairs?"

He grinned. "Maybe I don't want to wait that long." And then he was kissing her again, his mouth going from her lips to her chin, her jaw, her ear, her eyes. He moved his hand from her waist to the zipper at the front of her dress. "From the moment you walked into the English Room in this outrageous dress, I've been dreaming of what I'd like to do with this zipper."

She raised a brow. "And?"

He fingered the rhinestone pull. "And I'd like to draw it down slowly...so very slowly." His fingers followed the words. "And then I'd like to kiss each new, tantalizing bit of flesh as it's uncovered." He bent his dark head, and his mouth did just that.

Raine moaned, gripping his shoulders as the feeling and the words shook her. "Bently—"

He smiled against her flesh. And the zipper went lower.

Her breasts swelled, waiting, yearning. Still the zipper moved slowly, the cold steel of it brushing her flesh on its way down, the air catching in her throat when she tried to take a breath.

And then the zipper was down, and with a madness that equaled the previous sensual slowness, he unhooked the front clasp of her wisp of a bra, baring her, and took her breasts in his hands, burying his face in them, his mouth going from one to the other, using his tongue, his teeth, his lips to drive her to a frenzy of desire.

Weak with it, she fell back on the stairs behind her, taking Bently along. He moved his mouth up to her neck, one hand still on her breast, the other sliding up under her skirt, his palm running up her thigh, his fingers inching beneath the leg of her panties.

"Bently," she breathed.

His fingers swept across her lower belly and then his hand cupped her and she arched her hips toward him, a sound coming from her throat she'd never heard before.

"Tell me how much you want me," he whispered against her neck.

She moaned.

"Oh, baby," he whispered fiercely, his hand pressing harder, the heel of his palm moving in a slow maddening circle. "Hurry, baby—say it. I need to hear you say it."

Her fingers delved into his dark hair and she wrenched his mouth up to hers, grinding her lips into his. "I want you, Bently," she moaned. "I want you."

Pulling himself away from her, he struggled to his feet. Sweeping her up into his arms, he staggered up the remaining stairs, kicked open her unlocked door and tumbled to the bed with her—amid the cornflowers where he'd known he wanted to be from the first time he'd been in this room.

Her hands moved to his pants, tugging at his zipper, shucking the trousers down as far as she could. He rolled over on top of her, his hand pulling aside the silk that covered her heat while her hands freed him, touching him, making him harder than he'd ever been.

He moved against her. "Now?" he asked her through ragged breath.

"Yes!" she cried. "Now!"

And then he was inside her, swift and sinuous as a memory, as though it was something that had happened before, as though it was something always meant to be.

She was so hot, so ready, and greedy—as greedy as he. There was no time for exploration, no time for anything but this hot, wild thrusting that they seemed to need more than they needed breath. She cried out, clutching him, and he felt her release when it happened, felt her give over to the pleasure of him, to her need of him, and then the sound of his own need roared in his ears as he poured himself into her.

And he felt more than release. He felt love.

RAINE WIGGLED a little, trying to get out from under him.

"Don't move," he moaned into her breasts.

"I thought you were asleep."

He shook his head against her. "Are you kidding? I'm not missing a moment of this—I've waited far too long for it."

She stroked his head, her fingers sinking into the thick dark hair. "We haven't even known each other that long, Pierce."

"We've known each other forever. And don't call me Pierce—not in bed. In bed, I'm Bently."

She grinned. "Okay, Bently," she acquiesced, but that word caught in her mind—that word *forever*. She didn't want to think about forever. Tonight. She would have him tonight. She'd worry about tomorrow when she had to.

Finally, Bently slid off her, propping himself up on one elbow to look down into her face. "Have you any idea how beautiful you are?"

She shook her head, gave him a sassy little grin. "No—why don't you tell me how beautiful I am?"

"You're beautiful enough to make the wind sigh and the wolf howl—"

She laughed. "Pierce!"

He put his finger to her wide mouth. "Bently," he corrected.

She pushed his finger away. "Okay, Bently. Are you always so corny after you make love?"

He stared at her for a moment. "I don't think I've ever made love before."

She didn't know what to say. She was stunned, because she knew exactly what he meant, what he'd felt. It was the same for her. This fast, furious coupling was somehow sweeter, held more meaning, brought her closer to him than anything she'd ever experienced with Mick.

She brushed the hair from his forehead, staring into his dark, dangerous eyes.

He lowered his mouth to kiss her softly, slowly, taking the time he hadn't taken before, his lips moist, exploring, his tongue dancing with hers. Pulling his mouth away, he got to his knees, took her dress in his hands and pulled it up her body and over her head, taking her bra with it. She lay beneath his gaze wearing only a small scrap of ivory silk and a lacy garter belt holding up her pale stockings. She had wide, perfect shoulders, high, full breasts, narrow hips, long, shapely thighs. And all of it was wrapped in pale, translucent skin—and attitude.

Her mouth cocked, her brow lifted. "You about done, Pierce?"

"The name's Bently—and I'll never be done looking at you, touching you."

He shrugged out of his shirt and she reached up and touched him, smoothing her hands over the dark hair on his chest, caressing his smooth, muscled shoulders. She helped draw his trousers the rest of the way down his legs, his shoes thumping onto the floor when he kicked them off. He was on his knees next to her, his legs spread, his thighs strong and muscled. He was hard and proud, ready for her again. She touched it. Velvet over steel.

Closing his eyes and throwing back his head, he gasped and she reveled in the power she felt as she stroked him. "Make love to me, Bently," she whispered. "I want you inside me again."

She expected him to fall on her, the second coupling as fast and furious as the first. But he opened his eyes, a smile coming slowly to his face. "With pleasure," he murmured.

And then he touched her—slowly, maddeningly, taking all the time he hadn't before. The world seemed to hang suspended while they learned each other's secrets, quenched each other's desires. And when the time came for him to fill her body, he filled her mind and soul with words, whispered with the harsh softness of his passion.

"I love you, Raine. I love you."

Chapter Eleven

They lay spoon fashion, Bently's arm around Raine's waist, her fingers intertwined with his, resting on her belly. She was spent, peaceful; relaxed and fulfilled. And in love. She knew she had told him, called her love out in the heat of passion, when she felt her heart would burst along with her body if she didn't. It was out and now they would have to deal with it. But not tonight. Tonight she just wanted to rest in the shelter of his arms and not think about what might come tomorrow.

"Raine? Are you awake?"

"Mmm." She nodded sleepily.

His arm tightened around her, his lips nuzzled the nape of her neck. "Come home with me."

"What?"

"Come home with me, Raine. We'll look in on Cat together, then we can crawl into my big bed and make love again, wake up beside each other, have breakfast with Cat."

Lord, she was actually considering it. It sounded so wonderful, so right.

But it would never work.

She pulled away from him, bounding out of bed and grabbing her robe to wrap around herself. "You better go, Pierce. It's late."

He was off the bed in a second, standing naked and angry before her. "We just confessed our love, Raine. We've just made love like I've never made love with anyone before. And now you want me to leave?"

He grabbed his trousers, thrusting them on, then shrugged into his shirt. "Get dressed, Raine. You're coming with me."

She tossed her hair and thrust her chin up. "No I'm not."

He sat down and started putting on his shoes. "There's no damn reason for us to be apart. Cat loves you—I love you. We belong together. Now grab some clothes and let's get out of here."

God, she actually wanted to obey him. Just this once she wanted to accept his high-handedness and just do what he wanted—do what they both wanted. But where could it lead? And how would she stand it when Bently looked at her the way Mick had when she couldn't give him what he wanted, couldn't be the woman he needed?

She wouldn't stand it. Couldn't. Because what she felt for this man imperiously glaring at her went beyond anything she'd ever felt for Mick.

"I'm not going home with you, Pierce. Not now, not ever."

He stood, gripping her shoulders. "You said you loved me, Raine."

"And you said you loved me. But we both know that saying I love you in the heat of passion doesn't transfer into forever. Forever just never comes."

"Then I'll say it again, on my feet and fully clothed. I love you, Raine. And we can make forever come if only you're willing to try."

She pushed away from him, her words full of anger. "*Willing to try?* You think I didn't try with Mick? You think I didn't try with my mother? You think my father didn't?"

Bently shook his head helplessly. "But don't you see, Raine? I'm not your father, or your mother, or Mick. The fault lay with them, Raine, not with you. Forever comes for some people, Raine."

"Oh, yeah? Who? You and Caroline? And Cat? Cat's mother didn't even stick around long enough to name her."

Bently shoved his hands into his hair. "Damn it, Raine, that has nothing to do with us. I understand that you're scared, but—"

"Not scared, Pierce. Smart."

He pulled her into his arms. "There's nothing smart about throwing away what we could have together," he ground out. Then his mouth came down on hers— full of passion, full of promise. When the kiss was over, he cupped her face with gentle hands, his dark eyes studying her. "Ahh, Raine, you're such a cynic. Such a beautiful, stubborn cynic. But we *are* working on a forever kind of thing here, you know. It feels like forever to me." He kissed her again, tenderly, wistfully. Then he slung his jacket over his shoulder and started for the door.

"I'll see you tomorrow," he called over his shoulder.

"No, Pierce."

He stopped at the foot of the stairs and looked up at her. "Sunday deliveries, remember?" He blew her a kiss and disappeared into the darkness.

Raine slammed the door and turned back to the room. Damn him! Couldn't he see that she was trying to save both of them from a lot of heartache and disappointment? Why did he keep dangling Catlin in front of her, like a prize she could win if she loved him enough?

And, God, she *did* love him enough. And she loved Cat. But had Bently forgotten completely that she could never have children? He'd told her that he wanted brothers and sisters for Cat, and Cat deserved to have them. Raine knew far too much about lonely childhoods to want to condemn Cat to one.

She threw herself on the bed, burying her face in the tumbled sheets. His scent was there, mingled with hers, mingled with the scent of their lovemaking. "Bently, Bently," she groaned, "how am I ever going to let you go?"

SOMETHING WAS pounding in Raine's head. She dragged open her eyes, closing them immediately again against the assault of the morning sun. She couldn't have been asleep for more than three hours—thanks to Bently Pierce's sexy body and provocative words. Groaning, she rolled over, hoping to grab just a little more shut-eye.

The pounding started again.

She crawled out of bed, shrugging into her robe, and stumbled down the stairs. Whoever was breaking down her back door was going to be a whole lot of sorry.

Flinging open the door, she opened her mouth to complain. Before she got a word out, a tall, gangly kid thrust an enormous arrangement of long-stemmed yellow roses into her arms.

She stared at them, dumbfounded. "You sure you have the right place?" she croaked.

"You Raine Rogers?"

"Yeah..."

"Then I got the right place."

Raine watched him saunter down the alley, then shut the door, burying her face in the scent of roses all the way up the stairs.

No one had ever sent her roses before. She set them down on her desk and drew out the card.

I love you was all it said.

"Oh, Pierce, what am I going to do with you?" she muttered.

Before she could even begin to fathom an answer to that, the phone rang.

"Good morning, love. How did you sleep?"

She swallowed the lump in her throat, making way for the goose bumps rising on her skin at the sound of his soft, teasing voice.

"Never slept better," she replied defiantly. "And you?"

"I tossed and turned half the night, missing you, thinking of ways I'd like to love you, ways I *did* love you."

The words sent a shaft of heated response right through her. Whoever would have thought that the angry man she'd shared that holding cell with would turn out to have such an incredible body and such a fertile imagination? She closed her eyes and inhaled the scent of roses.

"Did they arrive?" he asked softly.

"Yes. And they're beautiful, but totally unnecessary."

"Oh, they're necessary, Raine. Yellow roses stand for the celebration of life, the celebration we began last night."

"Began and ended, Pierce. A one-night stand doesn't require roses on the morning after."

"But true love does."

"Lust," she corrected.

"Love, Raine. You said it, remember?"

She groaned. How could she forget?

"You better get over here."

"Look, Pierce, we're not going to...I mean, *I'm* not going to—"

Bently chuckled. "All I'm asking for is diapers, Raine. Cat's almost out. It's time for Cotton Tails to deliver."

Raine glared at the dial tone coming out of the receiver, then slammed the phone down. If Bently Pierce wanted diapers, she'd deliver diapers. But that's *all* she'd deliver!

"HERE ARE YOUR DIAPERS." Raine plopped the package on the kitchen table and turned to go.

"Ki-ki," Cat squealed, and Raine stopped in her tracks just inside the patio doors. The baby had crawled all the way across the floor and was now at Raine's feet, trying to pull herself up with one pudgy hand grabbing at the leg of Raine's jeans.

Raine bent down, offered her fingers and Cat grabbed them and hoisted herself shakily to her feet. "Cat! You did it! You're standing!"

Cat squealed with delight and promptly landed on her butt. Her eyes grew round and solemn for a second, then she smiled and giggled, holding her arms up to Raine.

Raine bent and scooped her up, kissing her nose. "How long has she been doing that?"

"Just a few days. We wanted to surprise you."

She looked at Bently's grinning face and had to bury her own face in Cat's neck to hide how overwhelming she found the two of them. She'd intended to drop off the diapers and leave, but how could she? How could she turn away from sweet little Cat?

"Something smells good," she said to escape expressing what she was really feeling.

"I'm making an omelet. There's enough for two."

She watched him at the stove, a pair of faded jeans riding his hips, a yellow T-shirt setting off his dark looks.

"Where did you get the jeans, Pierce?"

"Back of my closet. Just wanted to demonstrate how flexible I can be."

What he was demonstrating was how great he could look at ten o'clock on a Sunday morning after almost no sleep. He sauntered over to the table and set down two plates, each steaming with half a perfectly turned omelet. He went back for a basket of croissants, then pulled out a chair for her.

"Join me?"

What could it hurt? What could it possibly hurt to share breakfast for a change with two people she cared so much about? It wasn't making a commitment, it was eating an omelet.

"Sure, why not." She pulled Cat's high chair closer to the table, strapped her in, then sat down and dug in.

"This is great, Pierce." And it was. Beautifully browned, the omelet was bursting with herbs and cheese.

"I'm afraid omelets are part of a very limited repertoire, the only other items being coq au vin and chocolate mousse." Bently bit into his omelet. "How about you?" he asked between bites. "Do you cook?"

"Nothing so fancy as coq au whatever or chocolate mousse, but I make a mean pot of chili and a pretty good beef stew. I can do soups, too. That's the kind of cooking I always liked—big pots simmering on the stove all day while the bread's rising."

"You can bake bread? You mean using flour and yeast?"

"Yeah, Pierce, using flour and yeast. When my mother left, I kind of took over in the kitchen."

Bently put down his fork. "You were seven years old."

She pushed a forkful of omelet around on her plate. "Not too young to learn—not too young to try to please my father."

Bently shook his head. "You were only a little girl," he murmured. "It must have been rough."

She tossed her hair back but kept staring at her plate, grateful that he didn't try to touch her. "It was like growing up in silence. I never could tell what he was thinking—how he was feeling. And he hadn't a clue what to do with the little girl he'd been left to raise."

"No wonder you were lonely. Where is he now?"

"In Florida with my two half brothers. They run a construction company. Do a good job of supporting him."

"Do you see him?"

She shook her head, tearing at a piece of croissant with restless fingers. Finally, she looked up, her eyes full of mischief. "Did I mention that once I'd given up trying to please him, I went the rebellious route? By the time I'd graduated high school, he'd had enough of me. One day he packed his bags, said I could find him at my brothers' if I needed him and left."

"And did you ever need him?" he asked quietly.

"No, I'd learned not to by then."

"And your mother?"

She shrugged. "Never came back. Never sent a card. After a few birthdays you quit waiting."

Bently swore, taking her hand and raising it to his lips. "Raine—"

She looked at his dark head bent over her hand. His tenderness always caught her off guard, never failed to raise a lump in her throat. She allowed herself the indulgence of a few moments more.

She was just deciding it was time to pull her hand out of his when Cat squealed and threw her toast, hitting Bently soundly on the head.

"Hey, whose side are you on?"

Raine laughed, wiggling her hand out of his. "I have her well trained."

"I see that."

Bently got up from the table and pulled Catlin from her high chair.

"Ki-ki," Cat cried. Bently laughed and put her down on the floor, strewing several toys around for her to find and explore.

"And why were you lonely, Pierce?" Raine asked when Bently sat across from her again. "You had a mother, didn't you?"

"Oh, I still have a mother, somewhere. Europe, I think. She left me to the servants. Too busy with club work, charities, social functions. I guess that's largely why I've been so reluctant to hire a nanny. I want my daughter raised by me."

Raine looked at Cat sitting on the floor, squeaking a rubber ball. "She's lucky," she murmured. She watched the baby for a few moments, that lump choking her again, then she scraped back her chair. "Well, guess it's time I left." She stood. "Thanks for breakfast."

"Why don't you stay?"

She turned around, a wary look on her face. "Look, last night probably shouldn't have happened."

He put up his hands. "I'm not asking for anything but the afternoon, Raine. We'll be friends—you, me and Catlin—just spending the day together."

"I don't know, Pierce—"

"I'll make my chocolate mousse," he teased, his white teeth flashing in a smile that could coax the coldest heart.

"Tempting, but..." *He* was the real temptation—he and his baby crawling across the kitchen floor, grinning up at Raine as if there was no tomorrow.

But there was a tomorrow.

"Come on, Raine. I'll go to the store and get what you need to bake bread and make that fabulous chili you mentioned. We'll make a day of it." His hands went into the air, palms up. "And I'll keep my hands to myself—you have my word on it."

She shook her head, unable to keep a tiny grin from her lips. "I don't know, Pierce. Chili with chocolate mousse?"

"Hey, don't turn conventional on me *now*. I think it sounds fantastic!"

Catlin noisily agreed.

RAINE WAS STARTING to think that getting Bently to knead the bread dough wasn't such a hot idea, after all. The man had some pretty impressive muscles bulging out of that yellow T-shirt. She leaned against the counter, watching them flex, thinking about the night before. No wonder he was able to—

"Now what?"

Raine's face flamed. "Huh?"

"It's as smooth and elastic as a baby's behind, just like you wanted. So, now what?"

She watched his hands smoothing over the dough and she could almost feel them on her skin.

Get a grip, Raine.

"Now we have to form the loaves and let it rise again."

She started to show him how it was done, but he was too close, standing a little behind her, his breath on her neck, the heady scent of him rising over the smell of the yeast. He'd promised to keep his hands to himself, and he was. But it turned out that he didn't have to touch her—didn't have to do anything at all—to make her aware of him as a man. A man who'd loved her so thoroughly and with such passion that she'd no longer been able to deny the love she felt.

"Uh," she said, half turning toward him, "maybe you'd better stir the chili."

Cat had suddenly lost interest in anything that was on the kitchen floor. She threw down a stuffed clown, sat on her rump, rubbing her eyes and yawning, and started to fuss.

"Time for someone's nap," Bently said.

Raine immediately conjured a picture of herself and Bently lying together, snoozing through the rest of the day, his hand on her belly, her head on his shoulder. Then waking up, just as the sun started to sink, to make love slowly before getting Cat from her crib for supper.

She cleared her throat and slapped harder at the dough. What was she thinking of? He was talking about *Catlin's* nap. Besides, there wasn't even any sun that day. The gray clouds had started to drizzle an hour ago, and it was turning into rain, tapping on the roof, splashing on the windows.

Even better, thought Raine. Snuggled up on the sofa in the study with a fire crackling on the hearth, the smell of bread baking, their hands on each other, stretching out to make love—

"Would you like to put her down?"

Raine spun around. "What?"

"Catlin. Would you like to put her down for her nap?"

"Uh, sure." She turned back to the loaves, covered them with a linen towel and brushed the flour from her hands. When she took the baby from Bently, her hand brushed his chest. Solid, real, warm. Their glances caught for a moment, his eyes so dark, so watchful. Could he see what she was feeling?

"Stir the chili while I'm gone," she finally said, and headed for the nursery.

She changed the baby, then laid her in the crib. Almost immediately Cat's fist went into her mouth, her eyes closed. Raine watched her, smoothing the blanket over her, humming softly. When she turned to leave, Bently was standing in the doorway.

He came into the nursery, leaning over the crib to give Cat a soft kiss on the cheek. Raine watched him as he touched the baby's hair. "She's the sweetest thing that ever lived, isn't she?" he whispered.

Words caught in her throat as she watched him standing over his daughter, and it came to her that it wouldn't matter what he looked like or what he did for a living. She would have fallen for this man on the strength of his love for his little girl alone.

She swallowed hard, then turned away and left the room.

She was sitting in the kitchen when he came back and started the mousse.

Another mistake. His jeans were tight across his rounded, firm rear. The muscles in his back flexed against the thin cotton covering them as he beat eggs, stirred chocolate. Every time he went into the refrigerator, he brushed against her where she sat at the table. She could move, but she didn't want to. Despite herself, she wanted the contact with him. Craved it.

"So where did you learn to make chocolate mousse?"

"Our cook. It was my favorite when I was a boy. I used to watch her."

"Same with the coq au whatever?"

"Coq au vin. Yes. That was my standard dinner of seduction in college. Have a girl over to the crummy little apartment I shared with two other guys, then dazzle her with a gourmet meal."

Yeah, Raine figured he was a real dazzler, all right. Probably could have skipped the meal altogether and still gotten them into bed.

Geesh, couldn't she stop thinking about sex?

No, not if he was going to get all cute while he stirred in vanilla and tasted things on his finger. Not if that shock of hair was going to forever fall in his eyes. Not if his tight little rear was going to keep time

with the eggbeater. To hell with the damn mousse—
she'd like to throw him to the floor and devour *him*.

The trouble was, Bently Pierce no longer seemed
interested. Oh, sure, she was the one who had gotten
him to promise to keep his hands to himself, but he
was playing the role of friend as if he were going for
an Academy Award. He'd never before been able to
keep his hands off her, so why now?

"There." He stowed the mousse in the refrigerator.
"Why don't we go see what's on television while we
wait for the bread?"

Now it'll come, she thought, following him into the
study. *He'll get me on the sofa, turn on some smaltzy
old romantic movie, and—*

"Looks like we're in luck. One of those great old
screwball comedies is playing."

He turned on the tube and settled into a wing chair.
Didn't even go near the sofa. Raine sat on it, giving
him a glance now and then, but his eyes were glued to
Jean Harlow. Raine might as well not have been in the
room.

She stood and stomped over to the window, crossing her arms in front of her, staring out at the rain,
wondering why she felt angry and abandoned.

"Rainy Sundays are nice, aren't they?"

He spoke from behind her, close enough to hear his
breath.

"Especially when you're not alone," he added.

She whirled to face him, certain that he was moving in for the kill, but he was already turning back to
his chair and settling in again.

For two cents she'd throw herself into his lap and get his mind off Jean Harlow. But she wouldn't give him the satisfaction.

Besides, what if he threw her back?

What if he'd decided she'd been right all these weeks? What if he'd started to agree with her, that there couldn't possibly be a future together for them?

Or maybe now that he'd gotten her into bed, he just wasn't interested anymore. Maybe it was as simple as that.

She stared at his handsome profile, his long, straight nose, his long, dark lashes. That mouth that—

Oh, hell. "I'm going to check on the bread," she muttered and headed for the kitchen.

Bently watched her leave the room, his gaze going from her swinging hair to her long, long legs. Her scent lingered in the room like the remnants of some sweet, erotic dream.

He got up and started to pace. How long was he supposed to keep this up? Friends! Couldn't they be lovers *and* friends? Couldn't they even be *married* and be friends? It was done. Certainly.

But not by stubborn women who no longer believed in happy endings. How could she spend the afternoon with them and still not see that this is how it should be—the three of them together, every Sunday afternoon for the rest of their lives?

Except, if he had his way, they wouldn't be spending Catlin's naptime watching some old movie. They'd be in bed, listening to the rain, listening to the sound of each other's passion.

"Bread's in the oven. We can eat in twenty minutes."

He looked at her standing in the doorway, a smudge of flour on her cheek, a splash of chili on her T-shirt. He wanted to tell her that he didn't want any damned bread, he just wanted her. But he couldn't. She would only get angry again, fight him, leave. He had to hang in there and make her see how very right they were together. So he sat back in his chair and smiled. "Good, I'm starving."

Raine was just about to take the bread from the oven when Cat started to cry. She threw down the hot pad she'd been holding and ran for the nursery, colliding with Bently at the door.

"Oh, sorry."

"No problem. You want to get her up?"

Raine looked at a teary-eyed Cat sitting up in her crib and her heart melted. Then she looked at Bently. He was her father, after all. "No, you go ahead. I have to get the bread out, anyway."

"I'll do that. Go to her, Raine."

Bently left and Raine picked the baby up from her crib. She was warm and soft from sleep, her tears already forgotten in the sweet smile she gave Raine.

"How's my sweetie? Did you have a nice nap?"

Cat gurgled in delight. Raine held her for long moments more, loath to let her go—it felt so good to have her arms filled this way.

By the time she'd changed Cat and carried her into the kitchen, Bently was popping the shiny browned loaves of bread out of their tins.

"Mmm, that smells wonderful."

"They look beautiful, too." He looked at her standing there with his daughter in her arms and thought, *and so do you, Raine. You look so beautiful with Catlin in your arms.*

He wasn't going to be able to keep this up much longer. If only there was some way of forcing *her* to come to *him.*

"Here, give me Cat and I'll put her in her high chair while you ladle out the chili."

Quite by accident, his fingers brushed her breast when he took the baby from her, but he heard her quick intake of breath as she dipped her head. Surreptitiously looking through his lashes while he strapped Cat in her chair, he saw the evidence of how she felt through her T-shirt. Her nipples had gone hard. With just that slight, innocent brush, her body had betrayed how she felt.

Bently watched her at the stove, having all he could do to keep from grabbing her, he was so turned on by her sudden desire. A desire she was trying to ignore and would surely deny if he called her on it.

Okay, so he'd push her. He'd push her until there was no way she could stay out of his arms, out of his bed and out of his life.

She set a steaming bowl in front of him and he grinned up at her. "Smells wonderful, Raine."

Her heart flipped over. Those gorgeous white teeth, that sensually molded mouth. If her body hadn't already been throbbing, that would have done it.

"Mmm, tastes wonderful, too. Hot, spicy."

The words, and his low, sexy voice made her think of other things besides chili.

"This bread is marvelous."

She watched his hands tearing a slice in two, spreading butter slowly on one half, licking a melting drop from one finger, then another.

She shoved back her chair. "I'll fix Cat some baby food." She opened one cupboard door, then another, but her mind was too messed up to find anything.

"Here," he stood and came toward her, "let me help."

He reached up and over her shoulder to a higher shelf, his body pressed lightly against the back of hers, his bare arm brushing her face.

"Let's see, she had peaches just yesterday..."

He was pushing the jars around, taking his time selecting something. All the while Raine held her breath, feeling that hard body moving so slightly against hers, smelling the scent of his skin.

"Here we go—yes, chicken, I think." He'd moved on to a lower shelf, his arm reaching across her, brushing her breast again when he brought it back.

She closed her eyes and bit her lip as the feeling shot through her. Lord, she wanted him. Couldn't he feel it? Didn't he know?

He finally moved away and she turned around, but he was already back at the table, spooning up chili, acting as if nothing had happened. What the hell was the matter with him?

What was the matter with *her?* This was what she wanted, wasn't it? To be treated like a friend. To be allowed to be part of Cat's life—no strings, no future? Of course it was. It was just that her body was still humming from the night before. But her body would get over it—her body would forget. Just the way Bently's obviously had.

He did the dishes while she fed Cat, all the while watching him, finding it hard to keep her eyes off that body that had loved her so thoroughly the night before.

It was time she left.

"I'm shoving off, Pierce. See you for your Tuesday delivery."

"You don't want to stay and help with Cat's bath?"

Oh, she wanted to. She wanted to stay and tuck Cat in—then tuck Bently in, crawling in beside him, loving him, holding him. And then she wanted to wake up to breakfast again with them, and another supper, and another—

"Not tonight. I've got paperwork to do."

"We'll walk you out."

"No need." She slid open a patio door.

"Cat likes to wave to you, you know that."

Bently took the baby out of the high chair and followed her out.

The rain had stopped. The air felt fresh, warmer. Gray, misty clouds scudded across a clear, night blue sky. Tomorrow would be fine.

They reached the alley and the waiting van. Raine bent to give Cat a kiss. "Night, sweetie. See you tomorrow."

"Not tomorrow," Bently said. "Tuesday, I think you said, is our next delivery."

She looked at him. "Oh, yeah." She looked down, staring at her sneakers, wondering what was going on. was he telling her to stay away unless she had a package of diapers under her arm? Had he decided that if there was no future between them, he just didn't want her around anymore?

"Thanks for supper, Raine. It was delicious. We'll have to do it again sometime."

She thrust her head up at the words, just in time to see him bend his dark head to hers. She watched his mouth getting closer, felt her heart pounding harder. But all he did was brush his lips across her cheek.

She quickly turned away before he could see the disappointment and hurt in her eyes and swung up into the van. Cat was waving as she pulled away, but Bently was already walking back to the condo.

She drove the van to the end of the alley, then stopped before pulling into the street, glancing back over her shoulder. There was no sign of them.

"'We'll have to do it again sometime,'" she mimicked. As if she was nothing more than some damn friend of the family! She laid her forehead against the steering wheel. A friend of the family. Yeah, that's all she was.

Well, it *was* what she'd wanted, wasn't it?

Okay, so if Bently could put that fantastic night of lovemaking behind him, so could she. A friend he wanted, a friend is what he'd get. But wait until Tuesday to see Cat?

She swallowed hard. Every damn thing she'd been so afraid of was happening. She had no real hold over Cat, no real place in her life, and she was going to lose her. But she was going to lose Bently, too. And, surprise, surprise, the pain she felt at the thought of not having Bently in her life hurt as much as the thought of being without Cat. Just like her mother, her father and Mick, forever wasn't going to come. Only this time it was no one's fault but her own. Her fear of losing again, her stubborn need to stay independent and not trust in another relationship, was keeping her from everything she ever wanted.

Her head jerked up at the sound of a horn, and she squinted into the rearview mirror at the car behind her. It honked again and she shook herself against the lethargy that held her there, pulled the van into the street and headed home.

Chapter Twelve

"What's got you in such a lousy mood?"

Raine slammed the door of Marshland behind her. "Nothing, Dee, absolutely nothing."

"Right," Dee said, turning her attention to closing out the cash register. "Are you going over to see Cat today?"

Raine thrust her chin up. "If I feel like it."

"I thought you always felt like it."

"I do. It's just that her father seems to want me to only come on delivery days now."

"You sure about that?" Dee cut in.

"Sure I'm sure. He just about told me so last night. Treated me like I was no more to him—I mean, them—than a *delivery* person!"

"Well, he must have run out of diapers early, then, because he just pulled up in front of Marshland."

Raine spun around. "Oh hell!" She looked down at her ragged jeans and tattered sweatshirt. "Stall him while I run and change, okay?"

Dee smiled. "Sure, but I don't think handing over extra diapers calls for anything formal."

"Just keep him busy."

Raine bounded up the steps, taking them two at a time and sped directly to her closet. Yanking off her jeans and T-shirt, she tore through her clothes looking for something—anything—that would make Bently Pierce sit up and take notice. She'd show him that he couldn't dismiss her that easily! She was the one who was supposed to do the dismissing in this relationship!

She paused, her head cocked as though listening to another voice.

Raine, you're not making any sense.

"So what!" she spoke aloud into the empty room. "Women in love don't have to make sense."

Women in love, huh? So you're going after him, are you?

Was she? She grinned. "Yeah, just maybe I am!" The grin fled. "If it's not too late," she added. "Please don't let it be too late!"

She started tearing through the closet again. There was precious little to choose from. Finally, she spotted a dress Dee had given her last summer because nobody else had wanted it. It was long, almost to the ankles, scoop necked with little buttons all the way down the front. The floral pastel material was almost transparent. She tore off the tags, unbuttoned the first few buttons and pulled it over her head. Not bad. She unbuttoned some of the lower buttons, too, so her legs would peek through the opening as she walked. Bently was crazy about her legs. She intended to give him a good eyeful. The silver bracelet lay on her dresser in the same spot she'd thrown it the night he'd given it to her. She picked it up and fastened it around her wrist.

She heard footsteps on the stairs and quickly ran a brush through her hair before the knock came on her door.

She opened it. "Bently, what a surprise! Did you run out of diapers?" she asked sweetly.

He looked her over—couldn't stop looking her over. The dress skimming her body was a provocative combination of innocence and sex. He would have been jealous as hell if he hadn't seen her tearing out of Marshland in her usual jeans and sweatshirt just as he'd opened the door. The dress was for him and he knew it. And so was the bracelet glittering on her wrist. It was the first time she'd worn it since he'd given it to her.

"Are you going out?" he asked casually.

"I might later."

"What a shame. We thought you might like to go for some ice cream with us."

"Where is Cat?"

"Downstairs with Dee. She'll be disappointed, but if you have plans—" Bently shrugged and started to turn away.

"Well, not until later—maybe."

"Oh, then would you like to come?"

"Sure, you know I'd never miss a chance to be with Cat," she said pointedly.

He smelled the peaches as she passed in front of him, the dress swinging out to brush his hand, gossamer and light as the scent she wore. *Raine, Raine,* he thought, *this better work because I don't think I can stand much more.*

"LET'S TAKE A WALK while we eat," Bently suggested.

Raine shrugged. "Okay."

They turned down a side street from the ice-cream parlor, Cat in her umbrella stroller, Bently and Raine each licking double dips of chocolate.

Overhead, trees were beginning to bud. Somewhere nearby a power mower droned and the sweet smell of new-mown grass rose on the breeze. Neighborhood children rode Big Wheels, clattering down the sidewalk, and Cat craned her neck to watch them in awe.

"Look at her!" Raine exclaimed. "When she really starts talking, that'll be the first thing she asks for."

Bently shook his head. "The thought of her being that mobile daunts me. It's tough enough keeping up with her now."

"Guess it's time you found that nanny."

"I've been thinking maybe what I need is more than a nanny."

Raine licked a path around her ice cream. "What do you mean?"

"Maybe it's time I found a wife for me and a mother for Cat."

Bently walked several paces, pretending not to know that Raine had stopped dead. He had to wipe the little grin off his face before he turned.

"Something wrong?" he asked innocently. She was standing in the middle of the sidewalk, her tongue out, suspended in motion on its way to her cone, a blank, uncomprehending look on her face.

"Raine?" At the sound of her name, she shook her head as if coming back to reality and shrugged. "What could be wrong?" she asked lightly, a pleasant mask covering that earlier, bewildered look as she started walking toward him again.

Her skirt rustled with the movement of her hips, her legs peeking through the open slit with each long, lazy stride. The sun was behind her, and Bently could see the outline of her body through the gauzy material of her dress—the dip of her small waist, the slight curve of her narrow hips, the entire luscious length of the gorgeous limbs he'd once felt wrapped around him. Sheer torture, Bently thought, moving his gaze to her hair ruffling in the breeze, the sun sparkling off it turning it to gold.

She caught up with him and they started walking together again.

"Have anyone in mind?" she asked carefully.

"Hmm?"

Raine let out an exasperated sigh. "For wife and mother—have any candidates in mind?"

"Oh, well, one or two maybe. I'll need to start dating again." He slid her a sideways look, trying to gauge her reaction.

Raine threw the rest of her cone into a sidewalk trash can and crossed her arms belligerently. "Sounds more like you have *interviewing* than dating in mind."

"Well, it will be rather like I'll be filling a position." He grinned. "But I intend to enjoy every minute of the search."

She scowled at him out of the corner of her eye. Could he possibly be serious? How did he think he'd ever find anyone more suited for the *position* than she was? Had he forgotten Saturday night? Or was he crazy enough to think he could just hop into bed with any old *applicant* and find that kind of fire?

Her gaze ran over his baggy linen trousers, the fabric blowing lovingly against his muscular thighs. His tan cotton shirt was rolled at the sleeves, open at the throat, revealing his strong forearms and a mat of dark hair curling on his chest. Who was she kidding? Almost any woman would jump at the chance to hit the sack with a man like Bently Pierce. And Lord knew the man had enough technique to build a fire in anyone who was still breathing. Maybe she was the one who was crazy for thinking that she had somehow been special.

Sullenly, she walked beside him, staring at her feet, listening with growing irritation as he whistled a tune, happy as a dog at the prospect of the hunt. And what could she do about it? She could hardly blurt out that she wanted to fill out an application herself—not after spending weeks convincing him how wrong they were for each other.

Face it, Raine. It's too late. You blew it.

She hardly noticed when he stopped in front of a storefront building of Cream City brick.

"Well, here we are."

She looked up. "Where?"

"This is the building I told you about. I bought it this morning."

Raine squinted against the sun. The place was two stories, with two front entrances side by side, a huge picture window flanking each. There was a small lawn in front where two trees swayed in the breeze. Lilac bushes, just coming into flower, graced both front corners of the building, their scent riding the wind.

Bently carried Cat's stroller up the two cement steps to one of the doors and unlocked it. Raine followed him inside.

The space was flooded with sunlight shining off the polished oak floor and the wainscoting that ran halfway up the walls. The remainder of the walls were painted a cream color. Dark outlines here and there showed where pictures had once hung.

"I thought I'd use this side as my office," Bently said.

Yes, Raine could picture him there, his hair mussed as he bent over a big oak desk. To obliterate the image and the feeling it gave her that Bently was moving on and out of her life, she walked to the back wall and unlocked the door there.

The door opened onto an enchanting little courtyard, walled in on all sides by more Cream City brick. The grass was a tender, spring green. Perennials were already budding along two sides of the walls and there was a space of bare earth, big enough for a modest vegetable garden.

"This is wonderful!" Raine exclaimed, going out to stare up through a huge oak tree's branches, placing a knee on the wooden bench circling its trunk. "Cat's going to love it!"

Bently stood in the doorway and watched her, the dress, ethereal as the wind, blowing about her legs, shadows of oak leaves caressing her face. She was as beautiful as anything nature had made. It was hard to turn away from her, but turn away he knew he had to—so he did.

"The other office doesn't open onto the courtyard because of the storage area I told you about. That's why I chose this one for myself."

Raine came back inside and followed him to the connecting door. The room was a mirror image of the first one. "This is the office you plan to rent out?"

"Well, actually, I think I've changed my mind about that. I might want to use it for a secretary or something. I don't know that I'd care to be anyone's landlord, anyway."

Raine watched him turn away. So—that was that. He no longer saw them here together, no longer saw the other space as something perfect for Cotton Tails. And from what Raine could see, it would have been. Oh yes, it would have been.

"Come upstairs. I'd like your opinion on a few matters."

He carried the stroller up the stairs, Cat giggling merrily at this new adventure, and she followed him, feeling strangely hollow and lost.

The door opened into a huge kitchen with pine cupboards and a black-and-white-checkerboard floor. Windows opened inward above the sink and again in a corner perfect for a table and chairs.

"I'm thinking of having this section of cupboards taken out to make room for a dishwasher. What do you think?"

Raine walked to the sink and opened one side of the window. "I always wanted a window above a kitchen sink," she said. "When I was a kid, we didn't have one, so I hung a mirror. I used to make faces at myself while I did the dishes." She peered out. "You can see the tops of the trees from here, the sky, birds. I don't think I'd mind doing dishes here at all."

"But you, Raine, are hardly what you'd call an *average* woman." Bently shook his head. "A more normal woman might mind very much doing dishes, window or no window," he muttered, his finger tapping his lips. "Dishwasher, I think."

Raine turned to glare at him, but he'd already pushed Cat's stroller into the living room. She followed, biting back a sharp retort. What did he mean she wasn't a *normal* woman?

The living room faced the street. Three tall, arched windows recessed in a shallow alcove took up the far wall. Here the floors were oak like the offices, as was the woodwork. Bently flipped a switch and a ceiling fan came on, casting a slow shadow over the pale walls and high ceilings.

Raine could picture a sofa in the window alcove. She'd place chairs facing it for a cozy seating group and shelves on the far wall to hold books and pictures. Pictures of Cat as she grew. Pictures of Bently and—

And who?

"Now in here," Bently was saying, "I'm wondering about these floors. Do you think my future wife might like carpeting better?"

The thought of covering up those beautiful floors pushed Raine's mind away from the misty image of another woman at Bently's side in all those pictures of the future.

"And hide this gorgeous floor? Are you crazy?"

"Well, I don't know, Raine. Wood floors can be awfully noisy, and soon Cat will be running around, her little feet scampering to and fro. Anyone who isn't really her mother might find it rather annoying."

"If that's the case," she stated levelly, her hands on her hips, "I'd say you'd better move on to another applicant."

He looked at her, considering. "Well, maybe."

Leaving Cat behind in her stroller, he walked out of the room. Raine stared after him, her mouth open. What would be the point of marrying a woman to have a mother for Cat if she was the type who'd be *annoyed* by the noise of pattering little feet?

She hunkered down next to Cat. "You don't want any mother who's going to be so easily annoyed, do you?"

"Ki-ki," Cat gurgled, sticking a wet finger out at Raine.

"Right," Raine said, grabbing the finger and giving it a kiss.

"The bedrooms are through here," Bently called. "Are you coming?"

Raine piloted the stroller down the hall. More wood floors. Perfect. She could picture Cat barreling around in her walker, all the bedroom doors closed, making a regular little speedway out of it, squealing her head off. But Bently was right, soon she'd be walking on her own—and Raine wasn't going to be around to see it. There was no way she'd be able to stand by and watch Bently turn this place into a home with another woman at his side.

She pushed Cat past two smaller bedrooms to find Bently in the largest one. He opened the drapes on three adjoining windows that looked out onto the courtyard, and the room came to life with the sunlight. There was a long, padded window seat and she went to sit on it, gazing out at the tree's brilliant green leaves, finding it impossible not to picture what it would look like blazing with fall color or blanketed in a December snowfall. She willed herself to be as detached as possible, but, damn it, she kept picturing herself in these rooms, Bently going through the years at her side. Cat growing up.

Bently was finally giving her what she thought she wanted, but it turned out that it wasn't what she wanted at all. He seemed to have absolutely no trouble moving on, while she was stuck in some never-never land where dreams didn't die but never came true.

His voice cut in on her thoughts, as cool and detached as she wished she could have been. "I'm thinking of blinds for in here. What do you think? Vertical or horizontal? Which do women seem to want these days?"

The lump in her throat dissolved into anger. Who did Mr. Bently Pierce think he was? She stood up and turned around to face him.

"You're really something, Pierce, you know that? First you dump your kid on me, then you accuse me of kidnapping her. Next, you want me to be her nanny. When I refuse you manipulate me like a damn choreographer, dangling that sweet, wonderful baby in my face till I'm completely crazy about her. Then you decide it's time for me to fall in love with you and you get me to do that, too. And now, cool as a cucumber, you're moving on, determined to find yourself a wife so you don't have to find yourself a nanny. And to really take the cake, you want *my* advice on fixing up this place so it'll appeal to a cross-section of *types* for you to sample!"

She started advancing on him, her hands on her hips, her chin thrust up, her silver eyes glittering. "I may not be what *you* consider to be a *normal* woman, but let me tell you something, Pierce. I'm much too normal to want to advise you on what you should hang in the windows to darken the room while you make love to another woman. And I don't want to help you pick out a dishwasher to entice some society babe with a manicure to marry you. And I'm not helping you choose a color of carpeting so the future Mrs. Pierce won't have to be *annoyed* by sweet little Cat's pitter-patter when she starts to walk."

She was directly in front of him now. "Anything else, Pierce? You want me to help pick out the bridesmaid dresses? Maybe help you find a caterer? And then what? What else can I possibly do for you?"

"You can marry me," he said.

She blinked. "What?"

He smiled, one of his heart-stopping, teeth-flashing grins. The one that always got to her.

"I said, you can marry me."

"But I thought . . ."

"You thought what, Raine? That I was going to live here with another woman? How could I possibly make love to another woman in this room after seeing you at that window seat? How could any other woman stand at the kitchen sink, gazing out the window or sit in the courtyard now that you've been there, your dress blowing in the breeze, your beautiful face lifted to the sun?"

She swallowed. "Holy cow. I mean—that was beautiful."

He laughed and took her into his arms. "That was the truth, Raine. We belong together. I just needed a way to get you to see it. Now, are you going to marry me?"

Cat squealed, pounding her fists on her stroller, grinning up at Raine through her drool.

Raine shook her head. "You two make quite a pair, you know that? Quite an irresistible pair."

He tightened his arms around her. "Then quit resisting, Raine. Say yes."

She gazed at him for long moments. Then her mouth slowly moved into a cocky grin. "And if I do," she finally said, "is the office downstairs mine?"

He threw back his head and laughed, long and hard. "God, Raine, you *are* something. But you're *my* something. Yes, the office downstairs is yours. The back room belongs to Cotton Tails. I'll even put your name on the deed if only you'll promise me forever."

She looked up at him, and he saw the love shining in her eyes, saw the promise on her lips. He kissed her gently, thoroughly. "Say yes," he whispered into her hair.

She pushed out of his arms. "I can't."

"What?"

"I can't, Bently. Not yet."

He shoved his hands into his hair. "Why the hell *can't* you say yes?"

"Haven't you forgotten something?"

Genuinely bewildered, he spread his hands helplessly. "What?"

"That third bedroom? Those brothers and sisters you wanted for Cat?"

He stared at her. "Oh Lord, Raine, is that why you've led me such a dance? Is that why you think we don't belong together?"

"Well, you told me on that very first day when we were locked in that cell together that you had no intention raising Cat as an only child."

"I know, but—"

"We both grew up lonely, Bently. I can't condemn Cat to that. I love her too much. And I can't condemn you to never having another child. I love you too much."

He took her hand and pulled her close, cupping her cheek with his other hand, running his thumb across her mouth. "Don't you know, Raine, that if I have you it'll be all I could want out of life? You and Cat are enough."

Her eyes were a little desperate looking into his. "How can you be sure? How can you know that someday you won't regret it?"

"Remember the song we danced to, Raine?"

She nodded, her silver almond eyes wet and shining.

"When a man loves a woman, he can trade in old dreams for new ones. Do you think I would ever want to be without you, could ever turn away from you, no matter what the problems?"

She swallowed hard. "But what about Cat? How can we grab happiness for ourselves and make her pay the price?"

"What price, Raine? She'll never be lonely like we were because we're not our parents. She'll always have us. Besides, Raine, we can always adopt. There are more ways than one to give Cat those brothers and sisters."

Raine dashed at a tear slipping from the corner of her eye. "Adopt? You'd consider that? Mick always said—"

He stopped the words with a finger against her lips. "I don't care what Mick said. I'm not Mick. Mick wasn't willing to invest in forever. I am, Raine."

Raine wanted to believe him. She wanted to believe that the fantasy could come true.

"Say yes, Raine," he whispered again, his breath caressing her face, his mouth brushing her eyes.

She shook her head. "I can't. I need time. I need to think—and I can't, not with you doing that!"

He groaned. "I don't have time, Raine. I need you, Cat needs you."

"Just one night—give me one night to think about it. Please? I need to be sure. *You* need to be sure."

His hand tightened on hers. "I *am* sure, Raine."

"Please?"

He sighed. "All right, my stubborn, beautiful woman. But tomorrow morning—*not* afternoon, *not* evening. Promise to come to me first thing tomorrow."

She took a shaky breath. "I promise."

"And when you come to tell me *yes* tomorrow," he murmured, his mouth brushing hers like sweet punctuation, "wear this dress. I want the pleasure of unbuttoning every one of those tiny buttons when I make love to you to celebrate our engagement."

She pulled back, her lips twisting, eyes flashing. "Pretty sure of yourself, aren't you, Pierce?"

"Pretty sure of *us,*" he answered.

"CAN YOU KEEP Catlin for the morning?"

Jack raked the hair off his face and chucked the baby under the chin. "Sure, Ben. What's up?"

"I've got a date with a set of buttons."

Jack screwed up his face as he took Catlin into his arms. "Huh?"

"I'll explain later," he said, handing over Cat's diaper bag. "See you at lunch."

Bently had slept surprisingly well, waking early to the sun, debating whether to take Catlin over to Jack's. He was torn between wanting their little matchmaker there when Raine said yes, since she'd be saying yes to both of them, and wanting to be alone with her so he could get at those buttons and make love to her again.

The buttons won out.

He whistled to himself all the way across the alley and through the patio doors. He looked at the clock. Did he have time to run over to the store and get some chilled champagne? He was sure they'd have something to celebrate. He was sure she was going to say yes, simply because there was no way he was going to let her say no.

On the other hand, it'd be just his luck to run out for champagne and miss her arrival. He opened the refrigerator and rummaged inside, coming out with a bottle of Chardonnay.

It would do. He wasn't taking any chances.

The front doorbell rang and his heart leaped to his throat. She was early—it had to be good news. She was going to marry him. She was going to be his wife and Cat's mother.

He nearly ran to the foyer. But when he threw open the door, it wasn't Raine who stood there. The woman on his threshold was inches shorter, shades blonder, eons more sophisticated.

"Caroline," Bently breathed, hearing the distinct sound of a crack marring the smooth surface of the life he'd been dreaming of.

Chapter Thirteen

Raine clattered down the steps, her sandaled feet flying, the gauze dress floating around her. She ran through to the boutique, throwing open the door, announcing, "I'm going to be a mother!"

Dee dropped the beaded jacket she was holding. "You're what?"

"Bently and I are getting married!"

"Oh my gosh! Oh heavens! Oh, Raine! I knew it, I just *knew* you loved him. Oh, it's so perfect." Huge tears filled her eyes, but ever practical when it came to fashion, Dee dashed them away and exclaimed, "I have just the dress!"

"I figured you would. But I haven't got time now, Dee. Bently's waiting. I have to tell him yes."

Dee stopped rummaging through the racks. "You mean you haven't told him yet?"

"No, I'm going over there now."

"Wait, here it is."

Raine looked at the dress Dee held aloft. It was a long-skirted cocktail suit, the skirt made of soft, buttery silk in the palest dove gray with a long slit slightly off center down the front. The jacket was slick, shiny satin with wide horizontal stripes of gray and a pale lemon yellow. It was low cut, sophisticated, designed to fit tight to the waist then flare saucily over the hips. It was a knockout.

"Oh, Dee, you're right. This is it! This is *the* dress!"

"Unless you want white, of course. You can have that, you know, even if it *is* your second marriage. People do it more and more. You can have a big white wedding, lots of bridesmaids—with me as maid of honor, of course."

"No, absolutely not!"

Dee pouted. "You don't want me for maid of honor?"

"Of course I do. Who else? I just don't want a big white wedding. I want a small, fast wedding—one that will just make me Bently's wife and Cat's mother as quickly as possible."

"Then this is the dress," Dee gushed.

"Yup," Raine said, running her hand over the cool satin, "this is the dress. Now, find something for yourself—fast! Like I said, I don't believe in long engagements!"

She ran out the door and hopped into the van. It started right up, purring like a kitten. Well, maybe a lion cub. Anyway, at the moment it felt as if it was gliding on air instead of four worn tires.

"I MADE A MISTAKE when I walked out on all this, Bently. I'm here to do something about it."

Bently followed Caroline into the living room, impatiently watching as she picked up objects, touched furnishings. Her cool elegance fitted into the surroundings as easily as the Baccarat and the Spode. And why not? She'd orchestrated the entire room to enhance her own frail, pale beauty. But Bently had learned long ago that the frailness was as deceptive as the brocade sofa she gracefully lowered herself onto. Inside, under the gracious, lovely covering, was pure, hard steel.

Bently glanced at his watch. "Get to the point, Caroline. What do you want?"

"All right, Bently." She trailed a hand through her long, pale hair. "I'm here to negotiate a settlement."

He gave a bark of laughter, his dark eyes flashing dangerously. "A settlement? And just what do you think you're entitled to after walking out of this place, my life and my daughter's life without a word or a second glance?"

She crossed her legs, the narrow skirt of her blue silk suit riding up to show her knees, and calmly toyed with a figurine from the gilt-edged table at her side. "We were equal partners, Bently, and you know it. I might have walked out, but half of what's here is mine."

His brows lowered. "And does that include Catlin?"

She looked up at him, her pale blue eyes cool and blank. "Who?"

Bently threw back his head and laughed, his body relaxing for the first time since he'd opened the door to her. "I take it, Caroline, that you're not here to make a claim on *my* daughter, only on the crystal and china."

She smiled serenely, obviously not in the least offended at his remark. "I have no interest in *your* daughter, Bently. She always has been yours, and she'll remain yours." Her mouth lifted ruefully. "I only wish that you could have been the one to go through the morning sickness and the labor pains."

"So do I," he snapped, then repeated, a weary edge to his voice this time, "so do I."

Caroline regarded him for a moment. "You know, I think you really mean that. I also think you're probably the best damn father in the world."

"I try to be."

"Good for you," she said briskly and stood up. "Now, back to the crystal and the china."

"It's yours."

"I beg your pardon?"

"It's yours, Caroline. Always has been. I'm selling this place, moving on, and nothing here fits into the new life I have planned. You can have everything— except for the furniture in the study and the things in the nursery, of course."

"And the condo?" she asked carefully.

"I'll write you a check for your half today."

"I must say, Bently, you're being more than agreeable." She eyed him speculatively. "Could it be that you want something in return?"

"Yes, Caroline, I want something. More precisely, I want Catlin."

"But you already have her."

"Legally. I want you to sign away any rights to her."

She started to wander around the room again, and Bently couldn't tell if she was preparing to give him a hard time or deciding how all her little treasures should be packed.

Finally, she stopped, her pale eyes going from an empty Waterford vase to his face. "You've found someone, haven't you? Someone who wants to be a mother to your daughter?"

"I've found someone I love, Caroline. It just so happens that she also loves my daughter. And I don't want you interfering in the life I plan to build with her. Not now—not ever."

WHEN RAINE PULLED UP behind the condo and cut the van's engine, she just sat back for a moment, breathing in the fresh spring air. Every doubt she'd felt had been tossed and turned, pummeled and chewed over in the dark hours of the night. With the dawn came the realization that forever would never come if she was unwilling to try for it. Bently thought their love would be enough—and she'd decided to take the gamble that he was right. If she lost, then she'd go down fighting. But she would try because there was no way she was letting another woman fill those rooms she'd walked in yesterday, mother that baby she already thought of as her own or love that man who'd opened up her heart again.

She stared at the morning sun blinking off the patio doors. Inside they waited for her. A man who wanted her, a child who needed her, a life ready to unfold. Suddenly impatient to claim it, she threw open the van door, making her way up the stone walk, a confident swing to her stride.

She pushed open the patio doors. The kitchen was empty. No sign of Cat or Bently. She was just about to call out for them when someone came through from the living room.

It wasn't Bently.

The woman was beautiful, her smile sweet, her complexion creamy pink and flawless. Silky pale hair fell to her shoulders, straight and fine, held off her delicately boned face with a pale blue ribbon. *Alice in Wonderland,* Raine thought. Innocently beautiful, tiny and dainty. Raine immediately felt taller, bigger—gauche. The thorough, speculative way Alice was looking her over wasn't helping any, either.

"You must be Raine," she finally said, holding out her hand. "I'm Caroline."

In a blurred daze, as though she really were looking through distorted glass, Raine took the offered hand. It felt smooth, cool, boneless, in her grip.

So this was Caroline. She looked nothing like Raine imagined. And she *had* imagined her— imagined what the kind of woman who could walk away from Cat would look like. And it wasn't anything like this. This Caroline looked sweet and kind. This Caroline didn't look as if she could walk out of her baby's life without a second glance.

And apparently she hadn't. The fact that she was standing in Bently's kitchen at this very moment proved that she was back for a second glance.

"HERE'S YOUR CHECK. I called the bank. There won't be any problem if you—" Suddenly, Bently's head shot up. He'd recognize that sound anywhere—the rumble of the Cotton Tails van starting up. By the time he reached the patio, she was gone.

He stormed back into the kitchen. "What did you say to her," he demanded. "Why did she leave?"

"I didn't say anything to her, Bently. I just introduced myself, and she mumbled something about talking to you later and left."

"You told her your name?"

Caroline moved her shoulders in a helpless, delicate gesture. "That was all."

"That was enough! Don't you see? She probably thinks you're back to claim Catlin."

"But I never said—"

Bently shoved his hand through his hair. "You wouldn't have to. Raine's mind cannot conceive of a mother not wanting her child."

"Or maybe she doesn't love you, or Catlin, as much as you think she does," Caroline stated quietly.

Bently swung to face her, his eyes narrowed. "What on earth do you mean by that?"

"I should think if she cares that much she'd be more willing to put up a fight and not disappear at the first sign of competition."

"Fight?" He gave a bark of laughter. "You don't know the meaning of the word until you've tangled with Raine Rogers. She didn't take off because she was afraid of a little competition from you, Caroline. She took off because she thought you wanted back into Catlin's life. She'd do anything for my daughter—anything—even give her up if she thought it was the best thing for Cat."

Caroline smiled. "In other words, she's everything I'm not and never could be. You better go after her, Bently. She sounds too good to lose."

"She is," Bently threw over his shoulder on his way to the front door. "She is."

Caroline ran after him. "What about the release?"

"I'll have a lawyer draw one up and fax it out to you." He turned around just before getting into the Mark VIII. "And Caroline—thanks."

"Good luck, Bently. You deserve it. And so does your daughter."

THE DRESS was hanging in Raine's room. Dee must have put it there after she'd left; Dee, who was probably picking out her own maid-of-honor outfit right at that moment; Dee, who was probably furiously checking out caterers and florists, making plans for a wedding that would never take place. Caroline was back, and the forever that Raine had finally decided to gamble on was never going to happen. All bets were off.

Behind her, the door opened. She knew who had burst into her solitary misery without even turning around. He'd fought a good fight, but he was going to lose, anyway. Cat had to be the only winner in this war.

"Why did you leave?" he demanded.

Raine didn't turn around but reached out to touch the dress, her fingers gripping the soft silk when she answered. "Cat's mother is back. *She's back,* Pierce— do you know what that means? It means Cat gets a second chance. Do you know what I would have given for just such a second chance with my own mother? Don't ask me to stand in the way of Cat having her real mother, because I couldn't do it, Pierce."

He moved toward her. "But Cat's real mother is right here, Raine. You're her mother—her *only* mother."

Raine turned to face him. Her chin came up, her eyes glittered. "What do you mean?"

"Caroline isn't back. It's true she came to make a claim, but not on Cat. She wants her furniture, her artwork and her share in the condo. She's at my bank right now cashing the check, then she's heading back to New York on a noon plane."

Raine swiped at her eyes with the back of her hand. "But I thought once she saw Cat—"

He shook his head and closed the rest of the distance between them. "She didn't see Cat, Raine. She didn't *want* to see Cat. Cat's at Jack's. Caroline's going to sign a release so you can adopt Cat legally.

You'll be her mother in every sense of the word." He reached out and put his hands at her waist, drawing her to him. "And you'll be *my* wife."

She dipped her head, biting her bottom lip, and he nearly held his breath waiting for her reaction.

Slowly, she raised her eyes to his. Slowly, her mouth quirked into a cocky grin. "Maybe I wasn't even *going* to say yes," she said.

He grinned, his hands tightening on her, giving her a hard little jerk, pressing her body to his. "You were going to say yes," he murmured.

"You're always so damn sure of yourself, Pierce."

"I'm only sure of one thing, Raine. I don't want to go through life without you. Marry me."

He watched her wide mouth open, watched her sweet lips form the word. "Yes," she said.

He picked her up and spun her around, tossing her on the bed, taking just one moment to drink in the beauty of her tumbled amid the cornflowers before joining her there to start working on all those little buttons.

"What do you think you're doing, Pierce?" she asked him, her tone full of the old insolence.

He nipped her lower lip. "Bently. Remember, I'm always Bently in bed."

Grinning, she drawled, "Okay. What do you think you're doing, *Bently?*"

"I'm making mad, slow, passionate love to you, Raine. And when I'm through—"

"Yeah?" she drawled. "When you're through, what?"

"When I'm through, we're going to go pick up *our* daughter."

"Our daughter," she repeated, her voice barely above a whisper. And looking into his dark eyes, she glimpsed forever.

Relive the romance... This August, Harlequin and
Silhouette are proud to bring you

by Request®

Making Babies

Families by proxy!

Three complete novels by your favorite authors—
in one special collection!

COMPELLING CONNECTION by Karen Young
A FAMILY AFFAIR by Sandra James
EVER SINCE EVE by Pamela Browning

These not-so-average families will steal your heart
this August.

Available wherever Harlequin and Silhouette books are sold.

HARLEQUIN® *Silhouette*®

HREQ895

RUGGED. SEXY. HEROIC.

OUTLAWS and HEROES

Stony Carlton—A lone wolf determined never to be tied down.

Gabriel Taylor—Accused and found guilty by small-town gossip.

Clay Barker—At Revenge Unlimited, he *is* the law.

JOAN JOHNSTON, DALLAS SCHULZE and MALLORY RUSH, three of romance fiction's biggest names, have created three unforgettable men—modern heroes who have the courage to fight for what is right....

OUTLAWS AND HEROES—available in September wherever Harlequin books are sold.

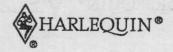 HARLEQUIN ®

HARLEQUIN®

AMERICAN ◆ ROMANCE®

®

*"Whether you want him for business...or pleasure, for one month
or for one night, we have the husband you've been looking for.
When circumstances dictate the need for the appearance of a man
in your life, call 1-800-HUSBAND for an uncomplicated,
uncompromising solution. Call now.
Operators are standing by...."*

I ♥ 800
HUSBAND

Pick up the phone—along with five desperate singles—and enter
the Harrington Agency, where no one lacks a perfect mate. Only
thing is, there's no guarantee this will stay a business arrangement....

For five fun-filled frolics with the mate of your dreams, catch all
the 1-800-HUSBAND books:

Coming to you only from American Romance!

HFH-1

THREE BESTSELLING AUTHORS

HEATHER GRAHAM POZZESSERE
THERESA MICHAELS
MERLINE LOVELACE

bring you

THREE HEROES THAT DREAMS ARE MADE OF!

The Highwayman—He knew the honorable thing was to send his captive home, but how could he let the beautiful Lady Kate return to the arms of another man?

The Warrior—Raised to protect his tribe, the fierce Apache warrior had little room in his heart until the gentle Angie showed him the power and strength of love.

The Knight—His years as a mercenary had taught him many skills, but would winning the hand of a spirited young widow prove to be his greatest challenge?

Don't miss these **UNFORGETTABLE RENEGADES!**

Available in August wherever Harlequin books are sold.

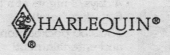 HARLEQUIN®

FLYAWAY VACATION SWEEPSTAKES!

This month's destination:

Glamorous LAS VEGAS!

Are you the lucky person who will win a free trip to Las Vegas? Think how much fun it would be to visit world-famous casinos... to see star-studded shows...to enjoy round-the-clock action in the city that never sleeps!

The facing page contains two Official Entry Coupons, as does each of the other books you received this shipment. Complete and return all the entry coupons— **the more times you enter, the better your chances of winning!**

Then keep your fingers crossed, because you'll find out by August 15, 1995 if you're the winner! If you are, here's what you'll get:

- Round-trip airfare for two to exciting Las Vegas!
- 4 days/3 nights at a fabulous first-class hotel!
- $500.00 pocket money for meals and entertainment!

Remember: The more times you enter, the better your chances of winning!*

*NO PURCHASE OR OBLIGATION TO CONTINUE BEING A SUBSCRIBER NECESSARY TO ENTER. SEE REVERSE SIDE OF ANY ENTRY COUPON FOR ALTERNATIVE MEANS OF ENTRY.

VLV KAL